LEAVING DEALLY

Brandianne Kroeker

This is a work of fiction. Any resemblance to real people or
circumstances are purely coincidental. Aside from obvious
historical references to public figures and events, all characters
and incidents in this novel are the products of the author's imagination.

For more information on the author and additional ordering information,
please visit the author's blog site, *brandianne.blog.com*
Additional correspondence with the author may be done via email:
brandiannek@hotmail.com

Cover photo credit: Katrina Elliott
Book cover design by Jeremy Cranmer
Author's photo credit: Shelby Stepp

Thank you to all of the people, family and friends, who gave your support, criticism, and praise throughout the process of writing and editing this novel!

I love you all, and I hope you enjoy the final product.

To my Best Friend, Jesus Christ- Thank You for Your creativity and encouragement, for all that You are to me.

PROLOGUE

Peering through the dense bush, I could see Marcus coming straight at me. I closed my eyes. If I can't see him, he can't see me. That was my theory, but the not knowing was causing my skin to dampen with sweat. It was still daylight out, and I worried my hiding place would be betrayed by the sunlight. I opened my eyes and saw Marcus was turned around, heading toward where my oldest sister was hiding. His dark hair was shining copper in the light. It was too bright out! I took a deep breath. I exhaled in relief, at least he wasn't looking my way anymore. He turned back. Had he heard my breathing? Or was it my heart racing that he could hear? Marc's steel blue eyes were looking vigilantly. There was a look of mischief about him.

"Carly? Is that you?" He walked slowly toward me again.

My breathing stopped. I was done for. Marc's hand reached into the bush, and I watched it come near my right shoulder. The bush rustled loudly about me as I jetted out of the back, through my own rabbit hole. I had not been touched. I ran toward the slide near the tall elm tree. That would be my safety. I turned back to see Marc fast on my trail. His arm was extended toward me. Running as fast as my nine year old legs would take me, I sailed past some kids sitting at a picnic table. There was a tree limb on the ground. I did my best to avoid it, but my clumsy feet failed me. I went tumbling down, tripping to my hands and knees.

"I've got you now, Carly!" Marc called as he jogged toward me. I felt him tag my shoulder. "You're it!"

All of my other siblings emerged from their hiding places throughout the park and surrounded us. I would now be the one seeking as they hid. I hated being the seeker. Usually, no matter who was supposed to seek, we could get Marc to do it for us. He was our big brother and he was a sucker for *please* and *thank you*. It didn't matter that he was the oldest of five kids- and the only boy besides the smallest child in our family- he still played around with us all the same.

Marc laughed a long hearty laugh as we all gathered around. He pointed at me and said, "Nice hiding place, Carly. I barely found you! But you've got some bush in your hair."

I began brushing through my hair with my fingers. Some green stuff fell out of the jet black mess. I had tangles too, and winced as my fingers pulled on them.

"Are you okay?" Marc saw my wincing.

"No… It hurts," I whined. Marc walked over to me and touched my shoulder. "Now you're it!" I yelled, punching him in the arm. I ran around the big elm tree as he chased close behind. Our sisters ran in different directions as soon as Marcus got tagged.

I kept running as fast as I could, widening my circles around the tree. I looked back and saw Marc's hand reaching toward me. I picked up the pace and-

"Oof!" I felt pain in my legs. My body flew forward and I fell in a tumbled mess on the ground. I could hear voices asking if I was okay, feet running toward me. I grabbed hold of my legs and assessed the damage as my siblings knelt beside me. The kids at the picnic table were staring at the scene.

I pulled up my pant legs and checked my shins. There was searing pain, and now I could see why. Bruises were already forming and the fall had afforded me a couple of skinned knees as well. The red and purple coloring was stark on my pale white legs, which made it feel even worse. I felt my eyes starting to tear up.

"That looks bad," Marc said. "We'd better go home."

"What happened?" I asked, looking back from where I had come.

Marc helped me to my feet and we all walked back toward a small marble plaque that was in the shade of the elm tree.

Marc looked at the plaque and read aloud,

"Carmen Deally loves to see smiling children. This park is for all the children of the town of Deally, that they might smile."

He spit on it. "Nobody believes Carmen Deally wants anybody to smile."

I heard gasps from the picnic table kids, who were still watching us.

Carmen Deally was a horrible woman, and everybody in town knew that. Nevertheless, respect and honor were important to Deally residents, especially toward Tom Deally and his wife, Carmen. Tom Deally founded our town, after all.

It was even a tradition in Deally to name your children after Tom. My parents plugged 'Deally' into the middle of each of their children's first and last names, mine included. My parents were particularly thankful to Tom for his

6

creation of "paradise". He was often at our home for meals, at the invitation of my parents. He was almost like an uncle to my siblings and me. Tom almost never brought his wife, Carmen, to these meals, but when he did, he had a continually pained look on his face. I couldn't really blame him for this.

Carmen Deally used to tell my friends and me horrible stories about how if we didn't attend church, or weren't nice to church elders, or said mean things to other children, or any number of things, we would be cast into a "fiery ocean". She was telling us what we had all been told before; after all, it was a common belief. Others in town would tell children these things as warnings, and generally in sugar-coated parables, but Carmen Deally told us all of the horrifying details of what we would experience in such an ocean of fire. Often she would end her stories with examples of different schoolmates we had which she believed were headed on this path. For years I was terrified of Carmen Deally. You might think a woman in her seventies would be a little mellower, but it seemed time did little to change Mrs. Deally.

Children growing up in Deally shared the fear of Carmen Deally and the fiery ocean supposedly awaiting them. I was like most kids in Deally, but there was one thing that separated me from most kids. It was rare for any children to leave town. My family had a connection to a big city, though: Grandma Freedom. My Grandma Freedom would drive in to town every couple of weeks and take a car full of grandchildren to her home in Elkston. The small rural town was nearly two hundred miles from Deally, and despite the drive, Grandma was adamant in her position that we needed to get out of Deally and see her. She was our only family outside of Deally, aside from a rarely spoken of uncle.

Most of my childhood, of course, was in Deally. I spent a lot of my time playing with my siblings at Carmen Park. After Marcus was taken away, however, I never went back. My sisters and little brother still spent sunny days there, and they tugged at my clothes and asked with pleading faces for me to come along. I always resisted their invitations. Eventually, they stopped asking.

ONE

I sat in the bedroom I shared with my two sisters. I had just awoken from one of my frequent naps. It had been three years since Marcus was taken away for "training". My siblings had spent the day at the park while I slept.

My mother came into the bedroom and informed me that we were all gathering in the kitchen for dinner. As we sat down, steaming vegetables and sliced beef on our plates before us, my father stood at the head of the table, as was the custom in Deally, to pray before the meal. He stood tall and broad-shouldered, wearing the bland attire of Deally, muted colors. I felt myself longing for the vibrant colors I saw in nature. Pushing those sinful thoughts aside, I bowed my head in reverence and waited for the prayer to begin.

"Dear God, thank you for this food. Thank you for the vision you gave your faithful worker, Tom Deally. Continue to bless his family, and allow us to become more a part of it." My father's voice grumbled over us all as we sat at the dinner table. "And forgive Emma's mother as she comes to you this day. Let us vouch for her misguided soul and beg your mercy on it." Hearing the weight of my father settle into his chair, we all lifted our heads.

Something was wrong. I watched in a daze as my family ate their food. I was still groggy from my nap, and I couldn't understand what my dad had meant in his prayer. *Emma's mother*? Why was Grandma Freedom mentioned? She was almost never discussed and certainly never prayed for. Her soul was beyond saving, I was told.

Those words ran through my mind more thoroughly. *Forgive Emma's mother as she comes to you this day.* I felt my chest tighten. I ate my food, knowing it would be sinful to leave it untouched. It was like ash in my mouth. No tastes could make their way to my tongue. I couldn't understand the feelings at the time, but I had a broken heart. I finished my dinner and went to take another nap.

I covered up with a quilt my mother had made me. The muted pastel shades of purple and brown covered me, and I recalled time spent at Grandma Freedom's home. My favorite person in the world had been Grandma Freedom. *Could she really be gone?* She never seemed sick, never near death. I shut my eyes and let warm tears stream onto my pillow.

I was able to talk with Grandma for as long as I wanted, about whatever I wanted. People in Deally didn't care to talk with children, but Grandma Freedom would sit with me on the front porch and talk for hours. I would tell her about my childhood dreams and aspirations, and she would tell me about her own childhood.

Another exciting thing about going to visit Grandma in her home of Elkston was that I got to eat at the most interesting places. Deally didn't have fast food restaurants. In fact, it didn't have any restaurants. It was understood in Deally that family came first, and if a mother was unable to provide home-made food for her family, she was a bad mother. To add to it, she was a sinner and in danger of that fiery ocean. I remember asking Grandma if my eating restaurant food was making her sin. She told me that when I came to her house, there were no sins. I loved Grandma's house.

I focused all of my energy on forming Grandma Freedom's face in my mind. The long, silver hair, the wrinkled skin, the big brown eyes. I could see her, but the picture in my mind was fuzzy. I let it go and drifted into sleep. Soon, my mother was by my side, rousing me from slumber.

"Carly," she said, touching my arm gingerly. "I understand you're upset about your grandmother. I am as well; she was the one who raised me for most of my childhood, of course. But I'd like to encourage you. Your sorrow will be less if you read some of the sacred texts and if you pray for her as well."

She looked at me with what seemed to be compassion, highlighted by the small creases in her face. They weren't as deep as Grandma Freedom's wrinkles had been. I studied my mother's face closely, being sure if she ever left me, I could recall her face in my mind. A long, thin nose, a lot like mine. Dark eyes. Sandy brown hair, not like my black hair. I kept staring. Her expression flashed from compassion to discomfort.

"Why are you looking at me?" She folded her arms.

I looked down at my quilt, but didn't answer her question.

Her hand returned to my arm. "Sometimes, if we who know the ways of God ask in prayer, people can be spared from the fiery ocean."

I wanted to believe her. At that moment, as I was about to bow my head and ask my mother to pray with me for Grandma Freedom, I remembered my grandmother's words. *At my house, there are no sins.* I had accepted both truths. There was a fiery ocean where sinners spent eternity. There were also no sins at Grandma Freedom's house. I suddenly understood the contradiction in my beliefs, and I resisted the temptation to pray.

My mother flashed a quick smile and walked out of the room. My youngest sibling, Jon, came into the room after she left. He was a pudgy little guy, and at that moment looked to have peanut butter on his face. He frowned at me and said, "Mommy says no more Grandma."

"I know," I replied, taking his hand in mine. "But we'll be okay."

Jon smiled slightly. "I will miss Grandma, but we'll be okay."

"Sure we will," I replied. I wished Jon hadn't come to me for assurance, but I was glad when he smiled and left me to myself.

~~~

It was soon after the loss of my grandmother that I turned thirteen. In church tradition, when a girl turned thirteen she was for the first time permitted to speak with a priest during office hours; usually this would be about finding a husband. That was not my intention. I wanted answers about my grandma's death, my brother being locked away, and the church in general. I had a lot of questions, some of which were merely feelings that could not be put into words.

I made an appointment with a fairly young priest named Liam. He had been a friend of Marc's years before. I sat across from Priest Liam in his home office. He looked confident behind his big desk. He had blonde hair, cut close to his face, which made his ears look large. I tried not to focus on the ears and looked into my lap. His wife and secretary, Charlotte, came in and placed fresh lemonade and store-bought cookies at a table beside the desk. She bowed and silently left the room, closing the door behind her. I looked up at Liam, searching my mind silently for all of my questions. Those pesky, inexpressible emotions tried to cloud my thoughts, but I pushed them aside as best I could.

"Would you care for any of these?" Liam asked, indicating the refreshment table. I couldn't resist smuggling a store-bought cookie to my side. It was a small, pale yellow cookie with a lemony scent. I wondered how Charlotte had gotten permission to buy pre-baked goods. They were not sold in Deally.

I sat silently. I knew I had to be addressed before I could speak to him. Another sin avoided. Liam looked at me with curious and searching eyes. I looked straight back into his brown eyes and made my face as business like as possible. I was standing my ground, though I had little ground to stand on, being a thirteen year old girl in Deally. Right as I took a bite of cookie Liam decided to address me.

"So, what would you like to talk about today, Carly?" He asked as I chewed. Swallowing was difficult at this point, but I chased the cookie with some lemonade and made my reply.

"I have some questions. They are religious questions." Clasping my hands in my lap, I began my search for answers, for truth. Liam sipped some lemonade and took his time in responding.

"Couldn't you have asked your parents these questions?"

"I thought you were supposed to be an expert. Why not ask you?"

"True enough." A satisfied grin appeared on his face. He grabbed a book from one of his desk drawers. It was one of the church's sacred texts. I recognized it right away.

"Ask what you'd like, Carly."

"My grandma was a really good person. She went to church, but not Tom Deally's Reformed Church. She never told me which church. She wasn't allowed to." I looked at Liam nervously. Other churches weren't good churches. I pressed forward rapidly.

"But I know it was good, because she was a good person. Yet, that book in your hands says that she's in the fiery ocean. Why should that be true? Why shouldn't she deserve to be in the Eternal Home of Glory? Who are *we* to say what's true? What if *she* is right? What if my *uncle* is right?"

I looked down at my shoes and waited for an answer. I hadn't intended to bring up my uncle. If Liam asked about it, I would have no answers; I'd never even met my uncle.

"You've got a lot of questions," Liam simply stated. "Perhaps there is no absolute truth. Perhaps your questions have no real answer, at least, not one that we can figure out on our own." He winked at me and looked at the sacred text in his hands.

"Did you look through the sacred texts before coming to me with such heavy inquiries?" I nodded. He sighed, and then with a gleam in his eye, asked, "Carly, do you trust your parents?"

What an odd question for him to ask. "Of course."

"And me? You must trust me to have requested Charlotte set up this meeting."

"You were friends with Marc," I said softly, feeling tears begin to emerge.

"Yes, I was. Marc is doing great by the way. When he heard of our meeting he asked me to tell you something. Would you like to hear the message?" I sat straight up in my seat, bobbing my head up and down.

Liam leaned forward a little and whispered, "He said to tell you that he misses you most. He wants you to wait for him to get out of his training so that you two can go visit Elkston together." He ended the message with a wink.

Going back to Elkston with Marc was the most brilliant and wonderful thing I could imagine. All of my questions were suddenly irrelevant. What did they matter if I could go to the city with my brother? I was enraptured with a moment of happiness like I hadn't remembered feeling in years. That is, until I remembered that Marc was still due for two more years of solitude. Not even a phone call was permitted. The happiness seemed to flee.

"Anyway, I trust my parents and you," I said blandly.

Liam seemed unsettled by my sudden change in attitude, but continued on in all professionalism. "When we tell you that the words in these texts are truly inspired by God and written by his faithful workers, Tom and Carmen Deally, why do you believe we are lying?"

I took a bite of cookie and chewed slowly. Liam did the same.

"I trusted Grandma too, though."

"Carly, she probably thought that what she believed was true. That's why Tom had to create this community, because no one was listening to God's message anymore. That outside world pollutes people's thinking. Carly, your grandmother was only one of many misguided souls." I remembered my father's prayer. Was Grandma Freedom really a *misguided soul*?

"What if it's the opposite?"

Liam opened the sacred text to a passage it seemed he had memorized the placement of. He began to read aloud, "If we are exposed to the outside world we are like sponges, absorbing each misguided thought and idea. We must keep the traditions of our parents alive. When we are worried about our faith, we must come before God with an open mind, and allow him to remind us of what is true. Flock, all you doubters who have been polluted as a sponge. Go to the wooded areas to expose yourself to God."

He closed the book and looked at me with a confidence that made me wonder what he thought had been accomplished by that reading.

"You should go into the woods and expose yourself to God," Liam stated.

I knew what that meant. It was a ritual. Someone with religious doubt was advised to go alone into the woods, and while there, literally expose themselves.

They were supposed to spend two nights in the woods, naked. My mother had told me of her own doubting as a young woman. She was commanded by her father to go do the doubter's ritual. She went, and for two nights she was naked in the woods. She had told me that God showed her where to find food and that she had seen a vision of her mother being attacked by gruesome-looking creatures. Her priest told her that the vision was a picture of what the world can do to a person.

My mother's parents had split up shortly after moving to Deally. Grandma Freedom said that the church wasn't right and they needed to move. Grandpa Sid did not agree. My mother and her sister, Hallie, were left with Grandpa, and Grandma took their son. The separation had given my mother all of her doubt. After the doubter's ritual, she stopped talking to her mother. That is, until Grandpa died, then they began to talk a little again, and that was when the trips to Elkston began.

"I'm not sure that's right for me," I told Liam.

"It's perfect. Doubters always do it and come back to our community with a renewed sense of religious pride. I think I'll recommend it to your parents." He jotted a note.

"Really," I said, raising my voice. "I get the point!" I got quieter and continued, "I shouldn't doubt. My grandma was just polluted...Like a sponge."

I didn't believe it. Maybe I should have, but I didn't.

"Are you sure?" Liam leaned over the desk toward me, studying my facial expression.

"Yeah. That passage out of the sacred text was pretty eye-opening," I lied.

"Is there anything else I can help you with, Carly?" I shook my head. It was pretty obvious he wouldn't be helping me.

"What about marriage?" Liam asked.

"I haven't been thinking about it," I said calmly. Marriage was almost as scary as the doubter's ritual. Even though it was normal in Deally to marry so young, I didn't feel ready. I barely knew any of the men in town. How could I have married one of them?

"Well, you are marrying age now. The custom is, if someone comes to ask for you, the marriage process begins. Unless, of course, there is a parental objection, but I don't imagine your parents objecting."

"Me neither," I thought aloud. Marrying age for males was eighteen. I tried to imagine the men in town who might ask for me as their bride. I felt sick.

"I'll worry about it when it happens," I laughed.

Liam smiled at me and replied, "Start worrying."

My jaw swung open and I looked at him for a few awkward seconds before any words came out of my mouth.

"What? Who?"

"Do you know a Gary Deally Wesson?" Liam asked, as he removed a manila envelope from his desk drawer.

I could feel tears coming again. I did know who Gary was. He was 21 years old, and I used to see him at the Carmen park all the time when I was younger. Marcus and Gary Wesson went to school together and seemed to be friends in those days. I didn't know him, though. He couldn't have been a very close friend of Marc's, because I didn't remember him ever coming to our home. He was essentially a stranger to me.

I silently begged God to let me wake up from a dream. Then, I remembered I was in between thoughts on God's existence, and I began to cry.

"I understand marriage is a big step," Liam said with a stern tone of voice. "Remember that lots of other girls have been in this situation, and you'll get through it just like any one of them." Liam folded his hands on top of the desk, as if to indicate the matter was not open for discussion.

I knew then that no one in Deally could relate to me. Nobody knew my fears, my anxieties, my doubts. I had to be the only one who ever had an original thought in Deally!

I suddenly became aware of my loneliness, and I longed for Grandma Freedom. She would know what I was going through. She had been here before, and she had gotten out of Deally. *Was she corrupted or did she find truth*? I wanted to sit on her front porch and talk with her. I regretted never asking her about these things before. Why did the questions have to come after she was no longer around to answer them?

If I was going to find the answers to my questions, I needed more than Liam or the reformed church that Tom Deally had created. I needed more than the sacred texts. I couldn't explain how, but I simply knew that I had to leave. If I stayed in Deally too much longer, I would go mad. I wasn't sure what kind of ritual they would have me do then.

TWO

If I wanted to leave the community of Deally, without sinning, I had to talk to Tom Deally. Pondering this, I made my way out of the house. My mother was sitting on the front porch, reading one of the sacred texts. She looked up for a moment to see me leaving.

"Where are you off to?"

"Just walking. I might go to the park or something," I replied. She smiled and went back to reading.

I wasn't going to the park. I had only been there once after Marc had gone. I suppose my mother would have known that if she had shown more than an occasional interest in her children's lives. She was like most parents in the community, too busy keeping traditions and trying to please elders to spend much time with family. She didn't even notice the increased napping after Marc had gone. At least, she'd never said anything to me about it. After Marc left, though, I began to realize it wasn't all that important to have a relationship with her anyway. Marcus had spent more time with our parents than any of their children, and he was basically given away!

It was the middle of the night when it happened. I think that was part of why it felt so wrong to me; nothing good ever happens after a knock on the door in the middle of the night. I was in bed, vaguely asleep. I could hear pounding on the door, so loud that it woke me up. I shot up in my bed. My sisters were both still asleep. *How could they sleep through that banging*? I heard my parents' door come open with a long creak. Then, footsteps, walking toward the front door. Voices. Males voices. My sisters seemed to be jostled out of their sleep now. They sat up. We looked at each other in the darkness, straining to see eachother's faces, straining to understand. Raye, the oldest, whispered to Caroline and I to go back to sleep. We laid down back down in our beds. I continued to listen. I wondered why they had pounded on the door, but once inside the house they whispered. I could hear my father's voice; it had a demanding tone. A few stray words hung in the air. "Spitting". "Priesthood". I sat up, hearing the voices cease, and footsteps come through the house, toward my room. The footsteps stopped in the hallway, just short of my door. I imagined right where the men stood, outside of Jon and Marc's bedroom.

When I woke up the next morning, Marcus was gone. I remember hearing the news from my parents, about him being selected for the priesthood. I ran to his bedroom. His bed was lying there cold, the sheets and blankets half on the floor. It looked to me like he had been ripped from sleep. Kidnapped.

My parents were happy. They said it was a blessing for our family, and for Marc. I was devastated. *How could a kidnapping be a blessing*? My siblings and I shared this sense of having been robbed, which we communicated in long faces and sighs to one another. We dared not talk about it. In Deally, talking against the church in any way was not acceptable. It was, of course, a sin.

It was an isolated existence that those training for the priesthood took on, living in the church's downstairs quarters. Marc was there with three other young men. The tradition was for the boys to spend five years in seclusion, only in contact with church elders, mainly Tom. They were to learn the ins and outs of the priesthood, memorizing sacred texts, and never laying eyes on a woman in all of that time, even at the cost of missing church services. They would not see the Deally newspaper, and certainly no television was permitted; televisions were rare in Deally to begin with. You had to have a permit to own a TV, or a phone for that matter. Don't even ask about computers- as far as I knew, they never existed.

I missed Marcus so much. I always looked up to him. He was always the leader of our little clan of siblings. We were depressed after losing Marc. If we had known what depression was we might have fought it, instead, we napped. I loathed my existence without Marc.

I rounded the corner on Main Street, making my way to the back roads which were not paved. Ahead of me, at a flower shop, I saw Gary! I ducked behind a trashcan. He was buying a bouquet of yellow roses. I knew what that meant. I sunk down a little more, to be sure I wasn't seen. Yellow roses were traditionally given to the parents of a girl, to ask for her hand in marriage. I once saw this happen. I was playing at my friend Becky's house when I was very young. Becky's older sister was fourteen years old. A man with a yellow bouquet of flowers came to the house and greeted the parents, who were on the porch. He handed the roses to the mother and was invited inside.

Becky and I were in the yard, scooping up dirt and pretending to serve each other ice cream. An hour later, the man emerged from the house with the fourteen year old beside him. They each held a duffel bag that appeared to be stuffed with the girl's belongings. I don't think that girl had ever met him before, but there he was, her husband. *He was an ugly man. Gary is handsome.* I scolded myself for the thought. I watched him a little longer, the tall brunette haired boy.

18

No, not a boy. Gary Dealy Wesson was a man. *And he wants to marry me?*

Watching Gary with those yellow roses made me feel hopeless. I had never felt such a sense of anxiety. I waited behind the garbage can, until Gary was out of sight. Then, I made the long journey to Tom Dealy's house.

I stood in front of the Dealy residence. I knew I had to talk to Tom; I had to try to leave that place. He was the only person who could make it happen. Of course, there were no fences, I could have walked out at any moment. The only fences in Dealy were the one's separating backyards, and of course the ones that protected houses with security systems. Tom Dealy's home had such a system. It seemed necessary; after all, he was God's servant. He and his wife were the faithful community founders who had written all of the sacred texts, being inspired by *celestial visitations*. They needed to be protected, though there was very little crime in Dealy. The occasional assault, theft, or apostasy was not unexpected. Usually these were committed by new members of the community, still struggling to leave the ways of the outside world behind them.

No other houses were near the Dealy's. Their home was actually quite a distance from the heart of the community. I looked up at the large three-story house, and it was daunting. No other houses I had ever seen were three-stories tall. I took a deep breath and tried to focus. I closed my eyes and I could see Grandma Freedom. I could see Elkston. That was where I wanted to be. It seemed so far away, but my heart was there, with Grandma Freedom. That would be my request, to leave Dealy and go to Elkston. I had never heard of Tom giving permission to someone my age to leave Dealy before, but I assumed it was because no one my age had ever made the request.

I opened my eyes and stared once again at the home of Tom Dealy. My way out. I shifted my weight nervously, listening to the gravel crunch under my feet. This man was like an uncle to me, what was I so afraid of? With another deep breath, I made my way to the door. The security gate was open, a sign that someone was home. The gate was only closed when they were not home and at night. With this open door, as it were, I walked toward my freedom. At least, I hoped it was my freedom.

"Hey Carly."

Tom Dealy was a few feet behind me. I froze. I was on the second step leading to his porch, almost to the door. I had wanted to make this meeting on *my* terms. *I* wanted to be the one showing up unexpectedly. That wasn't happening.

I listened for other voices. Mrs. Dealy, one of their eight children, anybody. There was only the ever increasing sound of Tom Dealy's feet on the gravel behind me.

"Carly, what are you doing here, Sweetheart?" I turned around to face him. He looked happy. That was good, I thought. There was a fishing pole in his hand. He was coming from Deally Creek, I imagined.

"Oh. I was just in the area, and I thought maybe Rebekah was here," I lied. Rebekah was Carmen and Tom's daughter, the child closest to my age. She was twenty and still lived at home. Everyone in the town whispered about her, speculating as to why she was still not married. It seemed to me that it would be intimidating to ask Tom Deally, that great servant of God, for his daughter's hand in marriage. She was the Deally's only daughter, and the only child still living at home.

"I'm sorry. Rebekah is in town, meeting with Priest Liam," Tom informed me. I almost laughed. That meeting wouldn't avail much.

"Oh." I tried my best to sound upset. The truth was I had never really liked Rebekah. She was a lot like her mother.

"Would you like a ride back home?" Tom was a church elder, therefore, he was allowed to have a car. I had ridden in a car with Grandma Freedom before, but never in a Deally resident's vehicle. I thought about it for a moment. Gary would probably be at my house, waiting for me. If I went now, without even asking for permission to leave, all hope of ever going outside of Deally would be lost forever. My existence would be that of a house wife, making bread and babies. I had to talk to Tom; I couldn't just leave without speaking up. I had to do it *now*.

"Actually, could I talk to you for a minute or two?"

"Okay. What's on your mind?" he asked, taking a seat on one of the ten porch chairs. I sat in the one to his left.

"Well, I-uh…" I stopped in mid-sentence and began to think about Grandma Freedom again. I had to do what she did. I had to get out of Deally.

"Are you alright, Carly?"

"Yes. I just need to ask you a huge favor. I know that this is kind of a rare thing, but…"

"What?" he asked with a smile. His eyes looked glassy in the sunlight.

"Can I have your permission to leave Deally?" I spat out the question with every word running into the one before it. I wondered if he could even understand me. He sat with a puzzled look on his face.

"Sorry. Did you understand that?" I didn't want to repeat myself.

"Yeah, I think I understand that, Carly. Look, you'd be surprised how many young girls come to me asking to leave Deally. It's always because of the same thing."

I was a little stunned. Had there been more young people like me? Had there actually been other members of Deally who wanted to leave? This was amazing.

"I think you should give marriage a chance," Tom went on.

I realized he was talking about nervous future brides. I didn't have that problem. Though, I did want to leave before I got into any of that marriage business. I wanted to tell Tom all of my doubts, all of my feelings of absolute desperation for truth. I wanted to do this, but I couldn't. I just nodded along with everything Tom Deally said, as if I was in total agreement. As if I were there because of worries about marriage. I hated it. I felt like a sell-out, and for the first time, I was glad Grandma Freedom was not around to hear about this.

"How about a ride home?" Tom asked with a satisfied smile.

"No. Thank you. I'm going to walk home."

Tom went inside, leaving me to my walk. As soon as I saw the door close behind him I ran. I didn't even really think; I just ran. After about ten minutes of running in a full-on sprint, I found myself at the Sadmen River. I sat on the bank. There was a huge, overgrown briar bush between my spot on the bank and the trail I had run down through. It was the perfect secret spot.

I stared out at the mass of twisting water. I wondered if the river was really called Sadmen. Did Tom Deally rename it where it ran through the community? It obviously extended out of Deally. It seemed to me at that moment that Deally was full of lies. Why would Grandma Freedom have left if there wasn't really something wrong with this town? What kind of a town is it that you have to ask permission to leave anyway? Grandma said she never had to ask permission to leave Elkston. Was Elkston normal, or was Deally normal? I couldn't get past the questions. But at least I felt safe here at the river. There were no people or houses around. It was just me and the trees. I watched the trees sway slightly with the breeze. They were so tall. They made me feel small. I ran my hands along the soft blades of grass on my left and my right, and I picked a dandelion from the earth. I looked at it for a moment, wondering if people outside of Deally called the little flowers dandelions too. I placed the flower gingerly beside me and began to cry. The warm streams of water on my cheeks were a long time coming. You didn't cry in Deally. My crying would only be acceptable during childbirth. Nothing else merited tears. At that moment, nobody was around to enforce such rules of conduct. No one was allowed to be around, because this river was sacred to the church. I didn't see what was so great about it. It was beautiful, but so was the plaque that Marc used to spit on. I leaned into the edge of the river and scooped up some water with my hands. I had been baptized here, like every other resident in Deally. It was when I was only three years old. I was afraid of the water then. I didn't understand baptism either; I didn't understand how pushing me under water was going to make me more spiritual, but it was a tradition and not to be questioned. I could remember crying uncontrollably when they told me they were going to "dip me backwards into the water, so that I could be seen as faithful to God and to the Deally heritage of faith".

I splashed some water onto my face. It felt amazing in the heat of the day. I wondered if I could swim out of Deally. I never learned how to swim very well, though. Grandma Freedom had taught my siblings and I all how to swim at one point, but she got too old to keep taking us swimming. She used to take us to pools, and sometimes we would go to rivers or lakes, but most of the time my siblings refused to swim there, knowing that in Deally, the river was sacred.

I must've sat by the river for hours. I pondered staying there overnight. After all, what did I have waiting for me at home? Parents who would be angry that I left without saying I would be gone all day, and a twenty-one year old man who wanted me as his own. Not exactly a fantasy. At least I had plenty of time to spend crying out there by the river. I had never felt so satisfied to cry. As the moon began to rise, the sun long gone, I got up and began to walk home. I decided that if I saw the lights on at my house, I would leave, walking as far as I could get. If the lights were off, however, I told myself, the darkness would signal no company- no Gary. So, I would creep inside, get some sleep, and leave Deally in the morning.

I could see the glittering town lights in the distance as I made my way down the dirt road, toward Deally's main square. Only minutes away from home now. I stared ahead at the lights, the town of Deally looked so quiet and beautiful at this time of night. I had never been out this late before. It occurred to me at that time that my parents might be up worried, in which case the lights would be on. I sighed. My lights-on, lights-off plan wouldn't work after all. I entered the square, wandering down the sidewalk, still looking at the lights. All of the homes were dark, but the shops had warm, glowing light emanating from their windows and doors.

I bumped into someone. Spinning around from the force of my collision, I squealed out an apology. I refocused my attention to see who I had hit. Before I saw the man's face, I saw what he held in his hands. A bouquet of yellow roses. I stood very still, lifting my face to meet the gaze of this man. Gary Deally Wesson. He looked at me through glassy blue eyes. At that moment all I could do was apologize once more. "I wasn't paying attention. Sorry."

Gary ran his left hand through light brown hair, gripping the roses with the other. He maintained strict eye contact with me as he said,

"Why weren't you there today?"

"What do you mean?" I forced my voice to waver with curiosity. He looked down at the roses in his hand and replied,

"Didn't Priest Liam tell you?" His voice cracked a little.

"Oh yeah. I guess he did, but I didn't know anything was going on today. I mean, where was I supposed to be today that was so important?"

"You know what these are, don't you?" He continued to stare at the roses.

"Well, yes."

"Carly," he began, "I...I..." He laughed nervously, a laugh that made *me* nervous. I took a step backward. "I saw you when I was buying these. *You saw me*. You knew I was going to be coming by today, and you took off."

Gary's eyes were still locked on the flowers. I thought he looked angry from what I could see of his face in the darkness. I suddenly became very aware of the darkness. It had to be past midnight.

"Well...I didn't know for sure. Some people buy flowers to deliver the next day, you know?" I wondered if that was a sin, delivering flowers the next day.

Gary lifted his face to look at mine. I could see he was holding back tears. I felt my stomach drop. This man was eight years older than me, I had hardly ever been around him, and he wanted to take me as his wife. I had no real reason to have sympathy for him, but he looked like a sad boy. Perhaps he was just as much a victim of Deally as I was.

"I understand if you don't want to marry me," Gary said sadly. His eyes went from me to the roses.

"It's not really up to me," I scowled. Arranged marriage was one of the many unquestionable traditions of Deally.

"This could mean trouble for me, but I don't want to force you into anything," he shook his head. "Anywhere else in the world you don't have to

23

deal with this. You can just date," he laughed to himself.

"What?" I asked, tilting my head to look at his face. He seemed to be magnetically attracted to those yellow roses. He met my questioning eyes with his.

"You know what a *date* is, right?"

"Today is the twelfth," I said.

He laughed at my naïve statement. "I'm not talking about a calendar date. The *date* I'm talking about is when two people, who like each other, go somewhere together, just to be together, and either one of them can decide to stop dating at any time and it's over."

I stared at him in astonishment. I had never heard of this before. *Dating*.

"What about marriage?" I asked.

"If the two people date long enough, and they like each other, they can get married. Marriage is pretty much the same, except you don't have to have any religious ceremonies if you don't want to. You just sign a piece of paper that says you want to get married and it's done."

"Wow. How do you know all of this?"

He was quiet.

"Wait, you didn't make all of this up, did you?"

"No. It's how my parents got together. They dated for three years before my dad asked my mother if she would marry him." I couldn't believe it. I had forgotten Gary was only a second generation community member. His parents had lived most of their lives outside of Deally. I suddenly thought Gary was the most captivating person in all of Deally. I wondered how much he, and his parents, would be willing to share about the outside world. If I couldn't leave Deally, at least I could marry into a family that knew something about the outside world. That was a poor consolation, but I held to it.

"So, where were you from? Were you from Elkston before you came here?"

Deally's education system wasn't much for geography and I tended to assume anyone from the outside was from Elkston. Gary didn't affirm my assumption, but was silent. I realized he was still holding the roses.

"I'm sorry I didn't go home today. I didn't want to make you feel bad, I just…" I wasn't sure what to say.

24

"I was there, waiting. I only left a few minutes ago. I had to tell your parents to forget it when you didn't show up. I was there for over three hours."

"Sorry…I was just scared. I might not know very much about what they do outside of Deally, but I know what marriage means. It means becoming property. It means being a servant, a cook, always at home. I was scared that if I went home you would be there and I would have to say goodbye to adventure, to dreams and wishes, to everything I love…" No reaction from Gary. "I guess it's pretty dumb."

Gary dropped the roses. I watched them fall to the ground, almost in slow motion. When I looked up he grabbed my hands in his and looked into my eyes. I was in a daze.

"It's not dumb. I'm sorry you hate it here so much. I wish I could show you the outside world."

"I don't hate it here," I laughed nervously.

"No, I can tell. Everything you just said is what I've been feeling for years."

Silence. Gary let go of my hands sheepishly and repeated, "It's not dumb."

I could hardly believe what was happening.

"Do you remember a lot about the outside?" I asked.

"It's like a sponge. How could I forget?" He laughed and I smiled knowingly. The old spongy outside world. "I do remember quite a bit. I lose some of it every day though."

"That's so horrible," I replied softly. I didn't want to forget my experiences outside. I looked at Gary and asked him seriously, "Would you leave Deally if you could?"

"Nobody leaves Deally, Carly. It just doesn't happen. There's something about this place. I can't explain it. Nobody leaves."

Gary stepped back a little and picked up the roses. "You can have these."

I took them. "Thank you…I know that people don't leave Deally. *Would* you leave if you could?"

He cracked his knuckles and sighed. "Yes. I would. You can't tell anyone I said that, though. If the church found out I wanted to leave, it would be all over for me."

I looked at him with questioning eyes. I didn't understand what the church had to do with anything.

"Well, you know what happened to your brother."

"He didn't want to leave Deally."

Gary laughed a little. "You didn't know? I bet you were just told he had *potential*, right? And maybe that it was God's will for him to be a servant of the church?" Gary put both hands on top of his head and let out a stressed sigh.

"Yes, they told me that, but I knew it was because he was setting a bad example for the other kids. He used to spit on the plaque at Carmen Park."

I searched Gary's face. Did he know something that I didn't? He had hung out with Marc sometimes, but I never realized that it was possible for Marc to have had secrets hidden from me.

"Marc wanted to leave. He and Liam had both talked about it, actually. Liam was taken away to become a priest only five years before Marc. It was because they had both planned on leaving Deally some day." His hands fell to his sides now and he shook his head. "Since Liam was old enough to justify taking under the church's authority, he was taken. Marc wasn't old enough, but the first chance they had, he was taken in. It was by request of Liam."

"What? Why would Liam request that if they were friends, and-"

"You don't get it. That five years does something to people. It's like their personality changes completely. The Liam I knew, the Liam that Marc knew, never would have done that. He was so determined to leave, and he knew Marc had always wanted out. It just, it changed him, being there for five years. When he got out, he was a priest, he had a wife, and an office. He was different."

"Do you think Marc is going to be different?" I asked through teary eyes.

Before he could answer, lights suddenly pierced our seclusion and a car pulled up beside us at the curb. My father jumped out of the back. Tom Deally and Liam were in the front. I instinctively hid the roses behind my back, as my father began yelling.

"Where have you been all day? You are never leaving the house again!"

He continued to say these types of things, questions followed by threats. Finally, Tom Deally stepped out of the car and stepped in to the situation. "Stop. Yelling at the girl will only make things worse. And we certainly don't want to wake up the neighborhood with all of your screaming."

We all stood quietly. Gary edged toward me and took the roses from behind my back. He stepped out in front of my father, and stretched out his hand, revealing the roses clenched in his fist. My dad looked from Gary to me and back again. He was clearly confused about how we could end up on the street together in the middle of the night. I was baffled by it myself.

"I don't know if her leaving home is a good idea after this," my father told him.

He was honestly turning down tradition, in front of Tom Deally! I was surprised, and kind of scared. I had experienced some kind of breakthrough tonight. I had connected with someone. He wanted what I wanted, and he seemed to understand how everything in the community of Deally worked. I didn't want to go home. I wanted to go with Gary, but not for marriage. I wanted to bring him with me when I made my escape. He would be a huge help to me. I took Gary's hand, squeezing it nervously. He looked back at me in surprise and smiled. I hoped this act of affection would bring my father to a new conclusion. If he would just take the roses and let me go with Gary, then we could use our two month engagement period to hatch a plan of escape.

"Well, would you look at that?" Tom began to reason with my dad. "They *want* to be together. Derek, you can't hold something like that back. It reminds me of when Carmen and I got together, years ago." He looked at me. "I told you it wasn't so bad."

I forced myself to smile at him.

"So, I should just let her go?" Dad asked. Tom nodded and pointed to Gary's still outstretched hand.

"Please, sir. I think that she can learn a lot from marriage, and I promise she won't get any more out of hand under my control," Gary assured him. I watched as my father took the roses out of Gary's hand and I was released from my childhood. I stood, frozen, my hand still in Gary's. I listened as my dad told me to come by tomorrow to pick up my things. Then, I watched him get back into the car with Tom and Liam and drive away. We watched the taillights fade into the darkness. When the car was out of sight, we both sighed in unison. Then, we laughed in unison. Was this really happening? I had barely processed it all when Gary took my other hand in his and asked,

"Do you really want to marry me?" I looked down at the ground. I closed my eyes for a moment and looked back at him.

"I want to leave Deally."

Gary looked at me with a piercing countenance. He seemed to search out every detail of my face, of my soul. Then, he laughed. His laughter was so loud and explosive, I was afraid he would wake up people in houses down the street.

"Carly," he said, wiping away laughter-induced tears, "I am so happy that you said that." He let go of my hands and embraced me tightly. I could feel his joy being poured over onto me as well. I knew I would leave one day, but I had no idea that it would be with a man. Everything was easier with a man to protect and help you. At least, that's what the texts that Carmen Deally penned proclaimed as truth. I laughed at the thought, remembering that those texts represented the very thing I was running away from. Gary laughed when I did. So, we stood there, hugging and laughing, for some time.

That night, according to tradition, we should have consummated our relationship. We weren't exactly following tradition, however. Neither of us were ready for marriage, especially marriage to people we hardly knew. We stayed up all night, planning. We planned on leaving *before* the marriage date. We wanted to get out of there as soon as possible.

"Where will we go?" I asked Gary. We were sitting across from each other at his kitchen table.

"I know you want to go to Elkston, but it would be the most obvious place. The first place they would go looking for us."

"You think people will come after us?"

Gary looked more serious than before. "Carly, how do you think I know all of the information I do? About why Liam and Marc were chosen, about the inner workings of the church? About the outside world?"

"You were friends with them. And your dad is an elder. And you lived outside of Deally for a while."

"That explains why I want to leave," Gary mused, "but the truth is, my dad was more than just a church elder at one time. My dad…Well, he is good friends with Tom. In fact, his father was on the original work crew that built Tom's house and the old church. Our families go way back. The only reason I haven't lived here all along is that my dad had a job that required us to live outside of the community. His job was to find people who left Deally. Don't you see? No one gets out of Deally, not unless Tom and the church elders want them to. After awhile they figured out a way to keep people here, and my dad's job wasn't necessary. Mind control is my guess."

"*Mind control?*"

"It's just what it sounds like," he told me.

"Okay…So, your dad told you all of this stuff?"

"No. If he knew I was in any way aware of this, I'm sure I would be training to be a priest right now. A lot of eavesdropping got me all of this information. Plus, my parents have a TV." My jaw dropped. A television? I never knew anyone who had one of those. The kids in Elkston had TVs, but I don't know that I ever saw them. We kids rarely played inside, or else maybe I would have.

"Your parents let you watch their TV?"

"No. I never could have watched TV without sneaking it. When my parents would go to parties, or when I stayed home sick on my own, I would watch. I had to sneak into my parents' bedroom. Once my mother got home earlier than expected and I had to jump out of their window and pretend that I had been playing in the backyard the whole time. My parents had an argument that night about who left the television on."

"So, what did you see on television?"

"When I was younger I would watch cartoons." I stared at him blankly. "Oh, cartoons are like…How do I explain this? Well, like a children's book, with all the colorful characters, acted out with moving pictures."

"Whoa. That's different."

"But when I got older I would watch the news. It was amazing. You know about the people who come here every once in a while to interview Tom, right?"

"Yeah."

"Well, they're on the news, and I've seen some of those interviews on the news too. Do you know how the rest of the world sees this place? They say that it's a fanatical religious group- which is *not* a good thing. They also say that Tom Dealy is a liar and that everyone who lives here is deceived. They say that our rituals and customs are wrong, too. I was shocked when I heard all of this, but it's what the outside world really thinks about this place. And, do you know how many people are in the outside world?"

"More than here. Like, maybe four or five thousand?"

"No Carly. There are *billions* of people outside."

"Billions?" I tried to comprehend billions. There were really that many people who thought this place was wrong? That was a wake-up call. It did more than confirm my feelings about Deally, it enhanced them- a billion times over. I could hardly believe it.

That afternoon, Gary and I walked over to my parents' house to collect my things. I had nothing packed; I wasn't expecting to be whisked off into marital life the night before. Gary and I sat in my bedroom, drinking homemade lemonade, as we packed up my childhood memories. We didn't talk most of the time. It was too tempting to speak of our plans, and we couldn't afford for my parents to have been eavesdropping.

"Well, we're done," Gary informed my parents.

My father and mother were sitting at the kitchen table drinking lemonade. My mother smiled slightly and called my siblings in from the backyard. Each of them hugged me and said goodbye. My two older sisters seemed to be jealous that I was leaving. They had not yet been given a proposal. Little Jon, on the other hand, was more than a little upset to see me go. I was the closest sibling to his age, his playmate. Those days were gone, though. As I embraced Jon, his pudgy arms wrapped around my neck, I realized how scared I was. I began to cry, and he followed suit as we continued in a long hug.

"Don't cry, Carly! If you stay here then I'll color you a pretty picture. It'll be really, really good," Jon assured me. I just looked at him through my tear-clouded eyes and smiled.

"I have to go, Jon. But I will come back and visit you, okay?" It was a lie. I knew it was, and when I said it, I couldn't help but be filled with anxiety. I asked myself a question that would be repeated in my mind many times thereafter: Was leaving Deally really the right thing to do? Everything I'd ever known was in that town.

"We love you, honey," my father said, still sitting at the table.

"We want to give you something," my mother said, before leaving the room. A moment later she returned with a statue of a goddess that the Deally church worshipped. She was a thin, lanky deity with long, flowing red hair. She was holding one of the sacred texts in her hands, as if to be reading it. The goddess was seated on a large, moss-covered rock. Though she was wearing no clothing, her hair was sufficient to clothe her nakedness.

"This is all that your grandmother left behind when she left Deally so long ago," she reminisced bitterly.

I realized this was my mother's way of acknowledging my relationship with my grandma. On the contrary, it seemed to have made a mockery of it. I wasn't even sure that I believed in Deally's god or goddesses. No one spoke out against the church, though. The last person to do that was Cynthia Fagetti. I vaguely remember her. She had told a friend that she didn't care to go to church anymore. The friend warned her to stop slandering the church, but when Cynthia simply stopped going to services, she also stopped being in existence in Deally. I was four or five when that happened.

"Thank you both so much," Gary said, snapping me out of my own thoughts. He took the small statue in his arms and thanked my parents once more.

As we walked home, each of us holding a box, I peered over the top of my belongings to look at Gary. He was a good guy. I still wasn't sure why he had asked me to marry him. Had he somehow known that I wanted to leave, I wondered. It was a question that gnawed at me ever since that first morning at Gary's. I had woken up in a strange bed. I was frightened for a moment, until the previous day flashed to my mind. I looked out of the open bedroom door to see Gary, still asleep on the sofa in the living room. At that moment I began to question him in my mind. He had been old enough to marry for some time, and I had only been old enough for a few days. Why me? Had I been picked out ahead of time? Had he been waiting for me to grow old enough? It didn't make sense.

Gary looked over the box in his arm and met my glance. "What?"

"What?" I answered back.

He rolled his eyes, and we continued the walk to his house. *Our* house.

31

THREE

The boxes laid on the floor in Gary and my living room. I didn't see the point of unpacking. I sank into the couch and paged through the Deally Chronicle. Our engagement had made the news. I looked at the grainy photo of Gary, holding the stupid yellow roses. They always took photos of the guys when they bought yellow roses. Next to Gary's photo was another like it of a guy named Swede Tyran. Swede had apparently proposed to Helen Mann's parents three days ago. I sighed and turned around on the couch to see what Gary was doing in the kitchen.

"Don't look!" yelled Gary playfully. "I told you that I'm going to make dinner, but it's a surprise!"

I turned back around.

"I'm so bored," I mumbled. "Besides, isn't this a sin?"

"Yeah, yeah. The fiery ocean is calling my name, right? Me cooking, instead of my wife, is going to kill my chance of an afterlife." He laughed.

I could hear him chopping something. I tried to imagine just what he was making. Men in Deally do not cook. The chopping stopped and suddenly it was very quiet. I could hear something on the stove boiling.

"Hey, Carly?"

"What?" I asked, being sure not to look back in his direction.

"I didn't mean to call you my wife just then. I mean, I know that's what everybody thinks, but I don't want you to feel awkward." I couldn't help myself from smiling when he said this.

"I didn't even notice." It was quiet again; just bubbling water. After a moment I heard the chopping commence once more.

In the end, the surprise dinner was spaghetti and salad. It was pretty good, too.

"So, how did you learn to cook like that?" I asked, as we washed dishes together. Another sin on Gary's part.

"Well, I always watched my mom cook and I used to taste the different spices and stuff. I guess I just sort of picked up on what went well together. When I moved out on my own, I had to fend for myself, so I had to make my own food." He scrubbed a plate and handed it to me to dry. His pinky finger lightly grazed my hand in the process.

"So, that's another peculiar thing about you. Nobody else in Deally ever just moved out on their own that I know of. How is it you got to leave your parents' house without getting a wife?" He handed me another dish, but our hands didn't touch this time.

"When I turned nineteen, my parents told me that I had one more year to find a wife. If I didn't find one, they said they would take me to Tom and see what he wanted to do with me. I didn't find a wife, obviously. On my next birthday my dad, after plenty of yelling, took me to Tom's house. I was terrified he would put me into the priesthood. So, I told him that I was waiting for my chosen girl to turn the appropriate age. The compromise was to let me move out on my own, into the house my parents had prepared for my future family, with the condition that I would have a wife within the next two years."

"So…Does that mean-"

"Look," he cut me off, "I didn't have a plan. I was just postponing the inevitable. My time was getting close. I know that my dad would have had me put into the priesthood. I had to choose someone who just turned thirteen so that my story would match up."

"Oh," I said, taking the last dish from him. I didn't know what to say. "But…"

"Carly. I don't want you to be upset. *Are* you upset?"

"It's just that I'm confused. You seemed so sincere on the street the other night. I thought…I don't know what I thought."

It was quiet as Gary and I stood in front of the sink, no longer any dishes to fill the silence. He sighed and walked into the living room. I watched him sit on the couch with his hands cupped over his face. He seemed frustrated. I didn't understand what had just happened.

I stood in front of the sink for what seemed like forever. I didn't know what to do. I had to pass by Gary to get to the bedroom, so going to sleep wasn't an option. I wanted to avoid him at this point. I sat at the dinner table, my back to the living room, and twiddled my thumbs together. I thought about Gary. Ultimately, he was just some random guy. I wanted to be indifferent. Just as I was trying to muster up some resentment, I remembered his pinky finger. It had

34

touched me when we were doing the dishes. It shouldn't have meant anything to me, but for some reason it did. It kept me from getting angry at him. He had only chosen me to avoid the priesthood, but I had looked past that, because of his pinky. I laid my head on the table and sighed. Gary appeared on the opposite side of the table.

"I'm sorry," he told me, sitting down. "I admit that I brought you into my life for selfish reasons. *But*, I believe that it's no coincidence things ended up this way. Obviously, we were meant to be together in this. I think if you could see it that way too-"

"It's fine, Gary," I interjected. "If we are going to get out of Deally, that's all that matters to me. And we're going to have to work together. Plus, you know how I feel about marriage. If you *did* like me, if you *were* planning on marrying me, well- it would only make me dislike you." Gary stared into my eyes, a contemplative look on his face. He then stood up and walked back to the couch. He laid down there and threw a nearby blanket over himself. I wished for a moment that we were going to get married, but reminded myself what we *were* planning was much better.

That night, I dreamt about our great escape. I woke up at around four in the morning, when Gary jumped into bed with me. I shot upward, and he covered my mouth with his left hand. His right hand's index finger rose to the front of his lips. I was confused and groggy. I would have screamed if it weren't for his hand covering my mouth. He whispered to me in the darkness,

"Someone is outside. I think they suspect we're not a real couple." I looked at him doubtfully. We had only been "together" for a few days. Why would anyone have reason to suspect we were faking our relationship?

Gary removed his hand from my mouth and I whispered back to him,

"What?" My eyes adjusted to the dim light and I could see he was looking around the room, listening for something. I sat still and listened as well. I looked over at the row of windows on the far wall. There was a light, like that from a flashlight. Gary's arm pushed me down onto my back. He laid beside me.

"Pretend to be asleep, Carly," he whispered. I squeezed my eyes closed tightly, lying perfectly still. My eyes were so tightly closed I almost didn't notice the light change around me. It went from dark to bright instantly. After a few seconds, it was dark again. I waited until Gary tapped my shoulder to open my eyes.

Gary was sitting up beside me, in that listening mode again.

"Do you think they're gone?" I asked quietly. He didn't respond. We were both quiet. I could hear my own breathing, my own heart beat. I was carefully exhaling when a crash arose from outside. It sounded as if someone had knocked over one of the metal trash cans outside. I jumped abruptly at the sound and embraced Gary.

"It's okay," Gary assured me, "They're leaving." Just as he said that I heard a car's engine start up outside of the house.

"This isn't good, Carly." Gary slipped out of my frightened hold and stood beside the bed. The light came on as he began pacing back and forth.

"We are obviously under surveillance," he said, his feet moving swiftly beneath him.

"Can they do that?" I felt dumb as soon as I said it. They could do whatever they wanted. In Deally, there was no such thing as a police officer. The church controlled everything, and by the roar of the engine outside, it was easily concluded that the church elders were behind this surveillance.

"Why would they think we weren't a real couple?" I asked.

"I don't know. Maybe Liam put it together somehow. He knew that I had talked about leaving Deally in the past, and he knew you had doubts. Didn't he recommend the doubters ritual to you? Isn't that what you said?"

"Yes, but if that were true, wouldn't he have recommended you for the priesthood like he did Marc? Forget about me, you would be in training right now."

"No, no, no," he still paced the room as he continued, "You don't recommend that a church elder, or anyone in his family, do *anything*. That undermines the authority of the elder. You can conduct an investigation though." He stopped pacing and shook his head with a look of distraction.

"What does this mean?"

"I don't know. I don't know." He rubbed his head like people do when they get a headache. "It means we just- we have to leave when nobody knows."

"But the plan was to get permission to do our shopping, and use that as our out. It's tradition for engaged couples to go outside of Deally to buy whatever they need."

"I know, but it just won't work!" He yelled. I shut my mouth. He took a cleansing breath and went on, "If we're under surveillance, you can bet we'll get followed out of town. I'd say we should leave in the middle of the night, but obviously there's a chance someone will be outside of our window. Then, if we get caught, there's no going into the priesthood. No making you my brain-washed secretary. No, it will be something much worse."

Gary let out a big groan and sat on the floor, against the wall.

"What's worse?" I asked.

"Remember Cynthia Fagetti?"

I was afraid he would say something like that.

"Let's leave right now," I suggested desperately. "Whoever was here left. We could get out right now."

"On foot? That would never work. The elders all have cars. It would only take them minutes to find us in the morning."

"Gary, I'm not waiting until this investigation is over. That could take forever, and what could we ever do to prove we're a *real* couple anyway?"

It was quiet. I could almost feel the anxiety in the air. "I don't want to stay here forever," I went on after a moment.

I was on the verge of tears. I crawled out of bed and went into the dark living room. I groped my way through the room and quickly found the statue my mother had given us.

"Do you see this?" I said, coming back into the room. "This is the only thing my Grandma Freedom left behind. She got out, Gary."

I let the tears slip out. I didn't want them to. I thrust my arm forward and let the statue roll off my fingers. I listened to it thud on the carpeted floor, and as if the sound was my cue, flung around face first into the bed, burying my face in the pillows. More tears flooded out.

"We'll get out, Carly. I will get you out of here."

I felt the bed shift as Gary sat next to me. Warmth covered my shoulder. I realized it was his hand. I sat up and looked at him, wiping my eyes thoroughly. I sniffed and leaned toward Gary with puckered lips, reaching for an embrace. As I leaned forward, the distance between us stayed the same. He was leaning back, to avoid me. I returned to a normal sitting position and reminded myself of Gary's not wanting to marry anyone, let alone me. I just looked at him, speechless.

"We'll get out, okay?" Gary assured me. I nodded, trying my best to pretend nothing had happened.

Gary went back to the couch and seemed to have fallen asleep immediately. I, on the other hand, could not get to sleep. I laid there feeling like an idiot. Why had I tried to kiss him? I felt like nothing would be the same now. I convinced myself there would be tension in the morning. Although, I hoped we could go on pretending nothing awkward had gone on.

~~~

There *was* tension in the morning. I knew I needed to address it before it got too uncomfortable.

"Look," I began, "I am really sorry about-"

I was interrupted by a doorbell. Gary sprang to his feet at the sound and whispered hurriedly, "Hold that thought."

He jogged on tip toe over to the front door and peered through the peep hole. I watched him jump backward at the sight of whoever was there. He then ran to the couch, scooped all of the bedding into his arms and threw it into the bedroom. I sat at the table. Frozen. Who could it be?

"Hold on!" Gary yelled to the door. Rather, the person behind it. He fluffed up the flattened pillows on the couch, then opened the door. Tom Deally was on the front stoop.

"Hey kid!" Tom sang happily. I tried to wipe the confused look off of my face before he saw me.

"Carly!" He hollered across the house. I waved. I meant to say the word, hello. A wave was as close as I could get to that.

"How are you Tom?" Gary asked, motioning for him to come in.

"I am great. I wanted to come by and see how you two are doing."

The two of them sat at the table with me. I found an extra glass and filled it with orange juice for Tom. Honestly, I was uncomfortable playing hostess, but I tried my best to emulate what my mother might do. Tom took the former egg plate and helped himself to the remaining pancakes and bacon.

"This looks great, Carly. You really lucked out with this one, Gary. Most new wives have no sense when they're in the kitchen."

I smiled as sincerely as I could, knowing Gary had made every meal since our "engagement" started. I didn't know how to cook, and I almost felt like an intruder in his kitchen. Cooking was like a hobby for him.

"She is quite the cook," Gary laughed.

We made meaningless small talk as Tom ate what was left of our breakfast. It wasn't until the last bite that the real reason for Tom's visit was revealed.

"Well, as you know, it is generally the tradition for new couples to go into one of the surrounding towns and pick up furniture, cookware, whatever they might need, really. Now, I have got a treat for you two," he said with a dry laugh, "Normally we arrange for a cab to come and take the couples into town, but you are very special to me. Gary, your family is very close to me, and your father is one of my closest friends. Honestly, I'm surprised you didn't end up marrying my Rebekah." I was slightly offended by that remark. I looked at Tom. He smiled at me, and I noticed syrup crusted around his mouth from the meal.

"Sorry, Carly. You are a fine girl. Your family is close with mine as well. Your brother has become very close with me through his training for the priesthood, you know."

I winced at the thought of Marc in the dingy church basement.

"My point is, I would like to take you two personally, in my car."

"Really?" Gary said, through a smile that looked pasted on. "We are honored. Why should *we* get special treatment?"

"For all the reasons I just mentioned," Tom stated coldly.

I began busily wiping down the table-top and clearing away dishes. I believe it's what a real Deally wife would have done at that moment.

"What do you think, Sweetheart?" Gary asked me.

I was standing at the sink, relishing the sound of the word *sweetheart* rolling off of Gary's lips, directed at me. Then, I realized I needed to answer him. *What would a real Deally wife say?*

"Absolutely," I responded cheerfully, spinning around to give an approving smile. Of course it was an act. I didn't want to go. Gary didn't want to go. There was no other option, it seemed.

"Great. I'll go warm up the car," Tom told us contentedly. He meant now.

Tom went outside to warm up his car, and we scrambled to come up with items to buy. We decided to buy a toaster that could take bagels. In addition, we would get a new bed. Frame, mattress, the works. Gary suggested that this would be wise, because it alluded to the idea that after sleeping in the previous bed together, we found a new one a necessity. Hopefully, this would convince Tom Deally of the validity of our relationship, though it had none.

After a long day of shopping with Tom Dealy, whom insisted we buy all sorts of things we had not discussed, we returned home. I went into the kitchen to set up the new toaster, and Tom helped Gary set up the new bed. I realized that if I was quiet I could listen to their conversation. I stood very still and lifted my eyebrows in an attempt to hear more clearly down the short hallway. The first voice was Tom's.

"So, how has it been with Carly?"

"It's been fine."

"Well, you're getting a new bed, what did you do to ruin the last one?" Tom laughed.

I felt my face turn red when he said that, and I started to fiddle with the toaster again. I couldn't help but wonder what Gary had said to his question, though. I let my curiosity keep me quiet enough to hear Gary explain that I simply preferred a plusher mattress. It was quiet after this, with only the sound of tapping. I suspect the tapping had something to do with assembling the new bed frame, or taking apart the old one. Aside from the tapping, it was quiet for a time.

"What are you doing?" Tom asked, suddenly.

"What do you mean, Tom?"

"Be straight with me. Do you and Carly really have the connection you thought you would?"

"Yes," Gary replied.

"Maybe I should rephrase the question. Do you two even like each other? The reason I ask is that there has been some concern that you two are putting on some kind of a show."

"Why would we do that?" Gary asked with a laugh.

"You would have to tell me, Gary. You see, I didn't believe the talk. I know you pretty well, and I know Carly. She comes from a good family, and you do too. That was part of why I came along with you today. You know, you never once held hands or kissed or anything."

"Well, Carly isn't comfortable showing affection in public," Gary rationalized. Quiet again.

"No. I think it's you, Gary. I see the way Carly looks at you, and smiles at you, and laughs at your jokes. She really loves you, but I'm worried you are having trouble adjusting to married life. I feel partially responsible for advising your father to allow you to be a bachelor, and live alone. You know, that was a privilege no one else has ever gotten. I want to encourage you to stick to it, and let her take over things- like cooking."

"What?"

"No newly engaged girl can cook that well. I knew breakfast was your doing. Look, it isn't a huge sin, but it is a sin, to keep your wife from her womanly duties."

"Yeah. Uh, thanks. I'll take your advise to heart, Tom."

"Good. Now, I'm going to leave you two alone. I think you can handle this bed without me."

"Thanks for the help," Gary said.

I heard footsteps in the hallway. I returned to fiddling with the toaster. Tom came into the kitchen.

"I'll see you at the wedding," Tom told me, as he left out the front door. I listened for his car engine to start up. I ran back to the bedroom where Gary was.

"What happened?" I asked Gary. I knew what happened, of course, but I wondered what he would tell me.

"Tom Deally is convinced we are a couple. Yeah, he said it was obvious that we loved each other a lot. I guess we did a pretty good acting job." He didn't make eye contact with me. I felt a little sick.

"Yep. I did some good acting," I laughed nervously.

"Yes, well…Let's get out of here," Gary asserted, leading the way to the kitchen, where we always did our planning.

"If we want to get out before church, we've got until tomorrow night."

"What are we going to do?" I asked. Leaving before church services was smart. There were all sorts of weird ceremonies that went on during engagements, and I wanted no part of them. Weird customs aside, I didn't want to step foot into another church as long as I lived.

"Tom Deally's car looked pretty easy to drive. I think I'll steal it," Gary told me nonchalantly.

"Um. You want to steal Tom's car?" It sounded like a horrible idea.

"Yes. I think I could pick up driving pretty easily. I was watching him today and it didn't look too difficult."

"How do you think you'll even get the car, Gary?" This was not at all what we had discussed prior to this moment. This was a totally new plan.

"Leave it to me. My family goes way back with the Deallys- as far as security system codes go," he said slyly.

"No way. You know their code?"

"The truth is, I picked out their code, and their son, Bradley, picked out my dad's code. I was like seven at the time, but I still remember it."

"Wait. Why not just take your dad's car? Wouldn't that be less dangerous?"

"Honestly? I'd just rather rob Tom."

"And you really remember the code after all of this time?"

"Well, I actually memorized it on purpose…I guess I always knew I'd need it somehow." His eyes looked distant, but I didn't question his thoughts at that moment.

"Anyway," he continued, "we'll get the car, go as far as a bus station, ditch the car, and get on a bus. If we pay a couple dollars we can go for miles."

"Really? Well, let's do it then. We can just go and go and never look back." I was thinking of all of the billions of people we could meet on the way.

The next morning my mother called. She missed having me at home and wanted to have lunch. Gary thought it was a good idea, to keep any suspicion at bay. We would be leaving that evening. Finally!

~~~

"How is everyone?" I asked my mother, as we stood in what used to be my kitchen.

"Jon misses you the most, but your sisters seem to have adjusted well in your absence. They like having more room to themselves, I suppose. As for your father, he would never admit it, but he misses you. He wasn't even this bad when Marc left us," she laughed.

I had to stop myself from asking questions about Marc.

I *did* have a question I wanted to ask, though. It was a question that I would never again have the opportunity to ask. I felt it was necessary to risk whatever reaction it might evoke from my mother.

"Mom." I had to pause. How would be the best way to go about this? "So, you know how Grandma Freedom left Deally when you were little? Well, I always sort of wondered what happened to my uncle. I know he's like the black sheep of the family, and it's not like I want to follow in his footsteps or anything, I just wonder what happened with him. I guess what I'm getting at is this: I'm a woman now, and I hoped you would indulge my curiosity. The rest of the family is great, but I feel like I'm missing a part of the puzzle."

My mother looked at me, her dark eyes almost flickering somehow. I wondered if I had gone too far. Her eyes dropped from me to her plate of food. She seemed to be intently studying her sandwich.

"Have you been pretty successful cooking for Gary? If you want, I can give you some tips."

"No, Mom. I'm doing just fine cooking, okay? Can't you just say so if you don't want to talk about my uncle? I mean, I guess I'll just talk to Hallie. She's always been the open one, anyway." I rose from my chair slightly, for effect. I knew I would be stopped. She was always competing with her sister, Hallie.

"No. Hallie won't tell you anything. You want to hear this from me. Believe me." She paused for a moment, and it seemed to me she was mustering up some sincerity.

"First of all, his name is Eric. He was only a baby when my mother took him from us. He moved with her to Elkston and grew up, being raised by her. They started attending a Christian church and got fanatical about it."

I had heard about Christianity, and it surprised me that Grandma Freedom had gone to a Christian church. When we studied religion in school we were taught that it was one of the most dangerous "false religions" of the outside world. Whenever Deally lost a member of the community, it seemed to be attributed to Christianity or atheism. That was another dangerous belief system, we were taught.

"Did Grandma always go to a Christian church?" I asked, slightly amazed.

"That was how she was raised, and when she left Deally, she went back to it. Eric was raised in it. He is convinced that *our* religion is false, and not his!" My mother had a huge smile on her face when she said this. I had never seen her looking as happy as at this moment when she told me of Eric's religious ignorance. She laughed a moment before continuing her story.

"Well, he would always send us letters. They started off nice enough. He

43

seemed like a good guy, someone who just wanted to know his family better. Eventually, his motives became clear. He wanted to convert us to his religion. I never understood it. Why would you want to convert someone to a religion that is so obviously wrong? You would have to be really stupid to follow a religion that says that God had a son, and that there is no goddess. If there's no goddess, how can there be a son? It's impossible. I wrote a few letters to him, trying to help him see how illogical it was, but Eric was so steeped in this theology it was impossible to change his mind. He kept insisting that we 'accept Christ in our hearts'. As if the Eternal Home of Glory could be attained by simply *accepting* something. The point is, he was crazy. I imagine he still is. He hasn't sent a letter in quite some time, I suppose because no one ever writes back." She stopped for a sip of lemonade before going on. "He ended up being a priest in the Christian church. Actually, they don't call them priests. *Pastors*? I think so. It doesn't really matter. Carly, I know he seems like a total idiot, but we must remember to pray for him. He is just another-"

"A misguided soul?" I asked, before she could finish. She nodded and took another sip of lemonade. Even though religion in general seemed to be a sham, I wanted to meet Eric. If he was raised by Grandma Freedom, he couldn't be that bad.

"Did you save the letters?" I asked.

"Yes, he is my brother after all. It's the only connection I have to him."

"So, would it be too much to ask to see the letters?"

My mother looked at me with eyes that said 'no' before her mouth opened.

"Actually, did he send letters to Hallie, too?" I asked, before she could verbalize the no.

"Hold on, Carly," she said, with a lowered tone. She walked out of the room briefly and returned with a small tin box. She open it up on the table before me, and revealed at least thirty letters inside.

"Do you want to take them home to look at later?"

I was shocked at the offer. I felt like she was testing me somehow. Her eyebrows slowly raised, and she wetted her lips. I shook my head no and laughed,

"I'm not *that* curious about the guy! I mean, he's obviously crazy, right? Why would I want to read his ranting?" I looked at the letters, shuffling through them, as if to be only semi-interested. I made a mental note that the last letter had a return address of a place called the Roman Chapel. I would ask Gary about it later. Maybe we could find some refuge there in our travels. After all, this uncle of mine wouldn't take me back to this place, thinking what he did of it. I hoped.

"This has been really nice, Mom," I told her sweetly. "We'll have to do it again soon. I have to go if I'm going to get dinner done at a decent hour for my sweetheart."

"How is that going, Honey? Are you loving it?"

"I really am, Mom. Gary is amazing."

I smiled and gave her a big hug before leaving. I wasn't sure at that moment if I would see her again. I imagined another tin box in her room, full of letters from me. I was on the front lawn when I had this mental image come to me. I wanted to turn back and hug my mother one more time. I knew she would be suspicious, though. She loved me, but she was not naturally loving, she was suspicious of people and their hidden motives. I just kept walking.

FOUR

I waited anxiously, staring out the giant window beside the front door. It was nearly 1AM. Gary had gone to Tom Deally's house, on a mission to steal his car. That was an hour ago. I knew it would take him a long time to get to Tom's house on foot, but I was hoping the time would fly by with all of the excitement. Just the opposite happened. Time seemed to stand still, the clock didn't seem to do anything. I actually changed the clock batteries in the process of waiting, because I was convinced it was running slow. I sat, tapping my right foot. All of my anxiety seemed to be concentrated in that one part of my body. After what seemed like a lifetime that wasn't my own, I finally saw headlights. I ran outside to see Gary in the street. Sure enough, he had done it.

I jumped in beside him with the backpack we had stuffed with clothing and money. I sat silent in the front passenger seat, watching Gary drive. I was afraid if I said anything I would somehow ruin the moment, somehow my voice would alert Tom Deally and all the church elders of what was going on. When Deally was well behind us, and Gary seemed to have the hang of driving, I had to speak.

"So, how did it go?"

"We're in the car, aren't we?" Gary replied, keeping his eyes strictly on the road ahead.

"Are we seriously here? We are in the car, Deally is behind us, and we are on our way!" I couldn't hold in my excitement any longer. I poked my head out of the open window and screamed,

"*Woohoo! Goodbye Deally!*"

Gary started laughing uncontrollably as we went down the dirt road. We were still in the countryside where Deally was so well hidden from the outside world. We would soon be in a place where we'd be free. I felt so liberated at that moment.

"Alright. Alright. We need to compose ourselves. I'm not sure this is safe. Driving, and laughing, and screaming in the middle of the night," Gary said, still laughing.

"Alright, but as soon as the sun rises, I'm starting another round of laughing and screaming."

"Fair enough."

When the sun finally rose in the purple-streaked sky was the next time I said another word.

"How did it go, really? How did you get the car?" I stared out the window at the houses that were beginning to pop up between the giant evergreen trees.

"I was right about the security codes. Nothing has changed. I just went to the outside keypad and entered the code. I deactivated the security system, and then I was able to pry the garage door open from the outside. When I got in there it was pretty scary. I thought I saw a dog or something in the darkness. I thought it was Mitsy."

"Mitsy?" I had to laugh. Mitsy was a shaggy yellow dog that the Deally's had a long time ago. Mitsy died before I was even born.

"I stood there for a while before I realized Mitsy wasn't alive anymore."

"Maybe it was her ghost," I teased.

"I think it was probably just my nerves, but it was still pretty scary."

We both stopped talking as a sign came into view on the side of the road up ahead. *Welcome to Elkston: Home of the Original Turkey Pot Pie*. I looked over at Gary to see him smiling. The first sign of outside civilization. We both took a deep, sobering breath of air. Air that *didn't* float around in Deally. Somehow, it was sweeter.

I stared out the window at the places that I so vividly remembered from my childhood visits. There was the old general store where Grandma Freedom used to buy my siblings and me ice cream cones. Then, a few blocks over was the road that led to the lake where I had learned to swim. I wondered if I could still swim; it had been a long time. In a few moments I saw a house that triggered lots of memories. It was a two-story home, painted white, though it was peeling in spots, with small windows every few feet along the walls. The front lawn looked unkempt and there were a lot of little yellow dandelions growing in the midst of the tall grass.

"Hey, Gary. Can we stop?" I asked, quietly, as we came by the house.

He must have been aware of what this town meant to me, because he seemed ready to pull over at any moment. We came to a stop in front of the house where sin did not exist. I got out of the car, and Gary followed behind me. The place looked abandoned. I looked through one of the small windows by the door.

It was very dark inside, and not much light came through the small windows, so it was hard to see what was going on inside. I could make out a few old chairs, but that was it. It looked so empty. Still, I almost expected Grandma Freedom to come around the corner into the living room with cookies and milk on a fancy silver platter. Then, she would invite me inside to eat with her. Maybe we would put together a puzzle. My favorite puzzles were of the bearded man she had so many of. Grandma had a liking for tan, bearded men, I had thought.

I stood at the window, playing over and over again that scenario of Grandma Freedom coming out to greet me with cookies and puzzles. When it didn't happen, I felt something within myself break. I turned to see Gary. He was looking down at his feet, seemingly bored, but patient. I allowed my knees to give, and the rest of me sank against the wall, leaving me sitting in a pile on the front porch. A deep sadness washed over me. I had never felt anything like that before, not even when Grandma Freedom died. Not even when Marc was taken away. I realized that what I dreamed of leaving was behind me, and what I dreamed of going to didn't even exist. This fountain of emotion showered down on me, and overpowered any sense of resistance I had had in the past. I began to sob right there.

Grandma Freedom was not coming. She could never know that I left Deally; she could never know that the statue she left behind was the same statue I left behind. She could never know. I had left my only family behind, and I suddenly longed for little Jon's embrace. I wanted to be sipping my mother's lemonade. I wanted to be fighting with my sisters. I wanted to go back.

Gary sat down beside me. I did have *someone*. He could be trusted; we had gone through this together. I turned to him and cried softly,

"This is my grandma's house. We used to sit out here at her table and talk about all the different kinds of birds that would fly by. Her favorites were the hummingbirds, but I liked the blue birds best." He smiled at me and remarked,

"Hummingbirds *are* the better bird."

I actually laughed.

"Where is she now?" Gary asked.

"She died. I guess she's… in the fiery ocean," I cried.

"No. She's not there," Gary said plainly, opening his hands palms up. "And, to be clear," he continued, "We don't have to believe that anymore. That stuff only applies in Deally. Not out here. Not here where your grandmother lived. She can't be in the fiery ocean, because she lived, and she passed away, out

49

here."

I remembered my grandma's words. *At my house there are no sins.* I studied Gary's face. He looked certain of his words. His blue eyes stared straight back at me and his mouth was set in a thin line. A convicting stoicism shown through his expression. So, it was decided. I believed Gary, and I believed Grandma Freedom. She couldn't be in the fiery ocean. Believing anything else was too painful.

"Well, we should get going," Gary said suddenly. "Tom will realize his car is gone soon. We need as big a head start as we can get."

"Yeah. Okay," I sniffed.

We drove for a few more hours until Gary decided it was time to find a bus and ditch the car. We ended up leaving the car in some briar bushes outside of a city called Kingston.

We got on the bus, for a handful of change, and rode as far as we could, to another bus stop. We continued bus-hopping, and by the time we were on our third bus we were exhausted and almost immediately started dozing into sleep.

I tried not to rest my head on Gary's shoulder and fall asleep. My eyelids were heavy. I kept my forehead against the window. Watching the road whirr by seemed to lull me further into slumber. I blinked my eyes, a few long, labored blinks and fell into a dream.

Suddenly, I was on Tom Deally's porch, pleading for my life. I was on my knees before Tom and many community members, some I did not recognize. I knew that Gary and I had been caught, and Gary had already been taken away. I was crying and trying desperately to speak. I was mute. No intelligible words came from my mouth- only cries and whimpers. I was continuing my struggle to speak when someone in the crowd shouted, "Kill her too!"

I knew for certain what fate Gary had found. I fell on my face before the people as they mocked and jeered. Still, no words came out as I pled for my life. I was suddenly short of breath. I gave up on my attempts to speak and labored to take a breath.

I woke from my dream, choking on the air. I was wide awake now. Gary was alive. I examined his face closely- he seemed to be resting peacefully. I took a few easy breaths and reminded myself where I was and what was happening. We were on a bus, far from Deally. I was safe. Gary was safe.

Gary snuggled into my shoulder. At least *he* was having a restful sleep. I shut my eyes and hoped to enjoy the same peace. It took some time, but I found myself in a state of rest once again. Sleep came.

I woke up every few minutes to look around and see how far we'd gone. I began to doze off again when the driver yelled,

"Last stop before we turn around folks!" Gary sat up straight in the seat and looked at me groggily.

"Let's go."

We sat at our forth bus stop together, in a city whose name escapes my memory. It was probably about 36 hours since we'd left Deally.

"I'm starving. Can we ditch the bus thing for a while and get some food?" I asked.

"Okay. We should probably try to figure out where we're going anyway. We'll find somewhere to talk," Gary replied with another yawn.

"Are you tired?" I laughed.

"Yeah, yeah."

We walked down the street a ways, looking for a restaurant. I could hardly keep my focus with all the traffic speeding by. I had never seen so many cars. They were all so beautiful. All the colors of the rainbow, and more, were represented on the busy street. The different styles amazed me as well. Some looked like boxes with wheels, others were shaped like beans, and some looked like buff bicycles.

When we got into the restaurant, a place called *Mary's Bakery*, I immediately noticed how different all of the people outside of Deally looked. I hadn't really taken it all in before. In the restaurant, though, I couldn't miss it. Everyone inside seemed to be around Gary's age and they wore a lot of black. In Deally, you only wear black when you're going to a baptism. They had crazy hairstyles as well. Some of them had brightly colored hair that shot into the air like blades of grass. One girl had multi-colored strands of hair, ranging from red to green to purple. In Deally there were not people who looked like this, and in Elkston there were no people who looked like this. I was surprised to see them; I had thought the folks in Elkston were a good example of what the outside world was like, but apparently it was only a small sample of billions.

"Wow. Can you believe the way these people look?" I said quietly. Gary stood beside me in the entry way. He smiled at me and said,

"This is just like TV."

We walked up to the counter and stared at the chalkboard with "Today's Specials" written on it. I had no idea how to order. I had eaten fast food in the past, but I never had to order it myself. Grandma Freedom always ordered the food for me and the rest of the grandkids.

"Hey. Can I help you guys out today?" the woman behind the counter asked. She was a round woman in her mid-thirties. She was a pretty woman, I remember thinking, but I wondered why she had a metal bar going through her lip. I assumed she was in some sort of accident, and I didn't ask any questions about it.

"I'm not really sure," Gary yawned.

"Sounds like you could use some coffee, Honey. How do you take it?" she asked with a chuckle.

"I don't know. However is easiest for you to make it, I guess." Gary seemed out of his element, but then we were in the same boat.

"Okay. Black coffee it is." The woman smiled and looked at me. "Anything else, for either of you?"

"What's good, food-wise, here?" Gary asked with a serious face.

"I'll just get you a couple of our sandwiches. The special today is ham and swiss. Now, go have a seat and I'll bring you that coffee," she told Gary.

"She was nice," I told Gary, as we sat at a table against the far wall.

"Yeah, but what do you think *coffee* is?"

I shrugged my shoulders. I thought maybe it was some kind of dessert. When Mary returned she had two sandwiches, wrapped in cellophane and a cup of hot liquid.

"Black coffee," she said, setting the cup in front of Gary. She placed a slip of paper beside the cup as well. The woman, whom I'd concluded was Mary, went back to her position on the other side of the bakery, behind the counter.

"Don't I need a spoon for this?" Gary asked, mostly to himself. It was obviously soup, this coffee, but no spoon was provided.

"You must not need one. She would've given it to you. It's slurping soup."

He looked around the restaurant and saw that no one else had spoons for their coffees either. He rubbed his hands on his pant legs anxiously, then lifted the oversized cup of soup to his mouth. As he set the cup down a bitter look crossed his face. I had to laugh a little.

"That's the worst soup I've ever tasted," he whispered.

"Maybe it's an acquired taste," I suggested. He offered me a drink, but I wanted no part in this coffee-soup tasting experience.

"Alright. Where are we going?" I asked, leaning in close over the table.

"I don't have any particular place in mind," he told me. I picked up the slip of paper Mary had left on our table.

"What is this, anyway?" I asked, disregarding the previous topic of conversation. I slipped the paper toward Gary gingerly. It was a receipt, to be paid off before we left the bakery. Unfortunately, we knew nothing of receipts, and when we left the restaurant, Mary was in the back, unaware of our departure without payment. We simply assumed we had eaten in a very benevolent woman's bakery.

"Who knows?" Gary said, pushing the receipt aside.

"Oh! Wow, I can't believe I forgot to tell you."

"What? What did you forget to tell me?"

"I have an uncle."

"That's good. I guess," he replied, with a confused look.

"No. I mean, what if we go and stay with him for awhile? He is a..." I trailed off, wondering if I should tell Gary of my uncle's profession.

"What?" Gary demanded.

"Well, he's a Christian priest, or a-"

"A *pastor*?" Gary asked.

"Yeah, I guess. But, maybe it's not a good idea. I figured as long as he's not in Deally it's *something*. Someone we can trust. I know he would never turn us in."

"You *know*?" he asked, with raised eyebrows.

"I don't *think* he would turn us in," I said, editing my previous statement. "If Christians are as against Tom Deally's Reformed Church as Deally residents are against Christianity, I think we're safe."

"You're right. He probably wouldn't turn us in. My only question: *Do you think he'd try to get us to become Christians too?*"

53

I remembered what my mother told me about the letters he'd sent her and the family.

"Yes. Not right away, though. He was in contact with my family for a while before he even mentioned religion, according to my mother."

"I suppose we'd only need his help for a while, until we find a way to make it on our own." Gary contorted his face around in funny positions, something he did when he was thinking. His lips pursed and moved from side to side, as his eyebrows waggled.

"Do you know where he is?" Gary asked.

"Yes…Well, no. I mean, I saw the letters he sent, and the last return address was a place called the Roman Chapel. I didn't catch what the city name was, but if we can find the Roman Chapel we should be able to find him. His name is Eric."

"Alright."

~~~

We asked around, and found that the Roman Chapel was a fairly well known place. It was in the town of Carl Hill.

We boarded a bus which would take us to Carl Hill. It was a much nicer bus than the others we had previously ridden on. It was a little costlier too. We only had a few dollars left in the blue backpack we'd been toting around. Had we not stolen our lunch, we wouldn't have been able to board the bus at all.

"This bus is really nice. There's even a bathroom in the back," Gary informed me.

"That's neat," I said, as I realized a bathroom break would be necessary.

"I'm going to use it," I said, getting out of my aisle seat beside Gary.

The bus restroom was rather cramped and smelled horrible. I plugged my nose and quickly took care of business. I had to unplug my nose to wash my hands. I squeezed some pink liquid soap into my palm and ran the cold water. Apparently there was only a cold knob on the sink. I started wondering when all this traveling would finally be over. I wondered when Gary and I would be independent and living in the outside world, with Deally behind us. That was when it occurred to me, right then as I reached for a brown paper towel, that we would probably go our separate ways. In a few years we might be able to pass by each other on the street somewhere and not recognize one another. For some reason this disturbed me. I felt very vulnerable at that moment, very alone. That feeling was short lived, because Gary came pushing through the door at that moment.

"What are you doing?" I squealed in shock.

"*Shh!* Liam just got on the bus," Gary told me in a quiet voice, closing the door hurriedly behind himself.

"What?" I felt my heart immediate begin to thrash.

"They must have found Tom's car. I don't know how they figured we would be on *this* bus." He rubbed his temples and suddenly got a disgusted look on his face.

"What did you do in here?" he asked, pulling his shirt collar up over his nose.

"Nothing. It smelled like this when I got in here, okay?" He looked at me doubtfully.

"*Seriously,*" I stressed, plugging my own nose.

"Okay. I'm sure it smelled even *worse* before you came in, right?" He laughed.

"Gary, what are we going to do? We can't stay in here forever." This was no time for jokes.

"I know. Liam didn't see me when he got on the bus, but he'll certainly be looking around for us."

"Unless he's got to use the restroom," I whispered sarcastically. I was trying to blame this on Gary in my mind, but it wasn't his fault Liam was on our trail.

We waited in that disgusting bus bathroom for so long we no longer needed to plug our noses. Slowly, my anxiety was losing its edge.

"I hope nobody comes back here." My heartrate was almost normal again.

"Yeah."

Gary seemed uncomfortable being trapped in that little space with me. At the time I was sure it was because he had grown embittered toward me. I tried to guess how long he'd felt that way, and how long we'd been in that tiny bathroom together. When I got bored with that thought, I began to guess what Liam might do if he found us. I wondered what happened to Cynthia Fagetti. I wondered what happened to all of the people that Gary's father had been employed to track down. I wondered why it was so horrible for people to leave Deally anyway. Why did it matter if someone didn't want to be a part of Tom Deally's stupid community?

"Gary?"

"What, Carly?" We both had sad tones to our voices.

"When did you realize you had to leave?"

He cleared his throat, and stared at his feet. "I don't really know. I think I just always kind of knew there was something else out there."

"Yeah. I know what you mean, but I had a moment when I knew I had to leave. I mean, did you have one of those *moments*?"

"Well, uh…I don't really know. I guess it was- Well, you know my dad is a church elder, right?"

"Yeah." He looked at me for a brief moment and returned his gaze to the floor.

"It's just…I had a sister who…" He seemed lost in thought, his sentence incomplete. I didn't know he had a sister.

"What? *You had a sister who…?*"

"She was a little older than me. She got taken away." His voice cracked and it seemed to stop him from going on. I remained silent. Gary let the silence sit for a while, and then continued, "She was five years old. I remember her, even though I was only three or four. She was my best friend, you know?" He looked as if he could cry. "All of the church elders have to give over their first-born daughter. Tom still has her, as far as I know. Everybody knows about Carmen, but nobody knows about his other *wives*."

"*The daughters?*" I said to myself. I was in shock. I had never imagined this could be what was going on in the underbelly of Deally. I had never imagined it. Never. But it had to be true. Gary had nothing to hide, after all.

"Yes. The daughters. And he takes them when they're only five. I can't get over-" He stopped mid-sentence again. A tear rolled down his left cheek, followed closely by many others on each side. He was crying, quietly.

"So, I guess that was my moment," he said solemnly.

Gary looked so sad, so broken-hearted. His story made me think back to the night Marc was taken away. Only, he would be out of the basement after five years, and Tom Deally's secret wives, well they never surfaced in the public

56

again. I looked at Gary, as he wiped the tears from his face. I thought that if we weren't in that bus bathroom that he would've walked away now. I had never seen him cry before. It was quiet for a long time, until Gary said,

"Carly, we are getting off this bus, and when we do, Liam is not going to take us with him."

We would have to confront Liam one way or another. The bus was only going to stop once, and then turn around. If Liam got off of the bus, we'd be getting off with him. If he stayed on the bus, we would be walking right past him.

"I guess we may as well go out there now. He's going to see us eventually," I told Gary.

"Let's go sit down. It smells in here anyway."

We walked out, and as we settled back into our seats he turned around to see us. He waved and smiled, as if greeting old friends. Liam stood up and walked back toward us. He took the vacant seat ahead of us, turning his body around, sitting on his knees, and facing Gary head-on.

"Hey you two," he laughed, "you wouldn't be on your way to the Roman Chapel, would you?" He looked directly at me and grinned.

"How did you find us, Liam?" Gary asked, with a resentful tone.

"Well, I just had to speak with Emma Samson. You know, your mother-in-law. She told me all about a chat she had with your *wife*."

"She's not my wife. *Surprise*," Gary responded sarcastically.

"Not now, but perhaps we can get that taken care of back in Deally," Liam said, still smiling from ear to ear.

"We're not going back," Gary assured him.

I was afraid to say anything, I just watched them go back and forth. None of the other passengers seemed disturbed by what was going on.

"Oh, that is interesting. According to the bus driver we've got about a half hour to talk about that."

"Liam. Level with me here. What's the point of bringing us back? We'll just leave again," Gary said.

"I don't think so," Liam answered with a smirk. "You see, Tom Deally has elected to take Carly into his care, and your father has agreed to see you go through a rigorous training program before entering the priesthood. I believe *ten* years of solitude was agreed on. Personally, I thought you ought to be put in prison, but your father seems to be rather fond of you."

I was really scared now. Since when did Deally have a prison? And who might be occupying it now? I didn't even want to consider what he meant by Tom taking me into his care. I felt tears surfacing. I had to keep my composure. Gary said we weren't going back. I had to keep my confidence in his ability to keep his word.

"The problem with your plan is that we're not going back," Gary said, echoing my thoughts.

"You're obviously not following. I am bringing you two back to Deally. Your consent is not necessary, nor is it expected."

"What makes you so sure you can get us back, all on your own?" Gary asked, defiantly.

"Oh. You think *I'm* the foolish one, then? Interesting. I've got Tom Deally, Priest Kaine, and your father waiting at the bus station in Carl Hill. It should be no problem at all bringing you back. *And her*," Liam said dryly, looking at me.

I averted eye contact, looking down at the back of the seat ahead of me.

"I will die before I go back with you," Gary assured him, through gritted teeth.

"You know, you two could have had quite the life in Deally. If only you'd have played by the rules. But I could see it all along. When I heard you wanted to marry *Carly Samson*- I knew there would be trouble." Liam looked at me with searching eyes. "You were always asking questions. No answer was good enough for you. Carly, you didn't know your potential. Your family was in such good standing with the church, with the community, with Tom. Aside from your brother, that is. Can you believe Marc tried to escape from the church?"

I looked up at him suddenly, new information hanging in the air.

"Oh. I guess you hadn't known that. Well, it's true. I never thought he was priest material. That is, not *voluntarily*. The beatings pretty well did the trick. He's the most spiritual one in the whole program now," Liam laughed.

My tears found an escape hatch somewhere, and without my permission, streamed down my cheeks.

"Crying won't change anything. He's nearly indoctrinated enough to serve in the church." Liam reached toward me, as if to wipe the tears from my face. Gary's arm intercepted his reach, grabbing and twisting it awkwardly backward.

"Let go," Liam whispered in anger, "You're only making things worse for yourself."

"Do not threaten me, and do not touch Carly," Gary whispered back. The intensity in his voice scared me, almost more than Liam.

I watched Gary begin to loosen his grip. Liam's face took on a look of relief, when suddenly Gary pulled Liam's arm back into the previously painful position. Gary leaned in close to Liam and whispered,

"This is what happens when you threaten people."

Liam laughed, mockingly. Gary shook his head with disapproval, and then pulled on Liam's arm so hard and fast, I am positive it was ripped out of the socket.

"*Ahhh!*"

Liam screamed loud. The bus came to a halt in the middle of the street. A cacophony of squealing tires and shouting people could be heard behind the bus. It was a wonder no vehicles slammed into us.

"*What's going on back there?*" The driver took a look at the scene and cursed a few times, I guess after realizing he would have to deal with a violent injury. Gary immediately rose from his seat, grabbed my hand, and ran to the front of the bus. I gripped his hand tightly, following behind him. He pried the bus door open and continued in a sprint down the street. The driver continued to curse as we exited, finding ourselves in Carl Hill. We didn't know where the Roman Chapel was, or if it was even a good idea to go there, now that everyone seemed to know where we were going. We disappeared into an alley nearby and watched as the bus made a sweeping U-Turn and left us behind.

"Gary!" I cried out, embracing him tightly. I was shaking. My heart revisited its thrashing exercises from earlier and my lungs screamed for air. It was suddenly, in that moment, very clear to me what leaving Deally really meant. We could possibly have been killed. Was it worth it? I gulped air.

"I told you. We're not going back. Whatever it takes. *We are not going back*," Gary whispered, in my ear, returning my embrace with a squeeze. My breathing regulated as he spoke those words. I hugged him tighter now.

"I trust you."

A woman in a blue dress walked past us, staring suspiciously. I closed my eyes and listened to her heels click, click, click away. Every face in that alley was dark and distorted, probably from the lack of lighting between buildings, but I convinced myself it was something more sinister.

"Carly, you've got to calm down. We've got to find your uncle."

I took a deep breath and let go of my grip on Gary.

"Okay. Okay. Let's go ask someone for directions or something," I recommended, with a shaky voice. We got out of the dark alley and asked a red haired woman down the street if she knew where the Roman Chapel was. She informed us it was only two blocks up, six blocks over.

As we walked, I couldn't help looking at every face and peering into the window of every passing car.

"Carly, it's going to be fine. You've got to stop looking around like that. You're drawing more attention to yourself than you realize." He took my hand in his, walking closely beside me on the sidewalk. It helped my nerves a little. I felt safer. I had just seen Gary use his hands as a weapon. Now, one of those weapons was wrapped warmly around my own *non-threatening* hand. It was comforting, but a little scary. That hand that was so warm and gentle now was tough and dangerous only a short while ago.

After a while, we finally stood in front of the Roman Chapel. I had stopped looking around so much by then, my focus on the hand covering mine.

"Should we go in?" I asked Gary. The place looked deserted. There was one red, boxy car in the parking lot. The church shared a parking lot with a similarly deserted house with the words *Real Estate* etched on its big front window. I assumed, in desperate pessimism, that the red car belonged to someone in that building, and we were not safe.

We made our way to the double doors and Gary pulled on the left door handle. It didn't budge. He pulled on the second door. Same story.

"I can't believe this! Hello?" Gary yelled, pounding his fists on the doors. "I guess we'll have to come back-" He looked at the bulletin board. "*Sunday at 10:30!*"

I followed Gary down the street. We were almost on the other side of the parking lot when we heard a man calling in our direction. My initial reaction was to run. It had to be Liam or one of the elders, I thought. Gary turned around to see a tall, black haired man standing in front of the church. I didn't want to turn, but Gary took my hand and spun me around. I saw the man holding open one of the double doors. As we returned to the building, I couldn't help but stare at the man. He had a very dark skin tone. He was black. In Deally, and even in Elkston, I hadn't seen anyone so dark.

"Can I help you folks?"

"Yes, we are looking for a man named Eric. We were told he's the pastor here," Gary told the man.

He looked at us with a funny expression. "Eric hasn't pastored here in almost a year. *I* am the pastor. Can I help you with something?"

"We really need to see Eric. Can you tell us where we can find him?" I asked.

"Yes, but what does this pertain to?" the pastor asked.

"Look, we just escaped from a fanatic religious group, which Eric was born into, by the way. And we need to see him. *Now*," Gary explained bluntly.

"I'm his niece," I explained further.

The man looked shocked, a little wide eyed. Who could blame him?

"My God. Lord, thank You," the pastor said aloud, seemingly to no one.

He motioned for us to come into the church. We followed him to a room I assumed was his office. He sat behind a large oak desk and motioned for us to sit at the chairs across from him. I noticed a painting on the wall that looked very familiar. I thought maybe the man in the painting was famous. Though, it crossed my mind that it wouldn't make much sense for me to recognize someone famous, having lived in seclusion all my life.

"My name is Pastor Michael Freeman. I must say, I am very thankful to see you here. May I ask, which of Eric's sisters is your mother?"

I wondered how he knew about my family.

"I'm Emma's daughter, Carly. And this is my friend, Gary," I answered.

"We were supposed to get married," Gary said with a slight laugh, then continued, "I should probably tell you something. There are some people in the city looking for us, and they know that we were planning to come here."

The pastor jumped out of his chair.

"My God, help us! Why didn't you tell me before? Let's drive to Eric's house, then. No need to stick around here." He led the way out of the building and toward the red, boxy car outside. Gary sat in front with pastor Michael Freeman, and I took the backseat. We pulled out of the parking lot and I couldn't

61

keep myself from staring into all of the passing car's windows. I knew Tom and the others would catch on to the fact something went wrong when the bus showed up late, with Liam, Gary and I all missing.

"Carly, your uncle is going to be so excited to see you. You as well, Gary. I know he prays often for his family, and the other residents, in Deally. Also, I need to ask: these people who are after you, they don't know where Eric lives, do they?"

"No. I don't think so," Gary answered.

"No. They shouldn't," I confirmed.

"Good," the pastor sighed.

I continually stared out the window at passing cars. The further we drove the more I felt like there was something swimming in my stomach. Every car that passed was a threat. I sunk down in my seat, turning to look out the back window as another car passed.

"There they go!" I doubled over and clutched my stomach.

Gary turned to look and saw the same thing I did- a car with a familiar face pointing back at us. I struggled to breathe, closing my eyes tightly. The swimming creature was making its way up my chest cavity and into my throat. I swallowed it back down.

"They are turning around," I heard Gary say. A car honked long and loud behind us.

"What? Who? The people from Deally?" the pastor asked.

"We've got to get out of sight," Gary insisted.

"Okay, okay," Pastor Freeman mumbled to himself. "Lord, help us. Cover their eyes, make us invisible, something…" He continued unintelligible mumbling as he drove.

I opened my eyes to see where we were going, and where Tom Deally and the others were. Only a few cars behind us now. The pastor got off of the main highway and drove through a big box grocery store parking lot. We almost hit a green SUV pulling out of its parking space. There was a honk. Tom Deally drove close behind, and he almost hit the same vehicle. I closed my eyes again. More horns. Pastor Michael Freeman must have known what he was doing, because within the next few seconds we were safely hidden in a dark garage of some kind. He had drifted the red, boxy car around the corner of the store building and into a narrowly opened door. We were inside a fairly expansive loading area. There was a bread truck to our left and a few men struggling with oversized packages. I looked back to see the narrowly opened door closing, as a blur of blue passed by-Tom Deally and the rest.

I let out a huge, staggered breath. "Are we alive?"

"Yeah," laughed Gary, "we are alive. I do not know how, but we are!" He sounded exhilarated. The adrenaline rush had gotten him pumped up, but made me a nervous wreck.

"Praise God," the pastor sighed.

The bread truck driver looked over at us from inside his rig. He looked a little confused, and equally annoyed. "Hey! This is truck parking only! Customer parking is in the front."

The pastor looked back at the closed garage door. "You wanna open the door back up for us then?"

The man hit the steering wheel with a fist, got out of his truck, and jogged toward the closed garage door. He pressed a button and jogged back as the door began to open again. We exited and continued a back roads journey to my mysterious uncle Eric's house.

The sun and moon were both visible in the sky when we arrived at Eric's home. Night was quickly approaching. The faces would begin to look sinister again. I shuddered.

"Here we are," Pastor Michael Freeman announced. We had driven up a long gravel driveway to get there. There were massive evergreen trees on each side of the driveway. When the house came into view, it was a beautiful two-story structure. It had an unpainted wood finish, and a huge window on the left side of the front door revealed what looked like the dining room. The wrap-around porch was sprinkled with lawn chairs, two of them set up beside an old card table.

When I stepped out of the car I could faintly hear water. I suspected there was a brook somewhere buried within the conifer trees surrounding the house. Gary stood beside me in front of the house. I instinctively reached for his hand as we walked toward the front door. Michael led the way. He knocked on the door and took a step back, waiting for an answer. I watched through the dining room window for any signs of life. There seemed to be no one home. The door cracked open, adverting my attention from the seemingly vacant scene in the window.

A little face poked out of the doorway. She must have been about six years old. Her face looked serious at first, but after seeing Michael at the door, it lit up. She burst out of the house like a ball of pure energy and gave Michael an excited hug.

"Hey Hannah! How are you doing tonight, Sweetie?" Michael greeted her.

"I'm great!" she exclaimed, still hugging his waist.

"Who's out there?" A male voice came from inside.

The little girl, Hannah, turned around toward the open door and yelled back,

"It's Pastor Michael, Daddy!"

She ran back from where she had come excitedly, leaving the door open. Michael walked inside slowly and waited for someone to greet him. I stood quietly, holding Gary's hand, outside. I hadn't thought that little Hannah had seen us.

The man whose voice had called out earlier emerged to greet Michael. They exchanged some words, which I couldn't make out from where I was. The man, who I assumed was my uncle, walked outside and stood before Gary and I. He looked at each of us for a moment before asking,

"Are you really who you say you are?"

"Are you Eric?" Gary asked. The man nodded. I took note of his appearance at that time. He kind of resembled Grandpa Sid. He had the same short, black hair and athletic build, though he wasn't very tall. Upon closer inspection, I saw he also had Grandma Freedom's kind eyes, complete with her thick, dark eyelashes.

"You're Emma's daughter?" he asked me. Michael was no longer in the doorway.

"Yes. I'm Carly," I responded, quietly.

"And you are?" he asked Gary.

"I'm Gary. We both wanted to leave Deally, so we did." I was surprised at Gary's matter-of-fact attitude when it came to our escape. Personally, I thought it was a pretty big deal- bigger than, *We both wanted to leave Deally, so we did*.

"Wow," Eric said, frowning slightly. "Well, come inside."

We followed Eric into the living room, where Michael was already sitting on an oversized couch, chatting with a plump, blonde woman. Hannah was playing with another little girl. They both looked like the blonde woman.

"Hannah, Joanne. It's time for bed," Eric told them. They both gave him a hug and scurried off to another part of the house. The blonde woman beside Michael stood up, smoothed out the front of her brown sundress, and turned her attention to Eric. I assumed Michael had told her who Gary and I were.

"Where is Jacob?" Eric asked the woman.

"He's doing some homework in the office," she replied.

"Could you tell him we have company, please? I want him to come out here when he gets done with his work."

"Sure, Honey." She hurried off in the same direction the girls had gone earlier.

"Have a seat," Eric directed us. I was still holding Gary's hand, and I suspected that I sat a little too close to him.

"How do you two know each other, again?" Eric asked.

"I asked Carly to marry me, in order to avoid the priesthood. She agreed to it, on the condition that we leave Deally together. We left a few days into our engagement period. If you're wondering, we are not involved romantically. That was just a con so we could get out of Deally."

I thought maybe we should stop holding hands after that, but we didn't.

"Eric, you are my uncle." *Well, that's obvious*! I stumbled over my own thoughts. I needed to explain why we were there in Eric's home, why he shouldn't have just turned me over to my parents. I needed a better reason than, *you are my uncle*. "Uh- Anyway, my mom told me about you, and I can remember seeing pictures of you at Grandma Freedom's house. And- well, this was the only place I could think to go," I told him nervously.

"Carly," Eric replied with a warm smile. "My mother- your grandmother- talked about you a lot. She would say that you liked to swim in the river, even though the rest of the kids didn't. She said you were very curious, about lots of things, too. I remember thinking that it was a shame I would never get to meet you. But here you are, the little girl that my mother loved so much." His smile extended to show his off-white teeth. "The point is, I am honored that you would come here. You are both welcome here."

This man seemed so sincere.

"I didn't know that she talked about me," I told him.

"Oh yeah. She did. She was always happiest when some of the grandkids were at her place. She said there was something special about you in particular."

"How come you never came over when we were there?"

"There were some rules, some stipulations, about you kids going to her home. One of them was that I could not come around."

"I miss her," I sighed.

"Me too," Eric nodded. His smile was gone now. Just then, the blonde woman reentered with a tray of sandwiches. She set them down on the short table between the furniture. She left the room again, and the next time she entered she had a tray of orange colored beverages.

"You must be starving," she said to Gary and me. She sat beside Eric on the couch. She smiled the same warm smile my uncle had used to make me feel a little less uncomfortable in this strange place.

"This is my wife, Beverly," Eric informed us. She shook our hands, forcing us to break grip with one another.

"We have no where else to go," Gary said, sounding business-like.

"I understand that, and we will make arrangements for you to stay here as long as you need," Eric promised. "I would like to know exactly what the situation is here, though." He seemed intent on hearing about how we managed to leave Deally.

Gary told most of the story, and I jumped in with details at times. By the time we finished, all of the sandwiches were gone, and the drinks were finished. I was thankful for Beverly's refreshments; we hadn't eaten for almost a day.

"Are either of you interested in more food or a refill of orange juice?" Beverly asked. Everyone was satisfied. She grabbed the trays and went away somewhere for a few minutes. I remember thinking that Beverly and her hospitable ways would be fitting in Deally. It reminded me of the security I had left behind, which I hated. I almost hated Beverly too. Thankfully, her sweet personality averted my attempts at disliking her, even a little.

"Eric," Michael yawned, "I've got to get going. My wife is going to have a fit here pretty soon if I don't get home."

"Use the phone on the way out, if you like," Eric offered.

"It should be alright," Michael said, standing to his feet. "It was good to meet you two. I wish you the best. God bless."

"Thank you, Michael," Gary said.

Eric walked Michael to the door. As they rounded the corner, out of sight, a thin teenage boy with dirt-blonde hair entered the room. He looked at us with confusion, and without a word, left the room. A moment later he came back, Beverly ushering him into a seat.

"This is my son, Jacob," Beverly told us. "This is Carly, and Gary. Carly is your cousin from Deally."

Eric came back into the room and I heard a car start up outside.

"No way. You're one of my cousins from Deally?" Jacob marveled. "Dude, how did you get out of there?"

I was a little thrown off by that word: *dude*. I looked at him and said, "Yes. I am from Deally."

"How old are you?" he asked.

"Thirteen," I told him.

"Oh. I'm older. *Fifteen*. What about you, Gary?"

"I'm twenty-one," he answered.

"Hey, you can drink," Jacob remarked with a laugh.

"Hey!" Eric said in a demanding voice. Jacob looked at his father with wide eyes.

"Just a joke, Dad." They both smiled at each other.

Meeting these people- my relatives- was strange for me. I didn't know them, but they knew about me and my family, about Deally. They seemed to even have a good gauge for the emotion I was going through. Everything they said seemed to ease my mind. Jacob had a way of diffusing tension with humor. Eric was a calm man, who seemed to be smart, and his wife was a pleasant woman whose sweet personality made Gary and I feel comfortable right away. I liked these people. I could get used to them being my family.

That night, Gary and I were put into different rooms. Gary's room was next to Jacob's, in a sort of storage room, attached to a rarely-used bathroom. An air mattress was set up for him. My room was across the hall in the family's guest bedroom. We didn't have those in Deally. I tried to think about the oddities of the outside world, in an upbeat sort of manner. This was to keep my mind off of the fact I felt uneasy sleeping away from Gary.

Beverly talked to me, as she showed me the luxuries of the guest bedroom. It was Saturday night, and she invited me to go to church in the morning with them. I told her I didn't particularly care to go. She understood. She said it would be fine if I stayed home in the morning, and Gary as well, if he felt the same way. They would bring home lunch afterward. I was surprised at Beverly's response. In Deally, no one was that casual about differing beliefs, especially religious beliefs. I recalled a time when Marc said he'd like to stay home from church- he was practically dragged there anyway.

I laid in bed, awake, not wanting to turn off the light. I noticed a painting on the wall. It resembled the one in the pastor's office. I tried to remember where I knew the man in the portrait from. I stared at it for a long time. A few minutes before I dozed off into sleep, I realized that man resembled the one in Grandma Freedom's puzzles. I still didn't know who the man *was*, though.

I dreamt about Grandma Freedom that night. I was helping her put together a puzzle, one of the tan, bearded man. Grandma Freedom was wearing a stunning red dress and shining black shoes. The room we were in was not one I remembered. It was painted a brilliant blue color, but out of the corner of my eye, the color looked purple and yellow in spots. I was just about to ask her who the man in the puzzle was when I shot up in bed. I was awake suddenly.

I had heard a noise. I peered around the room. The door was cracked ever so slightly. There was a shadow at the base of the door. The door opened a little more. I sunk into the bed, burying myself up to the eyes in a blanket. I listened to the door open further. My heart began to race as I wondered who could be at the door. I wished Gary was in the room to protect me. I imagined it was Tom Deally at the door, coming to take me away. Then, a quiet voice came from the door.

"Carly? Are you awake?"

It was Gary's voice.

"I'm awake," I answered through blankets. I could barely make out Gary's silhouette coming into the dark room. Someone had apparently come by and turned off my light after I dozed off. Gary sat beside my bed in a big wicker chair.

"I can't sleep," he whispered.

I thought he'd fall asleep more easily if he were lying in bed.

"Carly?"

"Yeah?"

"Eric told me he's going to call a friend of his tomorrow. He's a police officer. Did Beverly tell you that?"

"No. We just talked about church."

"Oh. Are you going?" he asked me. He seemed to forget the prior topic.

"No. Did *you* want to go?"

"I thought about it, but I don't know if I'm ready for religion to be a part of my life again so soon. You know?"

"Yes," I responded rather loudly. I forgot how late it was. I turned to look at the digital clock beside the bed. It was nearly four in the morning.

"We should probably stay out of the public for a while anyway," Gary reasoned. "I'm sorry I woke you up."

I could hear his weight shift on the chair.

"Wait," I whispered. He leaned back in the chair again. "I wanted to say thank you. For everything, Gary. Everything that you've done for me."

I couldn't see his face in the darkness. He didn't say a word. I wondered if he was having second thoughts about leaving Deally. Second thoughts about getting involved with me. I opened my mouth to ask him if that was the case. Before any words came out, though, he spoke.

"I would never have been able to do it on my own."

With that, no more words were said. I got a glimpse of Gary as he left the room, the hallway light played on his face.

FIVE

"Carly?" Beverly sang, standing in the doorway of my room. "Hey, I just wanted to let you know that we're heading off to church. I didn't want to wake you, but I thought I should remind you in case you got worried."

"Thanks Beverly," I replied sleepily. The door closed, and I pondered sleeping in a bit longer. After all, I'd never really slept in before. In Deally, it was a sin to sleep in. Laziness was a sign of disobedience to God and the community. I can remember when I was about eight years old and I had accidentally slept through my parents' calls to wake up. I was awakened rather harshly after that. My father threw some cold water over me and quoted the sacred texts. The quotes were about washing away laziness and disobedience. That whole day I was squeezing water out of sheets and pillows, and soaking up water with a sponge.

The memory was too fresh in my mind. I got out of bed and looked through the only piece of luggage Gary and I had packed- the blue backpack. I had three shirts and one pair of shorts. I looked at the clothes in disgust. I hated the bland looking clothes. Deally's one clothing shop got all of it's items from outside shops and boutiques, yet nothing they sold looked even remotely like the popular styles worn outside. The people outside of Deally wore bright, bold, exciting clothing. Deally only had dull items to offer. I wished I had something else to wear.

Reluctantly, I pulled on some dull clothing. Faded green shorts with no pockets, a pastel yellow sweater, and my only pair of shoes, which were plain and white. I had only changed clothes one time since we'd left Deally. Though the clothes were bland, it was nice to have fresh clothes on. Gary had packed one extra pair of brown khaki pants. I wondered if he wanted them. He hadn't changed since the night we left. I walked across the hall to Gary's room and knocked. As I waited for him to open the door I took one last look at my clothes. I found myself tugging at the yellow sweater with contempt.

"Good morning," Gary answered, with a mysterious red toothbrush hanging out of his mouth. He motioned for me to come in.

"Where'd the toothbrush come from?"

"Eric showed me where some extras were at," he answered, making his

71

way through the small room, and into the bathroom. I followed him and stood outside of the open bathroom door.

"Do you want these pants?" I asked, the khakis in hand.

"No. I'm okay," he answered, standing in the same outfit from days ago. I shook my head and wondered how he could be so gross.

"I need some more clothes," I informed him.

"What? Three outfits won't do for the rest of your life?" Gary laughed.

"No. No, it won't do," I sighed. Sarcasm was not attractive on him.

"Do you want to go find something to eat?" I asked. Gary smiled at me and shook his head vigorously. I rolled my eyes.

After venturing downstairs, we found a fresh plate of waffles on the kitchen table, with a note beside them from Beverly:

Enjoy the waffles. If they're cold when you

get to them, feel free to pop them into the toaster.

-Bev.

I had two waffles, and Gary ate the rest. It was a substantial plate of waffles, but somehow, he managed to eat every one of them. He stained his shirt with syrup in the process as well.

"Are you just going to walk around with a syrup stain on your shirt all day?" I asked him, with a light laugh.

"It doesn't bother me. It'll be something tasty for later," he said, while waggling his eyebrows cheekily.

"Wow. That is disgusting. You should really find another shirt."

"Why do you care? It's not your shirt," he said with a hint of annoyance.

"Yeah, but I have to look at it. Why don't you borrow one of Eric's shirts? I don't think he'll mind."

"No, Carly. It's not a big deal." He seemed on edge now, which didn't make any sense to me.

"You are really annoying," I said under my breath.

"Well, you're extremely irritating. You sound like my mother or something. You're like twenty years younger than me!"

"Try *eight* years, stupid." I am not some little kid, I thought. I left the table and busied myself with dishes.

"My name is Gary, not Stupid. *Stupid.*"

"Okay, my name is Stupid now?" I asked, with a high pitched voice, as I scrubbed an extra syrupy plate.

"It must be. It fits you perfectly," Gary proclaimed.

I turned around to face him. He was the stupid one, I thought. I looked at him, without a word, then looked at the half soapy, half syrupy sponge in my hand. I took about two seconds to consider my action, then threw. The sponge bounced of off his chest and landed in his lap. He slowly looked down at the sponge, and then back at me. I couldn't help but laugh.

Gary tried to look seriously at me, but when I didn't stop laughing he finally cracked a smile.

"Fine. I see how it's going to be!" he laughed. He stood up with the sponge in his hand and walked toward me. I ran into the adjoining living room, screaming in delight. He chased after me. I ran around to the back of the couch, and waited for him to come toward me, then I moved to the other end of the couch. We did this little dance for a few seconds until finally Gary jumped over the couch all together and grabbed me around the waist.

"I've got you now!" Gary called out with a cackle. I squirmed to get free, but he wrestled me to the ground and rubbed the sponge into my hair.

"Stop! Stop!" I squealed. He dropped the sponge beside me on the hardwood floor and put his hands in the air, as if to say he had nothing to do with what had just happened.

We sat on the floor behind the couch, both exhausted from our little chase. I attempted to run my fingers through my hair, but couldn't.

"Sorry," Gary laughed, touching the syrupy strands of hair I had in my hand. His fingers gently caressed mine as he felt the syrupy mess of hair. I instantly remembered the night he made spaghetti, and how his pinky finger had grazed my hand when we washed the dishes. My mind then flashed to the bus ride when Gary rested his head on my shoulder to sleep.

I bit my lip and tried not to lean forward. I so desperately wanted to kiss him. I thought that I loved him. I almost thought that if I could kiss him, he would suddenly understand how I felt. He would feel the same way too.

"Gary?" I whispered, as if any sudden noise would ruin the moment.

73

"What?" he asked happily, standing to his feet. He reached for my hand to help me stand. I took it. I looked at him and sighed.

"I have to go wash my hair," I told him.

It wasn't what I wanted to say. It was true, but I wasn't planning on saying it. I wanted to say something beautiful and romantic. But I was thirteen, and I didn't know anything about romance. I knew that I got a fuzzy feeling when I thought about Gary. It was nice, but I didn't understand it enough to know if it was worth pursuing. More than that, I had no idea how to tell if Gary felt the same way.

"Go wash your hair then," Gary laughed, "and I'll finish the dishes."

I washed my hair and tried my best to push those fuzzy feelings aside. I avoided Gary as much as I could until my family got home that afternoon.

They returned around one o'clock, with chicken and fried potato wedges. I ate silently, listening to them talk about church.

"What did you girls learn about in Sunday School?" Beverly asked the two blonde girls. Hannah answered,

"We learned about how when Jesus died he had only one disciple who was still his friend. All of the rest of them left him and told people that they never knew him."

"Oh. So, did you learn about Peter, then?" Beverly asked.

"Three times!" Joanne called out, with potato in her mouth. She held up three fingers, all matted with potato mush.

"That's right," Eric laughed. "He denied Jesus three times, just like Jesus told him that he would."

Joanne and Hannah both nodded knowingly. I wondered what all of it meant.

"What about you, Mom? What did you learn in big people church?" Hannah asked. She was very cute, I thought. Joanne, on the other hand, reminded me of my little brother Jon. She was cute too, but I didn't like to look at her. I didn't know if I'd ever see my little brother again.

"We learned about how to tell people about Jesus," Beverly informed her.

"Well, I coulda' told you howda' do that!" Hannah laughed.

"Hey, Dad," Jacob began, talking to Eric, "Did you notice that new song in worship today? It was so cool. That guitar part was awesome. I'm gonna' ask Francis how he does it. I think I could pick it up pretty quick if I knew the tabs and stuff."

I wondered what Jacob was talking about as well. I didn't regret not going to church, but I did wish I knew what they were saying.

"Are you the pastor at the church you go to now?" Gary asked Eric.

"Yes. I am the *youth pastor* there, actually. That was why I left the Roman Chapel. This church was in desperate need of a youth director to come in and help out their outdated program. The Roman Chapel was doing well, and they had an assistant youth pastor who could do the job without me. I felt like moving out to Holy Haven was the right thing to do."

"What is a youth pastor, anyway?" I asked him. There were no *youth priests* in Deally.

"Basically, I'm a pastor who works specifically with the young people. We have services every week, aside from Sunday mornings, that cater to their generation. It's more set up in a style that they like, and hopefully is more attuned with what they need spiritually too," he explained.

"Yeah. Youth group is pretty sweet. I get to play guitar in the worship band. It's awesome. I can play the drums too, but we have a few other drummers, so it's better if I stick with guitar. Worship is always the best part of youth group, plus we do video game tournaments every month that are really cool too," Jacob informed us.

"Sure, and I preach too, but it's kind of lame," Eric joked.

"Pretty much," Jacob laughed.

~~~

Gary and I were sitting in the dining room, in front of the huge window. Eric was getting us ready to talk to his police officer friend. After a while, a knock came at the door.

"That must be Ian," Eric said, leaving to answer the door.

We sat in the living room and told Ian our story. I didn't want to at first, because he looked like he couldn't be trusted. Something about his demeanor reminded me of Tom Deally, and it scared me. After a while, though, I was able to look past it and I poured out my story. I don't think he needed all of the information I gave him, but I did give it to him. Detail by detail, heartache by heartache. I told Ian the whole story, and I spared no detail.

75

"Well, this is quite the story," Ian marveled.

"It's all true," I reminded him. Gary nodded in agreement.

"I believe it. I really do. We've been stacking up evidence for a federal case against Tom Deally and the other upper members of the Deally commune. So far, there's not a lot of testimony, though. We've got Ms. Freedom's old interviews on record and now this," he said, indicating the notes and recording he'd taken. "Your story has confirmed a lot of Ms. Freedom's own account."

"When do you think you'll have enough for some real action to be taken?" Eric asked.

"You know, we gather evidence and present it over and over to our people. So far, it's just not been hard enough evidence. We don't want to go after Tom Deally with a flimsy case, or speculative charges. He does still have quite a few connections on the outside, and powerful ones at that."

"We'll certainly keep praying," Eric assured him.

Suddenly my time in Deally was worth something, not just a haunting memory, but *evidence*. Getting the story out was cleansing enough, but to give it to someone who could really use it to take action- that was comforting.

Ian looked sullenly into his cup of coffee. "You know, Pastor Michael Freeman, he was pretty severely injured this morning. It seems he was locking up the church when someone confronted him."

The officer looked up now and kept his face emotionless. "We haven't been able to find any witnesses. He was staying late at the church without anyone else. I believe it was most probably Tom, or Liam, or one of them. Definitely someone from Deally. That's the only logical conclusion."

"Well, how is Michael?" Eric asked.

"He's in the hospital, and until we can get cleared by the medical staff we won't be able to find out all of the details. I'm told his condition is getting better, but he did have some broken bones. A neighbor of the church found him knocked out cold on the church steps."

"Wow, I'm so surprised we haven't heard from Margie or one of the kids," Eric said. He seemed to slump in his seat. "This is awful."

I felt myself taking staggered breaths. I imagined Tom Deally beating that pastor, but only after forcing him to reveal where Gary and I were hiding. He could be banging down our door any minute if that were the case. "Um, officer Ian?"

"Yes, Carly?"

"What if it was Tom Deally or Priest Liam, like you said? What if they know where we are?"

"Yes, that's part of what makes this so difficult. We don't know what information someone may have gotten from Pastor Freeman. So, as a precaution, we are going to post two of our officers at either end of the property. We're hoping to speak with Pastor Freeman tomorrow and get more specific information. Just rest easy for now, and we will get back to you."

"Should we stay home until then?" Eric asked.

"Yes. That would be wise."

SIX

I saw shadowy figures at every corner. I knew Tom Deally was just lying in wait to reach out and grab me. I slept with the light on. I couldn't stand the darkness. I couldn't stand the fear. I wondered if leaving Deally was worth all of this. Someone had gotten hurt because of my leaving, someone who was innocent.

"Gary, do you want to go for a walk?" He was sitting at the kitchen counter. "I just need to talk to someone."

"Yeah, sure." He hopped off of the kitchen stool, and we began to walk toward the door.

"Hey, Gary! Come look at this," Jacob yelled from across the house.

"Hold on, Carly." Gary jogged toward the sound of Jacob's voice.

I sat at the counter and waited. I had so many thoughts running through my mind; it wasn't hard to keep myself occupied. I wanted to go find that brook I had heard when we first arrived at Eric's home. Water had such a calming effect on me in the past. I needed some calm. Talking with Gary was another thing that had a calming effect. I still waited for him to return.

"Come on, Gary," I muttered to myself.

"What?" asked Hannah. She had snuck into the room somehow, or more likely, she came into the room normally, and I was too consumed with thought to realize.

"Oh, hey. I was just talking to myself."

"Oh," Hannah laughed. "That's silly. I guess I kinda' do that sometimes too, though. Especially when I play with my dolls."

"Yeah, I guess that's true." I forced a smile.

"That's still pretty silly," she laughed again. I laughed too, to my own surprise. Hannah was a sweet little girl. I hadn't really let her charm get to me before.

"So, what were you talking to yourself about?"

"I don't know. Nothing important."

"Oh, okay. Well, I really wanna play dolls now." Hannah laughed some more. "But I need some juice first!" She grabbed a small box of juice from the fridge and left the room with a bound in her step.

I sat for a moment, smiling. Then, the image of a bloody, broken pastor came to mind. What was taking Gary so long? I walked to Jacob's bedroom to see what was going on.

"Gary?" I called through the door.

I heard some rustling, and the door opened. Jacob stood there. I could see Gary sitting at a computer desk, eyes glued to the screen.

"What's up, Carly?" Jacob asked.

"I was waiting for Gary to come back."

"Oh. Well, I was showing him a little video I made. Do want to see it? We can start it over."

"No. I was just waiting for Gary; that's all."

Jacob looked disappointed. He looked back at Gary, then at me. "Yeah. Okay. Gary, Carly is waiting for you for some reason."

"Okay. I want to see the rest of this. Can you wait a few more minutes?" Gary asked, without turning to look at me.

"Forget it, Gary." I would just go on my own. He was obviously too involved with whatever Jacob wanted. "I'll just go on a walk alone."

Jacob began to shut the door. "Alright. Coolness. Thanks for stopping by, Carly."

I took a deep breath and rolled my head back and forth. Now, I would have to go out on a walk alone, not knowing if Tom Deally had gotten onto the property while a police officer let his guard down! What did it matter? If I was in danger, if I got hurt or killed or taken back to Deally- well, that would make them sorry. It was irrational, and maybe even dangerous, thinking. I was a bundle of nerves and emotion. I needed to find that brook.

I walked onto the back deck and listened. I could faintly hear the water running. Walking toward it, I was careful to keep my eyes scanning back and forth. There were lots of shadows around. There was a massive amount of evergreen trees and little shrubs all over the property. My Uncle Eric was essentially living in the forest. It was really a beautiful place. It lent to my uneasiness in a very serious way, however. Every tree was a hiding place. Every shrub was a cover-up. Something was out there, lurking. I was halfway between the water and the house when I had an all out panic attack.

Everything seemed to be swirling and spinning around me. My stomach suddenly seemed to drop. My palms began to clam up and sweat, my eyesight seemed to blur and my knees went weak. I needed a hiding place. I scrambled to my hands and knees and began to crawl toward a clump of small pine trees. If I could get into the little hiding place they formed I could get my composure back. I could get my breath back. My heart was beating so fast. I couldn't catch my breath. I continued toward the little pine tree hiding place until I finally made it. It was not a calming place after all. I felt it closing in on me. I shut my eyes and tried to slow down my heart beat. Little green and red dots were pounding and pulsating on the inside of my eyelids. I had no success regaining my normal function. I felt like I might die.

I began shaking violently. I felt my arms being scratched by the tree limbs. I began to weep. I didn't dare to open my eyes but a tiny bit, to let the tears run out. I still felt someone or something was watching me, lurking in the shadows.

I wept and shook and waited for something horrible to happen. I waited to die or to be grabbed by the strong arms of some Deally church elder. Slowly, I ran out of tears and felt my heart beat return to normal. I was drenched in sweat when I opened my eyes and looked around. I hadn't made it to the sound of the water. I had barely made it away from the house. I could still see the porch. I had probably only gotten twenty feet away from the safety of the house before I fell apart.

You should never have left, I heard a voice say. I looked around for the person who had said it, but no one was there. I felt a cold chill run up and down my spine. I had to get back to the house. The brook was no longer a priority. I needed to regain my sanity and get to a safe place to rest. I was exhausted. That was Monday.

~~~

Pastor Michael Freeman was stabilized and able to speak coherently on Tuesday. A police sketch artist took Michael's information and composed a striking image of his attacker. Gary recognized him right away when shown the picture.

"Oh, yeah. That's definitely Marcus." Gary looked from the sketch to me, and back again.

81

"I think you're right," I said slowly. "But, this doesn't make sense. He's still supposed to be in isolation for the priesthood. And he would never do this. He doesn't hurt people…"

"I don't understand it either, Carly. But, there's no doubt in my mind this is a picture of him." Gary's voice was unwavering. He really didn't have a doubt.

"Alright. Thanks, Gary." Officer Ian put the sketch back into his bag. A black man in a black suit sat beside him, quietly looking at each of us and taking notes. His face looked stoic, and he made me nervous.

"Would you like something to drink?" Beverly asked, entering from another room.

"No thanks, Bev. I'm going to be quick," Ian answered. She smiled and disappeared again.

"Apparently, Marc is more zealous than most these days," Gary said with anger in his voice. "He used to want to leave Deally. I don't understand what they've done to him."

Officer Ian had no answer.

"How is Michael? I've been trying to reach Margie but the phone's always busy." Eric leaned forward with concern. Ian did have an answer for this question, and quickly replied.

"He's got some recovery ahead of him, for sure. I think it was two cracked ribs and a few broken fingers. His face was pretty bruised when we spoke this morning as well. Everyone I spoke with seemed encouraged by his progress, though."

Eric leaned back and wiped his brow. "Good. Good. And what did Michael have to say?"

"It seems the man who attacked him was looking for these two." The black man interjected, motioned toward Gary and me. "He called them *turncoats*. He was pressing Pastor Freeman pretty good for information about their whereabouts- and about you, Eric. Freeman says he didn't give up any information. Apparently, that's why he was beaten so badly."

I felt a knot developing in my stomach. Gary asked if we were safe. It felt like someone had turned up the thermostat. I inhaled slowly and tried to concentrate. The black man continued,

"Yes, you're as safe as you can be right now. The local police have been instructed to come by the house every four to five hours, to report and investigate any suspicious activity, and to look at all visitors with suspicion in town. The best news in all of this is we seem to have definite grounds for an arrest. We're going to focus in on this Marcus guy, and we're looking into the testimony about Tom Deally's child brides as well. It's too bad about Pastor Freeman, but the truth is this outside violence may turn out to be just the break we need to get in to Deally and poke around."

"By the way," Ian announced, "this is FBI Agent Jones. He's come into the Deally investigation as of late, and it's a good thing. It's all been politics and red tape trying to take Deally down, with almost no cooperation from any agencies outside of our own force."

"Well, the truth is Tom Deally has always run a top notch organization and only lately have things gotten sloppy. Before now we've had no reason to go in, but your testimonies and this incident with Pastor Freeman have changed things." Jones crossed one leg over his lap and made a note on his legal pad. The agent showed no emotion.

"Too bad it had to happen this way," Gary commented. He looked at me; a smile flittered on his face momentarily.

"Yeah. It is," Ian said. "Hopefully we can deal with the situation tactfully. I realize Marcus is important to you both."

"He was a friend of mine as a kid, and he's Carly's oldest brother." Gary didn't elaborate or ask for mercy on Marc's behalf. I would have, if I had the stomach to say anything at all. The thought of Pastor Freeman in the hands of a brutal attacker was bad enough, but putting Marc's face to it made me feel even worse. Something was swimming in my stomach again, and it was eating away at my own delusion that all this time Marc had been fighting to find a way out of Deally. I remembered what Liam said about his dedication to the faith.

"Unless you have any more questions or pertinent information regarding Marcus or Tom Deally, we need to get going." Agent Jones poised his pen over the yellow paper and waited for any last facts. There were none.

Eric stood up to see Officer Ian and his FBI associate to the door. "Alright. We'll call you if anything comes up."

"I'm glad that's over," Gary sighed.

"That pastor got hurt because we left Deally."

Gary sat close to me and sighed. "I know."

"And Marcus did it?"

"I guess so." Not what I wanted to hear.

Eric sat down across from us now.

"I'm sorry that your friend had to get hurt." I said to Eric. I felt my eyes getting teary. "I don't know what's gotten into Marcus. He would never hurt anyone. Not when I knew him…"

"That's not your fault, Carly. Plus, if it's any consolation, I know Michael well enough to know that he would take a couple of cracked ribs for your freedom any day."

"Right." Gary said, "Most people are willing to take a bullet for perfect strangers; a beating is like loaning your buddy a dollar."

"I'm serious. He's a good man and he's serious about loving his neighbor. He'd lay down his life for a friend. That's the way he is."

"I never should have left," I said, echoing the voice in my head.

"It's better for bad things to happen in order that people find freedom than them happening randomly, without purpose," Eric said.

"I guess," I whispered. I felt a tear stream down my cheek.

"I know you're freaked out right now, but things will get better. Ian and Agent Jones are going to take care of things. Don't worry about anyone else getting hurt. Everything is working out for good," Eric said to us.

"I just get the feeling that we've done something that is never going to stop affecting people." I was trying to hold back sobs.

"You're right, Carly. What you and Gary have done will change things for ever. Deally may finally come down because of what you two have done."

"I hope you're right," Gary responded quickly. "I want to see that place destroyed and Tom Deally put away for good."

"That will come," Eric assured him. "And it will come so much faster because of you and because of Carly. You two are brave."

"Brave? I don't feel brave. I've been really *scared* lately…" I trailed off, finding it hard to go on. When I admitted my fear I found it coming back on me.

I put my face into cupped hands and cried. I didn't want this to happen. I wanted to be strong. I wanted to be brave. Gary wrapped an arm around my shoulder. I tore away from him and stood up to leave. He grabbed me in a bear hug.

"I'm sorry, Carly. I get it." He swayed a little with me in his arms. "I'm sorry about everything that's going on. I can't believe this thing with Marc. But I can promise you that even if you can't be brave, and even if you're scared, you've got me." He pulled out of the hug and looked over at Eric. "And you've got a family. Eric's right. Everything is going to work out."

"You both have a family here." Eric rose and gave each of us a squeeze. "And you don't have to *feel* brave to *be* brave. I can see it in both of you. Despite fears, you keep going. That's bravery. If it wasn't scary, well, I guess bravery wouldn't be necessary."

"True enough," Gary agreed.

I turned to see Beverly standing in the kitchen doorway with tears streaming silently down her face.

SEVEN

Eric and the family were at church. It had become ritual for them to go and leave us behind. I looked forward to my time with Gary each week. It was peaceful without the kids around, and it was nice to get to talk with Gary, without Jacob interfering. He was always dragging him away to his room to show him things on the guitar and watch movies. Now, we were sitting silently in the living room, only the sound of rain outside between us. I was enjoying the melodic sound, gentle rumbling on the windows, when it occurred to me that I felt happy. I hadn't felt that way in a long time.

"I feel good, Gary. *Happy*. I think this is new for me."

"Yeah…I think I know what you mean," Gary responded with a slow nod. "I feel it too, I think. I don't have to worry about being taken into the priesthood, or God knows what else. Maybe that has something to do with it. We don't have to be afraid of any of that Deally stuff any more."

"Yeah..." I winced a little at the mention of the priesthood. Marcus was now a powerful, menacing leader, with enough prestige to go outside of Deally on his own. It had been three weeks since Marcus beat up Pastor Michael Freeman. No one had reported seeing him since, and his sketched image was being well circulated. The police hadn't gone into Deally yet, however, something I didn't understand. "Well, I feel safe again." I tried to laugh, "Maybe for the first time."

"Me too." He went back to reading a book that Eric had given him. The rain tumbled about outside. I felt a frown developing.

"But, I also feel kind of disappointed," I sighed. Gary set the book down and looked at me, without saying a word.

"I mean, I thought it would be better. I *am* feeling good. I'm happier. I just feel let down. I imagined being happier than this. I thought I would be *really* happy, and I would feel *really* good," I explained.

"I see," Gary said slowly.

"Do you know what I mean?"

"I do, but *I* don't feel that way. I knew leaving Deally wasn't going to be

87

something magical that made everything better. It has changed a lot, and lots of things are better, but it'll never be perfect."

"I didn't think it would be perfect. I just thought it would be better. It just feels like something's missing," I sighed.

"Something that you had before, or something that you never realized was missing before, but now understand to have always been missing?" Gary asked.

"I think it's the second one," I answered with uncertainty.

"Are you sure it's not just that you miss your family?"

"I do miss them... But it's not that. I'm not sure what it is."

"It seems to me that everyone has something that fulfills them. You're still young. You have time to find what that is, and then you can do it, and you'll feel better."

"Maybe that's true," I replied. He called me young. That bothered me. In my mind I was trying to make us the same age. Somehow it was more comforting if I were older, or if he were younger.

Gary started to pick up the book again, but I stopped him with more talking.

"What is the thing that fulfills *you*?" I asked.

"Right now, it's reading. When I'm not interrupted anyway."

I shot him a look. He smiled.

"Really," I insisted.

"I'm not sure. I think I'll find it eventually. For now, though, I'm enjoying this book."

"Fine. Read your book," I conceded.

I watched him read for a moment, and wondered what the book was about. *Bible*. What kind of a name was that for a book? I figured it was a character's name in the story. I imagined a short, chubby boy named Bible, running amuck in some rural town, solving mysteries or something like that. It made me smile.

"Boredom?" Gary asked suddenly, without lifting his gaze from the book before him.

"Huh?"

"Maybe you feel like something's missing because you're bored. You haven't done anything since we got here." He looked up.

"Yeah, I have."

"What have you done besides sit around and talk to Beverly or me?"

"Uh, I've talked to Eric and the kids!" I said.

"Okay. See, you need a hobby or an activity to keep yourself occupied."

I sighed. I had never had a hobby before; why should I have one now? I was going to ask this question, when everyone piled inside of the house from the nearby front door. The little girls shook their hair with their hands, spraying water all over. It was very rainy outside. I could hear squeaking from shoes being flung off of feet. Jacob was the first to enter the room, and he sat beside Gary.

"Hey, readin' the Good Book, huh?" he asked Gary, seeing the book about Bible resting in his lap.

"Yes. It's pretty interesting so far."

"Are you reading it from the beginning?" Jacob asked, with a surprised look.

"Yeah," Gary answered.

I wondered what was wrong with Jacob that he would question the intent of someone who reads a book starting with the beginning. It was very odd.

"Well, how far are you? Still in the Old Testament?" Jacob continued his questioning.

"Yeah. I suppose I am. I'm in Isaiah. Is that Old Testament?"

"Sure is. But you're almost to the good stuff," Jacob answered with a smile, "Jesus comes in soon."

"Hey," I interrupted, "don't spoil it. I might read it after him."

Jacob smiled and looked as if he was holding back laughter. Gary did the same. Now, Eric and the rest of the family came in. Hannah was holding a bag in each hand, and Beverly was holding two bags also.

"Tacos. As requested," Eric announced.

"Let's eat, dude." Jacob grabbed the bags from Hannah, who sat down right where she was, on the floor, and resumed fiddling with her wet hair. Beverly sat the other bags on the coffee table and escorted both girls into another room with a wave of the hand.

"So, Jacob, what is a *testament* anyway?" Gary asked, picking up the earlier conversation.

"Oh," Jacob spat out in a dumbfounded way, reaching both hands into a fast food bag.

"You know, like the old and new ones you were talking about," Gary reminded him.

"I know what you're talking about. I don't really know how to explain what a testament is though."

"Mind if I take this one?" Eric asked Jacob, who nodded. Jacob held his hands up, palms out, as if in surrender.

"The word *testament* has a few different meanings. First, it's just a testimony, or a retelling, of events. It can also speak of a contract; in this case, between God and man. So, the Old Testament is a contract, as well as a collection of stories and accounts of what happened under that old contract between God and man. The New Testament is simply a newer collection of accounts, and a new contract."

"Yeah. That's what I meant to say," Jacob laughed, now finished with one taco.

"Alright. So, does that mean the Old Testament is no longer relevant as a contract, since there's a new one?" Gary asked. I can't say I was wondering the same. I was still trying to figure out where little Bible and his mysteries fit into this whole thing.

"Yes and no. The old covenant has to do with what's called the Law. It's basically the ten commandments that God gave Moses."

"Yeah. That makes sense," Gary nodded.

"Then, the New Testament has to do with what we call Grace. It is sort of a resolution to the old contract."

"How so?" Gary asked.

"Well, have you read up to the ten commandments yet?"

"Yes. They all seem pretty good to me," Gary replied.

"That's good," Eric laughed.

"So have you followed all of them, then?" Jacob asked, with eyebrows raised and a new taco in hand. Gary grabbed one out of the bag now, as did Eric. They continued talking.

"Well, most of it," Gary responded.

"Like what? Out of curiosity," Eric asked, seeming to catch on to what Jacob was getting at with his line of questioning.

"Well, I've definitely never killed anyone. I haven't stolen...I don't remember all of them," Gary laughed.

"Well, how about this," Eric began, "have you ever lied? Disobeyed your parents, maybe?"

"Well, yeah. I forgot about those ones."

"So, you can't enter into the old contract, right?" Eric asked.

"I'm not sure," Gary said, drumming his fingers on the book.

"Well, let's say God asks you to sign a contract that has the ten commandments on it. The terms of the agreement are that you have to go your whole life without breaking any commandments. Then, you will be granted a place of rest after death and have relationship with God. The question is, can you sign the contract?"

"I could sign it, but I wouldn't be able to live up to it. I've already broken it," Gary explained.

"Exactly," Eric said in a chipper tone.

Beverly and the girls came back into the room. Hannah and Joanne had dry hair now.

"Grab your food, girls," Beverly told them, "We've got to eat at the table in the dining room." The girls each grabbed a taco, with a discontented sigh, and left the room.

"Alright," Eric continued, "The thing is this: nobody can live up to the contract. God knows that. So, He made a way for us to be able to co-sign the contract with someone who could live up to the standards of the Law."

"You just said that nobody can live up to it, though," Gary pointed out.

"Yes, I did. But, there came one man who was able to do it. He became the way that we all could sign the contract."

"Hmm. So, who is this man who came along to co-sign?" Gary asked.

"I told you guys not to spoil the book!" I shouted out. They all laughed, knowing that the book was not about a young mystery solver named Bible. They didn't tell me. They just stopped talking about the book.

"Well, I guess you'll find out when you get to that part," Eric told Gary with a wink.

"Sorry, Carly. We don't want to spoil it for you," Jacob said with a huge smile.

"Thank you," I answered, returning his smile with my own smaller version.

A police car pulled up out front and Eric gave the officer a thumbs up through the window. This had become rather routine. At first the officers would come inside and chat, look around the property a little and be on their way. That had quickly gotten to be too much, and Eric insisted that he could signal them from the house that everything was fine. The officer returned the thumb signal and made his way back down the driveway.

"Hey, Dad. Did you talk to Ian about the youth conference?" Jacob asked. The officer's vehicle was out of sight behind some pine trees now.

"Yes, and everything is a go."

"Sweet! That calls for another taco," Jacob laughed.

After the tacos were all eaten, mostly by Jacob, I set out to find a hobby. I wasn't sure where I could find one, so after some aimless wandering of the house, I found Beverly. She was in the girls' shared bedroom, watching them play with some plastic dolls.

"Beverly, what should I do for a hobby?" I asked.

"Uh," Beverly laughed, "That sort of depends on you, Honey."

"Okay. But I have no idea what to do, and Gary says I need a hobby."

Beverly looked around the room and squinted her eyes like someone does when deep in thought. I looked, too. I wasn't sure what we were looking for.

"Puzzle?" Beverly asked, her eyes fixed on a shelf across the room.

"I don't know," I responded.

"Well, you'll know when it's right. So, that can't be it…How about beads? You know, jewelry making?" she asked. I shrugged my shoulders. She looked at me now as she had the room.

"You know what? Something every girl likes is shopping. At least, every girl I've known."

"I've never really shopped before. Not as a hobby anyway. There weren't many stores in Deally, though."

"I know. Please forgive me. I am a horrible person. Look at you, wearing *my* clothes. I've been trying to save up a bunch of money, but I think we need to go now."

"What are you talking about?"

"Okay. So, I didn't intend on you wearing my clothes forever. You're thinner than me anyway, and not a lot of my stuff from the thin days are left for you. I have been putting away money for you to get a new wardrobe. It's not much now, but you deserve *something*."

"Oh. Wow. I've never gone shopping for my own clothes before." I felt a smile spread across my face.

"I'm so sorry I made you wait. What time is it?" She looked at her cell phone and confirmed the time. "It is much too late now. Tomorrow we will get an early start. I'll call the babysitter and that will be that."

"Okay," I said excitedly. Shopping for my own clothes was sounding like a great hobby.

EIGHT

I held a yellow sundress in front of my self, showing Beverly from across the store. I got a thumbs up and threw it into my basket. Shopping was so much fun. I decided that it would be the perfect hobby for me. I intended to tell Beverly this on the way home. I thumbed through racks and racks full of beautiful clothing. There were neon colored tank tops, and rhinestone studded jeans. I had never worn a pair of jeans before. In Deally, all of the women wore skirts or shorts with wide, skirt-like legs. Beverly never wore jeans, as a personal choice, of course. She said she didn't care for the feel of them, so I hadn't gotten to wear any at all, even when I was sharing clothes with her. I *wanted* some jeans! I ended up with my very own, and a smile too.

"Did you ladies find everything you were looking for today?" the checker asked.

"Well, that and more," Beverly laughed.

"Of course," the woman laughed, knowingly. I laughed as well, not fully understanding how addictive shopping was in this new culture I was living in.

"Well, that will be four hundred and fifty two dollars, and twenty seven cents," declared the cashier. As Beverly swiped her green bank card through the little machine on the counter, my new found hobby died. I realized this was a hobby that took a lot of money to maintain. It was nice while it lasted, though.

Beverly treated me to lunch on the way home- a placed called *Fat Nance's*. The waiters were friendly, wearing shockingly bright orange polos, and encouraging each customer to try the Fat Nance Burger. Beverly and I declined, opting for some not-so-greasy alternatives.

"Thanks again for the clothes," I began, "And the food. And the place to live." I paused. "You really have done a lot."

Beverly smiled sweetly. "Honestly, Eric and I are more than happy to do it."

Now *she* paused, and laughed to herself. "We should have expected it. Eric and I prayed so much. For you- your whole family. The whole community, really. I guess you two are the first fruits. God does some strange things with our prayers." She laughed again, "We should have seen this coming."

95

I smiled. I was amused at the thought of them praying, thinking their God would do some kind of miracle for them. I was the one who got out of Deally, and as far as I could tell, it was without the aid of God.

"Well, in that case, I wish someone would have been praying earlier. Maybe I wouldn't have been born in Deally at all."

"I know what you mean, Carly. Sometimes the timing does seem off, but God knows when He should do things." She refolded the napkin on her lap.

"I don't mean to be rude, Beverly. I mean, you've done so much for me, and I don't want to seem ungrateful or anything like that…" I crossed my legs and waited for the words to come.

"Sweetheart, you don't need to hold your tongue with me. Just speak from your heart. I promise I won't get offended." I was caught off guard by that. In Deally, adults demanded respect, and if your heart felt the wrong way, you could be damned for speaking from it.

"Well, I was going to say that Gary and I left Deally." I waited for more words. "And, well, I guess that's it. We just left. And God didn't seem to have a part in it."

Beverly didn't look offended, but I could tell she wasn't sure what to say.

"I know this can be hard to understand, but a lot of times when God is working there is no burning bush." She laughed a little, obviously realizing I missed the allusion. "What I mean to say is that many times God is working and we really don't see it. A lot of times, we don't understand His hand in things until the very end. It's like if you were to look at a painting early on in the artist's working with it. It would look a lot like a sloppy mess in the beginning, but if you saw it at the end, you would know that the artist had created it with a plan in mind for its end result."

I must have looked as unconvinced as I felt, because Beverly frowned. "Maybe it's just too soon for you to see where God has had a hand in things."

"Yeah, that could be it." When Beverly refolded her napkin again, I rolled my eyes. Beverly reached for her purse and began rummaging through the contents.

"I've got something to give you, Carly." She pulled out a blue pen and a tube of lipstick before finding what she was apparently searching for.

"You just bought me a new wardrobe. I think that's enough for quite a while," I told her.

"No, no. This isn't really from me anyway. Actually, Eric was supposed to give it to you, but he thought it would be better if I did it." She cupped something in her hand. "Gosh, I hope it fits."

I held out my hand and received the gift. A well worn, but still beautiful, gold ring rolled out of Beverly's palm and into mine. I drew it to myself and examined it closely. A turquoise stone the size of a dime sat poised atop the gold band. I recognized it easily. I had admired this ring on my grandmother's finger many times.

"How did Eric get this?" I asked, mouth agape.

"His mother gave it to him before she died."

"Wow." I felt tears brimming up in my eyes. "But, why?"

"I think that at the end of her life, she was able to see what we couldn't. She gave it to Eric so that one day he could pass it on to you."

"What?" I looked up at Beverly, not believing what I was hearing.

"It was strange. Eric kept going over how he could possibly send it to you or bring it to you, but he's not exactly welcome in Deally. He had been writing to your mother for some time. But after a while, his letters began to come back, unopened. Honestly, we thought she wasn't thinking clearly at the end."

I slipped the ring on my finger and examined it in the light. It had lost most of the sparkle it once had, but it's value had increased considerably in my eyes. "I don't know what to say."

"You don't need to say anything."

Beverly watched me admire the ring. When I looked up she was smiling wide.

"I've got something else for you, too."

"What? This is more than enough, really."

"This isn't much, but I thought it could start you on a new hobby." She pulled a small plastic bag out from under the table. I hadn't noticed her bring it in to the restaurant.

"Thank you, Beverly." I pulled some items out of the bag and laid them on my lap to examine. A sketch book, a fat gray eraser, some black drawing pencils, and a small pencil sharpener. I remembered drawing as a child. Drawing the fiery ocean. I wondered if Grandma Freedom was there, drifting.

"What do you think?"

Beverly's voice shook me out of my thoughts. I looked up.

"It's great. I used to draw when I was younger."

"Same here. I got it in my mind I was going to be a great artist when I was young. I bought all kinds of art supplies and headed off to an art institute."

"Really? I didn't know you were an artist." I began to place the items back into the bag carefully.

"Well, I'm not. That's the rest of the story. I realized when I got into the institute that I was really not as passionate about art as I had thought. After a few weeks I got tired of it. I still have all of the supplies, though. Anything you need, I've got it."

"I'm sorry it didn't work out for you at the art school."

"You know, it was really okay. I got into another school and got a degree. In the end it worked out great. God brought Eric into my life soon after that, and then I found what I was really passionate about."

"What was that?"

"Having a family. That's been the greatest joy of my life."

I smiled weakly. I wished things had worked out with my family. If only my mother had loved to take care of her family. If only our family had been a joy.

As if she could sense my longing, Beverly spoke in a whisper to me, "I'm so happy to have you as part of the family, sweetheart."

~~~

We were both quiet on the ride home, and I went to the guest room immediately to fold up and put away my new clothing.

"Finally got some clothes, huh?"

I turned around to see Gary in the opened doorway.

"Yep," I said, with a grin. "I got you something, too."

"Really? What is it?" He came and sat in the wicker chair beside the bed, where all of my clothes were now sprawled out.

"Well, I saw this and it made me think of you," I informed him, as I dug through a big brown shopping bag. I pulled out a yellow scarf.

"Not that," I laughed. I rummaged through another bag, and felt cold plastic on my fingertips. "There it is," I said, looking at Gary.

"Well, give it here," he urged.

"Okay, okay." I pulled out a plastic case and handed it to him.

"*Whoa*," Gary exclaimed, opening the case. He put on the sunglasses I had picked out for him. They were bright red and had a black design on each side, where they went back toward his ears.

"These are really cool," Gary said with a smile, "Thanks, Carly."

"Sure. Like I said, they reminded me of you."

Honestly, the glasses were probably a more accurate picture of something Jacob would wear. Gary was sharing his clothes, after all. Though, a few days later, when Eric took Gary clothes shopping (I suspect out of guilt, after Beverly had taken me), his choices weren't too far off from Jacob's style. I think he had grown comfortable with what Jacob had him wearing for so long.

"I really do like them," Gary assured me, placing the gift under another inspection, rolling them around carefully in his hands.

"Dinner's ready!" came a call from downstairs. It was Eric. He had made some sort of famous chili that night and insisted no one be late to dinner, because supposedly it would be gone quickly.

"Let's go," Gary declared, excitedly. He made his way out into the hallway, and I followed him. As I got passed the doorway, he turned and gave me a hug.

"Thanks again, Carly. I really should be getting *you* something."

"It's all good." I laughed, finding myself using one of Jacob's common phrases. Gary turned again and we went downstairs to eat. I sat across from Jacob at the table, and he began talking to me immediately.

"You know, you and Gary should come with the youth group to the youth conference we're going to next week."

"Jacob!" Hannah whispered urgently, putting an elbow into his left rib. He set the bread on the edge of his bowl of chili and looked at Hannah with raised eyebrows.

"Yes, Hannah?" he asked, with exaggeration in his voice.

"She doesn't believe in God," she whispered, almost quietly enough for me to miss the words.

"That doesn't matter," Jacob told her and then turned his attention back to me, across the table.

"What's a youth conference?" I asked, trying to shake off the embarrassment I was feeling. A little girl, in a house full of religious people, had just announced that I didn't believe in God. I was slightly uncomfortable with that sudden segregation between me and them. Then again, I always had Gary. Hannah didn't mention *him*, though.

"It's a meeting with a bunch of other youth groups, and there will be music and special speakers and stuff. It's always really fun. We're going to stay in a hotel in the city, and there will be a swimming pool there too."

As Jacob informed me of this, Hannah was taken silently by the hand into the other room, where I could see Beverly initiate a conversation.

"I think that sounds pretty fun," Gary said thoughtfully. I was surprised at his response. Neither of us had attended church, or youth group. We had been invited every week, but we'd never gone. Now Gary was considering going for days at a time, without any escape, to a youth conference? It was odd.

"What do you think?" Jacob asked me.

"Uh, I don't know," I began uncertainly. "It would be fun to go swimming, I guess." I looked at Jacob's face when I said this. He was advertising God, and all I got out of it was a few hours of swimming. That was really what caught me as a positive, though. I missed swimming, and it reminded me of Grandma Freedom. Jacob smiled, and said with finality in his voice,

"Great! I will sign you guys up. We leave next Friday, at noon."

"Oh. That's pretty soon," I said. Hannah and Beverly returned to the table now, Hannah hanging her head dramatically.

"What else have we got to do?" Gary asked me with some sarcasm.

"Nothing," I sighed. I wasn't quite sure about all of this.

"You kids will have a great time," Eric promised.

That was when I remembered he was the youth pastor.

"So, are you and Beverly going, too?" I asked Eric.

"I am going, but Beverly is staying home with the girls. Somebody's got to be here to give the thumbs up to the local police, right?"

100

Before I knew it I was packing my things, including a borrowed Bible. That was an embarrassing item to pack. Eric handed it to me when I was in the living room on Thursday night and told me I would need it. When I asked him why, he told me the different speakers would be using it for teaching, and I finally realized what it was. That evening I skipped dinner so that I could read some of what it had to say. It was pretty interesting, but I didn't understand what any of it meant at the time. I felt like I was reading one of Deally's sacred texts, though there seemed to be less talk of damnation in the Bible.

I read the whole book of Genesis, which took some time. Then, I remembered what Jacob was saying about the New Testament, and I found where it started by searching the table of contents. I ended up reading Matthew and most of Mark before I passed out, face first, into the open Bible on my bed.

I was asleep, with my face in the opened Bible. I woke up at exactly midnight. I remember looking at the alarm clock beside the bed. I had fallen asleep with the lamp next to the bed on. I sat up, groggily, and leaned over to turn off the lamp. As I reached out my arm, I stopped and left the light on. It was because I saw something. Or some*one*. The picture of the bearded man on the wall. But he was not a painting anymore, and he didn't look quite the same. It's so strange to recall. The man was moving. He was looking at me, and his eyes, which were brown in the painting, were now this amazing blue color. When I looked into them, it was like looking into an endless ocean of clear blue waters. The eyes were sort of sparkling, too. I rubbed my eyes, I blinked, and I even slapped myself, to get this *delusion* to go away. I was trying to get the man to become a picture again. He didn't. Finally, I ran into the bathroom and washed my face, rubbing my eyes with cold water. When I returned, walking into the room slowly and holding my breath, I looked at the picture. It was a painting again. I was relieved, but something overcame me, and I started to weep uncontrollably.

It was the strangest thing I'd ever experienced. It was as if I had an epiphany that I was in turmoil, and I wept and wept. I laid with my face buried in pillows and cried myself to sleep.

When my alarm went off in the morning, I immediately looked up at the picture. It looked totally normal. I pushed my pillow away and sat up. The pillow was soaked with tears. I didn't feel turmoil anymore, though. It was like I cried it all out. I felt really peaceful now, actually. I sometimes wonder if I was momentarily delusional, if reading about all of the miraculous things in the Bible had caused me to have some kind of strange dream. It was very odd, and maybe it was a dream, but it *felt* real, and it had an effect on me like nothing else I'd ever experienced before or since.

NINE

The first night's special speaker, at the Christian youth conference, was named Tom Beck. I was sort of apprehensive about hearing him speak at first, just because that name, Tom, sort of hit a nerve. He was a very charismatic man, though, and he won my attention by way of a few funny stories about his infant sons.

Now, he was talking about the very thing my own mother had pointed out as being ridiculous about Christian belief. The Son of God, sent by the Father to save our souls. He had read some scripture from Matthew, which I recognized from my night's reading. It was about Jesus, of course. I had read the same things the night before, and I did not understand them. This man, Tom Beck, did an excellent job of explaining the Gospel. I understood it, finally. I understood that Jesus was not just a nice man who helped people. He was not a crazy man with odd, incomprehensible teachings either. He was God, come from majesty and comfort to live among the sinners. He had to die to be a sacrifice, a perfect life, free of sin. I found out that the brutal way he died was not just a horrible ending to a nice man's life, but that it was the very act that gave humanity the ability to be reconciled with God.

"Jesus defeated death. He went to Hell after He died, but Hell could not hold Him!" Tom yelled with excitement. The teenagers in the crowd all joined in with shouts that sounded full of joy and victory. I sat quietly, listening and twirling Grandma Freedom's gold and turquoise ring on my finger.

"Look, you go to Hell for sin. Jesus had *all* sin upon Him at the time of His death, but it wasn't His sin. *He was innocent*. Hell had no legal right to keep Him. And Jesus rose on the third day!" More shouting.

"Jesus took people out of Hell with Him, and the Bible says that He and the saints of old rose from the grave. So Jesus has won the victory!" People jumped to their feet now and raised their hands, others went running to the front and kneeled in front of the stage. A few more people joined Tom on stage now, and began to pick up instruments. They began to play music. It was loud and pounding at first, and then it lightened up and got very soft. I looked up at all of the stage lights that were shining. There were purple lights shining on the crowd, dancing their way into various seating areas. There were brilliant lights doing the same dance, washing over the musicians as they played with awesome intensity.

The other instruments dropped out, and the keyboard player remained the only person creating sound. Tom spoke again,

"It's already been done. Jesus won the victory. If you want to take part in it with Him, then this is your chance to join the party." He laughed.

"Young people! Wake up! Jesus is calling you. He's knocking on the door of your very heart. That's why you're here, young people. It's not because your friends conned you into it, or because your parents made you come. It's simply because the Holy Spirit of God drew you here; He's knocking. Are you going to answer? Do it, and you will not only share in the victory over sin, the victory over death, the victory over the world, and the enemy of your soul- but you will walk into a destiny greater than what you can even imagine." He paused for a moment and then yelled,

"Wake up!" He was quiet, and the whole room stood still, waiting for him to speak again.

"Young people, how long will you ignore the call? God has such great things for this generation. You are a chosen people. You have an inheritance with Christ, and if you will accept Him- Well, it will change your life. Some of you are ready; I can feel it. There are young people in this room; some of you have never even been to church before, and some of you have been hurt by "religion". Well, look, I'm not trying to sell you religion. I am introducing you to the best friend, the greatest parent, the mightiest God you'll ever know! This is about relationship, not religion, or tradition, or old wives tales. I want you to be in love with Jesus. I don't care if you're in church five days a week and doing charity work. No, I want you to be sold out, in love, absolutely wrecked for your God!" Everyone screamed again as he yelled out this statement. "And then, nothing else matters." He paused and looked with serious, squared eyes, out into the crowd. "Come on. You feel Jesus tugging at your heart. Come to the front if you want to meet Jesus. Come to the front if you want to know the Savior of your soul- the One whose blood covers all sin. Come down and meet your God." His voice was full of genuine compassion as he gave this invitation.

A wave of people from every place in the auditorium moved toward the front. I felt myself wanting to go up with them. I wished the wave would just wash over me and carry me like a current up to the front. It didn't happen, though. I waited for my legs to do something. I just couldn't go. I looked over at Gary who was a few seats down. He was talking with a girl from the youth group. They had somehow just missed the amazing, enlightening message that *I* had heard. I started to wonder if maybe I had been fooled somehow, if it really wasn't as great as I had thought. Maybe the emotionalism of it all- the music, the shouting, the lights- was what made me feel the way I did.

Even with my doubtful thoughts, I still felt the urge to go up front. Tom was praying aloud, with the kids up front echoing. I continued to fiddle with my ring, thinking about what Beverly had told me. Grandma Freedom had seen something no one else could. Did she really have some glimpse into the future? Perhaps Beverly was right when she said I would understand God's intervention after more time had gone by.

Tom Beck said goodnight, and the youth group was gathered together and thrown into two fifteen passenger church vans. The whole ride back to the hotel I wanted to talk to Gary and find out what he thought of Tom Beck's talk. It looked like he was only interested in the girl he was talking to. Jessica was her name. I couldn't talk to him in front of her. I didn't want to.

"What did you guys think?" the driver, a volunteer named Philip, yelled to the back of the van full of kids.

"It was amazing!" yelled out one boy, named TJ. He was one who went to the front to meet his God. I was a little jealous. A few others also called out in agreement.

"Good," Philip replied.

"What's the plan now?" a girl asked.

"We are going to the hotel for pizza, swimming, and sleep," Philip said.

When we arrived at the hotel, I spent no time on pizza, going straight for the pool. It was nice to be in the water again. I hadn't swam since I was a very young child. The last time was in a small pond, barely deep enough to invite swimmers. Grandma Freedom was sitting on a picnic blanket beside the pond, finishing a crossword puzzle. My sisters were there too, eating potato salad and chicken, refusing to swim in what might be sacred water.

"Canon ball!" TJ shouted.

I looked up from my position in the hotel pool and saw he was jumping in my direction. I swam away as quickly as I could, but didn't miss the massive wave his canon ball produced. This was no longer a peaceful swim. My memory faded. TJ emerged from the water with a smile on his face and asked everyone how big his splash was. A girl standing at the shallow end of the pool told him it was a lame splash. He immediately swam over toward her, and a chase ensued. I heard another splash behind me and turned around. I expected someone's head to pop up from beneath the water, but instead I felt my leg being pulled on, and I yelped in surprise. I struggled for a moment, to free myself, before I realized it was Gary and kicked him in the stomach with my free leg. He came up from the water with a bitter look on his face.

"Ouch, Carly!" he exclaimed.

"Sorry. You shouldn't have scared me like that."

"You didn't have to kick me, though."

"Yes, I did."

"Whatever. I'm done swimming," he told me.

"Are you really that upset?" I asked, worried I had ruined his night.

"Nah. I'm just really pruney." He showed me his wrinkly fingers and swam to the edge of the pool. I followed, wanting to talk to him about Tom Beck's message.

We sat beside each other, wrapped up in hotel towels, and began to talk. It started off pretty generic, just small talk. Mostly, we discussed how nice it was to go swimming after years without the ability.

"Yeah, I could definitely get used to swimming," Gary said, watching the others playing some kind of game in the pool.

"Me too."

We both watched the other kids in silence for a moment.

"So, are you having fun?" Gary asked, turning his attention back to me.

"Yeah, I guess. It's sort of odd, but I don't really know anyone besides you and Jacob."

"And Eric," Gary reminded me, motioning to Eric, who was at the other side of the room reading his Bible.

"Yeah. Eric too."

"Yeah. The religious stuff is weird, but I like the swimming and food." He smiled at me, looking for agreement.

"I guess," I laughed uncomfortably.

"It looks like they were right about one thing in Deally- Christianity is definitely weird."

I looked back at the kids and sighed. I saw Eric, reading his Bible, and wondered if maybe I should talk to him about my feelings. I regretted not going

106

to the front and meeting God. I wondered what God would be like. Surely, he would be kind and loving. After all, he sent his Son to die for me. That was the difference between this Christian God and Tom Deally's deity. Tom Deally's "God" had no love, just tradition and ritual. I remembered there was a lot of fear in Deally. It was just sort of there. If you didn't stop what you were doing and look around, you might miss it. It just hung in the atmosphere. Fear of God, fear of the elders and church leaders, fear of your own family and friends. You never knew who would be in danger of damnation next.

As I sat by the pool, pondering that fear, Gary said something to me and ran back to the pool. I watched him jump in and start wrestling with Jacob. I was still in thought. I remembered one time when I was very aware of the fear in Deally. It was the first time I really felt it, the first time I realized it was so thick.

I was about five years old. Marc and I were playing around in the backyard. The other siblings were all inside the house, doing something. I had insisted that Marc take me outside and play in the fresh mud puddles with me. We each had a rubber duck and were making quacking sounds, pushing them through the water. I remember we were just playing, having fun, when we heard angry voices inside the house. Suddenly, our other siblings were pushed outside. Marc jumped up from his spot on the ground beside me and went inside to see what was going on. I remember calling after him that he had some mud on his pants. He disappeared into the house and there was a silence that was too silent.

A man named Ralph, one of the church elders, came outside and joined us in the backyard. He told all of us that he was going to lead us in some fun church songs. I was confused. I didn't know he was in the house until he came out. We all sang and were challenged by Ralph to sing louder and louder. It *was* fun. The songs were silly and common to all of the children in the community, who learned them in church and school. After a few songs, another elder poked his head out of the door and motioned to Ralph.

"See you kids in church!" Ralph said happily, before going inside.

The next day, my mother and Marc both had marks on their faces, like they'd been beaten. When I saw that they were hurt I wanted to hug and kiss them. Instead, a heavy blanket of fear came over me and I went into the bathroom, to be alone, and cried to myself. That fear was always there; it never left. I always questioned that day. Had my dad beaten them? Was it the other elder, or someone else who was in the house? I dared not ask these questions. The fear was too thick to ask such questions.

I pulled the hotel towel tighter around my body. It was all I could do to comfort myself at the thought of the fear that inhabited that place. I looked up at

Eric again and wondered how I should ask my questions. I considered my meeting with Priest Liam in Deally. Hopefully, my meeting with Eric would be more profitable.

I sat, wrapped in my soggy hotel towel, for quite a long time, thinking about how and what I should ask. I figured I would start off by finding out if the things I learned about Christianity and God were the same things that Grandma Freedom believed. I looked at the ring on my bony finger again and felt a smile stretch across my face. I walked over to Eric, who was deep in his reading.

"Eric?" I said, rousing him from concentration.

"Oh. Sorry, I didn't see you there. What's up, Carly?"

"I was hoping I could talk to you about some things."

"Yeah, sure," he answered, pulling a nearby chair toward me.

"Okay," I began, sitting in the green chair, "I get the whole God and Jesus thing. I just wanted to ask an expert some stuff."

"Well, I wouldn't call myself an expert, but you shoot me some questions and I'll do what I can."

"Okay." That was odd. No Deally priest ever showed signs of being humble. It was refreshing.

"Go ahead," he urged, excitedly. His eyes glittered a little, actually.

"Well, first of all, I want to know if the things I've heard tonight are the same things that Grandma Freedom believed in."

"They are. She raised me up right, and I have carried on her legacy of faith in Christ."

"So, then she is in Heaven, and not in some fiery ocean, or Hell?"

"Absolutely. The Bible says clearly that those who call on the name of the Lord will be saved. She was a firm believer in Jesus and never wavered in her faith."

"That's good."

Eric laughed.

"What else do you have questions about, Carly?" He cocked his head to one side and looked into my eyes. I could tell he was enjoying my questions.

"Well, I would like to know what you meant by 'calling on the name of the Lord'. Is that like what Tom Beck was telling people to do, by going up front?"

"Yes. But you don't need to go up front in a church service or conference in order to do so."

"Really?" I asked. I'm sure I sounded skeptical. I was not used to a God who was so informal.

"Sure. I got saved in a dance club."

"Wait. I thought you were carrying out Grandma Freedom's faith."

"Yes, but I wasn't totally sold on it until I was in my twenties. I knew in my mind that Jesus was the real deal. I was even aware that if I drank too much and ended up dead somewhere, I could very well wake up in Hell."

"Wow. So, you just took that risk anyway?"

"I did. I wasn't too smart," he laughed uneasily.

"I guess not. How did you finally meet God?"

I felt like I could relate to Eric at this point. After hearing Tom Beck speak, I knew in my mind that Jesus was the Son of God and I needed to accept Him in my heart and life, but I wasn't doing anything about it. I supposed I was in the same position Eric was in when he was young. "I finally accepted Christ, like I said, at a club. I had been drinking a lot in my college days, so I was at the club almost every night. Honestly, I see now that I was really just using the alcohol to try to hide from myself."

"What do you mean?"

"Well, I really didn't like who I was. It started with drinking with my college buddies and it spun out of control pretty quickly. It effected my school work. I was cheating a lot just to pass my classes. That led to my being a liar and, of course, a cheater. I knew it was wrong and dishonest, but I was at a point where I couldn't just stop and go straight. If I did, I would flunk out of all my classes and lose my scholarships. Basically, I had convinced myself that the only way I could make it was to cheat, and the only way I could keep myself from thinking about my dishonesty was by drinking. I knew better. My mother raised me to know better. I had turned my back on Jesus at this point, and the drinking helped me forget about *that* too." He paused and a faint smile appeared on his face.

"So, one night I was out doing my typical drinking, and Beverly came and sat next to me at the bar. This was the first time I'd ever talked to her. I had

had a few classes with her, but we never spoke."

"So, this is when you met her, and when you met God?" I smiled too.

"Yeah. In hindsight, it was probably the best night of my life," he replied.

"Okay. Go on."

"Beverly came in and sat beside me. I watched her to see what she would order. I was picking up girls most every night, and I knew by what she would drink how I could be most successful in bringing her home with me." His smiled escaped him now. He continued, "I watched, and she ordered a cranberry juice with lime. No alcohol. I was stumped, actually. I had never seen a girl sit down at that bar and order juice. I just looked at her and said, *Can I buy you a real drink, honey?* She laughed at me and said no. I walked away. I couldn't stand the rejection. A girl had never laughed in my face before. I wasn't drunk yet, so I felt the sting of it."

A few kids who were sick of swimming had gathered and began listening. There were about three of them. They were nodding along in recognition of the story.

"I tried to forget it, but I couldn't. I didn't even want to drink. I just wanted to take this girl home with me. I wanted to prove to myself that I was still irresistible, still a player, still a skilled womanizer, basically. I had walked to the other side of the club before I got up the nerve to go back to her. When I got back she was gone. I remember seeing her juice glass, with a gutted lime slice laying beside it on a napkin. She was gone. I wasn't going to give up, though. I went outside to find her. I mean, she could have been long gone at that point, but I was sure she was nearby.

"When I went outside, sure enough, she was out on the sidewalk. Her friends were trying to talk her into going over to the café across the street. She kept saying she had to get home, but finally they talked her into it. So, a few minutes later, I went over to the café. This was after a few more drinks, mind you. It was a waste of money, though, because when I talked to Beverly, it was pretty sobering."

"I love this part," a girl wrapped in two towels said to herself.

"I went over there and invited myself to join her group of friends. I was sitting next to her in a booth, blocking her from escape. I kept throwing out these lame pick up lines, and finally her friends just told me they were leaving. I stood up, to let Beverly out of the booth. I had admitted defeat. But Beverly didn't leave. She just sat there and told her friends she would catch up later. I was

110

blown away, and my ego was pretty inflated, too. Her friends took off and I sat down across from her in the booth. I was just ready to invite her back to my apartment when she asked me a question that threw me totally off guard. She just said, *Why are you running from God?*"

He paused and gave everyone time to wonder what would happen next.

"I was sort of freaked out." He continued, "I thought there was some kind of a prophetess sitting in front of me. I didn't like that. If God was talking to her about me, she probably knew too much. I really wanted to leave, but I was so shocked that I just sat there. She asked me again why I was running from God. I wasn't sure what to say. Right there she laid out the Gospel message. The same one you all heard tonight. I *knew* it was true. I knew about Jesus. I guess I needed to be reminded, though."

"But I thought you said you were saved at the club," I blurted out.

"Let me finish," Eric laughed.

"Sorry. Keep going."

"Well, I told Beverly that she was nothing but a tease and that she didn't know anything about me. I even called her a false prophet, and then I stormed out of there. I went back across the street to drink some more booze. I drank and I sulked and I thought about that stupid girl. I kept drinking, but it seemed like I just couldn't get drunk. One of my buddies saw how much I'd been drinking and told the bartender that I needed to be cut off. So, I wasn't getting anymore alcohol, but I wasn't drunk. I didn't even feel a buzz. There I was, sitting at the bar, sober, and really angry at God. I started speaking aloud to God. People were looking at me, assuming I was drunk. I didn't care about the looks I was getting; I was too angry.

"I told God that I was angry that He would tell someone else things about me. I told Him that I was angry He had allowed me to become a cheater and a liar and a womanizer and a drinker. I yelled at Him for not stopping me from going down the path I was on. I told Him that my mother's prayers should have been enough for Him to stop me from getting to the place where I was. I really just blamed Him for everything that was going wrong in my life. But I wasn't an idiot. I knew it was *my* fault. By the end of my ranting at God, I was no longer yelling, I was weeping. I was repenting. I was begging God to forgive me, and I was asking Jesus to come back into my life."

"In front of all of those people?" I asked, truly amazed at the idea.

"Yes. I didn't care who was around. It wasn't important, because if I

111

couldn't have God back in my life, if I couldn't know Him like I knew Him when I was a kid, nothing mattered. I had reached the bottom, I was empty, and I needed Jesus."

Gary, Jacob, and Jessica all came and joined the circle of listeners.

"So, that was it. I never went back to the club. I never picked up another girl, and I barely passed my college courses, by the grace of God, with very low Ds. Needless to say, the cheating was over. I turned everything around as best I could, and I knew something was different in me."

"So, what happened with Beverly? How did you end up with her in the end?" I asked.

"You know, I am still amazed that we ended up together. Believe it or not, I was still mad at her for asking me why I was running from God that night. Her asking me that was the catalyst for my reconciliation to Christ, for my turning things around, but I didn't understand that. I was still angry at her. We never spoke again until five years later. We were introduced through a mutual friend, and then we became close friends. After a while we got married. It's a pretty amazing story. To this day I wonder what made God decide to pick me out for such a great testimony, such a great life. I've got to believe it was my mother's prayers."

"Grandma Freedom," I said to myself. That name was always comforting. I felt the ring on my finger and closed my eyes. I could see her wrinkled face in my mind, forever smiling.

"Well, I think it's about time all you kids got to bed," Eric announced. Everyone sighed and grumbled.

"See? You're all cranky- you need sleep," Eric laughed.

The next day, I settled into my seat, right on the end of the pew. I knew this was the best spot for me to make my way to the front. I was so excited. I kept going over Tom Beck's words in my mind. I watched the big screens, scrolling various announcements. I listened to the booming music playing over the sound system. I waited for the musicians to go on stage. The sooner we finished worship, the sooner Tom Beck would be on stage, the sooner the alter call would come. I felt my heart race with anticipation. I was going to meet my God!

What I didn't know was that a different man would be speaking. A guy named Dustin Mitts spoke that night instead, and frankly, he wasn't great. He was more of a comedian than a preacher. That was not what I was looking for. There wasn't even a call to go up front, not even a prayer of repentance. I was sorely disappointed. Again, I was left with a knowledge of God, of Jesus, but no salvation. I felt cheated and I wasn't sure what to do. We all left for home that night. It was dark outside as we began the drive home. As we neared the house, the clouds broke up and a huge yellow moon appeared in the sky, full and round.

TEN

The fifteen passenger van I rode in was eerily quiet. It left me with a lot of time to think. All of the kids were half asleep. All but me; I was wide awake, and it was not because I was well rested. That weekend was a time when everyone was running on sugar and caffeine. I should have crashed like all the others, but my heart was talking too loudly, or maybe it was the sound of knocking. If Jesus truly knocked on hearts, I am certain He was doing just that while I sat in the van, staring at my grandmother's ring and going over the whole weekend in my mind. Time flew by, and soon, I was standing in my room, unpacking.

I stood over the unpacked bag on my bed and sighed. I wasn't sure what to do. I was still in shock that Dustin Mitts, and not Tom Beck, spoke that night. I placed my hands on my hips and decided I wasn't going to let that stop me. If God could receive so many people at one time at that conference, surely he would have no problem receiving just me in the guest room. This is a time of salvation. I closed my eyes and tried to formulate a prayer.

Just as I was about to say my own prayer, Gary knocked on the door. I opened my eyes to let him in.

"Hey. Jacob and I are going to watch a movie. Do you want to join?"

"Uh, no. I'm pretty tired," I lied.

"Alright." He began to leave the room but turned around.

"What?" I asked, slightly annoyed with his presence at what was supposed to be my time of salvation.

"What was Eric talking about at the pool last night?"

"He was telling the story of how he became a Christian."

Gary got a sullen look on his face. I felt my annoyance leave.

"What's wrong?"

"I was reading the Bible today. All of the guys at the conference did a Bible study this morning at the hotel."

"Yeah, so did the girls. What's your point?"

115

"I don't want to lie to you anymore. I haven't stopped feeling guilty since the Bible study, and I need to tell you this before I lose my nerve-"

I cut him off. "What are you guilty of? What are you lying about?"

I stood up as straight as a board, ready to guard myself against something horrible.

"Here's the truth. I prayed with Jacob about a week ago to accept Jesus." We were both quiet. Gary wouldn't look at me. It reminded me of the night we met on the street in Deally.

"You're probably pretty mad at me, right?"

"No. I think... Well, yes. Yes, I am mad."

"That's what I thought, but I can't deny Christ. I had to tell you. It's been eating me up inside." He stuffed his hands into his pockets. "If I deny Christ, what stops Him from denying me?"

"That's not even it. I'm not mad that you accepted Jesus. I'm mad that you didn't tell me about it until now."

"Really?"

"Yes. I wanted to go up front last night, when Tom Beck was speaking... Then when we were at the pool and you told me that Christians were weird, I felt like maybe I was crazy to feel that way."

"I'm so sorry, Carly."

I sighed and scanned the room uncomfortably. My eye was drawn to the picture of the bearded man on the wall.

"Who is he, anyway?" I asked Gary. I wanted to change the subject.

"It's a picture of Jesus," Gary said quietly. I looked at Gary, then back at the painting.

"No. Jesus is different." That painting and the man I saw in my vision, they were different.

"Well, I guess nobody really knows what He looks like." Gary stepped between me and the painting, redirecting my focus. "Look, I really am sorry. I should have told you."

"It's no big deal. I'm not going to hold it against you or anything."

"Alright," Gary said, as he walked into the hallway. I stood there, looking at the painting a few more seconds, and then I called after Gary.

"What?" He turned back to face me.

"Uh, never mind."

"Okay…" He folded his arms over his chest and stood still. "I should have told you. You deserved to know. I mean, you're like my best friend."

I wasn't sure what to say. He turned around to leave again.

"Wait, Gary." He turned back again.

"What?"

I felt my heart beat fast. My palms got clammy and warm. I knew this was my time. It felt right, and now that Gary was being open with me about this, I knew I could be open as well. I stopped to take a breath or two. Gary looked around nervously. I wiped my hands on my jeans and motioned for him to reenter my room.

"What's up, Carly?" Gary asked, as I shut the door behind us.

"Do you just want to yell at me?" Gary asked with his shoulders straight back. "I can take it."

"No. It's not that at all." I shut my eyes for a moment and waited for a wave of courage to pass over me. I could hear Gary shifting his weight back and forth. Opening my eyes, I finally let it out. "Could you pray with me to accept Jesus, too?"

He was quiet.

"I just don't really know what to do," I added.

"Yeah. Of course. I mean, it would be an honor." He smiled.

"Alright, so what do I do?"

"Well… This is kind of weird. Okay. Just say something. God is everywhere; He sees us right now, so just tell Him that you want to accept Christ as Savior."

I felt a smile sprout on my face out of nowhere. "Okay, God," I began, looking up slightly. "If you are here, I want to say that I believe in Jesus, Your Son…So, thank You."

I caught a glimpse of the painting of who I now knew was Jesus. "I hope to see You again soon, Jesus."

117

I lowered my eyes to the floor. A sense of embarrassment came. I looked at Gary. I saw that he was still smiling, and I felt my heart leap within me. A sudden rush of what felt like electric heat flooded through me. It overtook the embarrassed feeling I had received earlier.

"So?" asked Gary.

"I feel good."

"Good but disappointed- like something's missing?" he asked.

I thought for a moment. "No. Just good. Not disappointed at all."

"Maybe you don't need a hobby after all," Gary laughed.

I remembered Grandma Freedom. This must have been the moment she had always prayed for. I was out of Deally, I was with family, and I had become a Christian- I was now carrying on her heritage of faith. I looked down at the ring on my finger and shook my head in disbelief.

"This is what she saw," I whispered to myself.

"Wait. What?" Gary followed my eyes to the ring. He grabbed my hand and lifted it to examine it for himself. "Nice jewelry."

"It's more than that," I laughed. Tears were trying to make their way out, but I stopped them with some blinks. "This was my Grandma Freedom's ring. She gave it to Eric, and he gave it to Beverly and she gave it to me…"

Gary filled the silence. "Cool. It's like a family heirloom."

"But Grandma Freedom saw something that I couldn't see."

"What do you-"

Gary's question was cut off by a piercing scream. It cut through the atmosphere like a dagger. I dropped immediately to my knees. Gary squatted down beside me and held my hand tightly. There were more screams and then silence.

I prayed that laughter would follow and all would be well. I prayed that the family was only playing a game downstairs. The silence was too silent. I could hear heavy footsteps in the hall and whispers that sounded like male voices. Gary held a finger to his mouth, a sign to be silent. He led me by the hand into the guest room closet. We hid.

Huddling close to Gary, fear flying all around us, I felt like a scared little girl again. I shut my eyes and listened. The feet had made their way to the guest

118

room door. The knob clicked, and I knew the door had opened. The footsteps were heavier now, and circled the room outside of our hiding place. Gary wrapped both of his arms around me and I felt him kiss the top of my head.

"It's not going to end this way, I promise you," he whispered. I couldn't see his face in the dim light, but I knew what it had to look like. My mind pulled up the image of his determined countenance on the bus. He was willing to do whatever it took to get us out of harm's way. I knew this time would be no different.

"I trust you. And I trust God," I whispered in reply.

Before any more could be said, the closet door was being slid open. Light slowly gathered around us, and I let go of my grip on Gary. I knew he would want to fly into action quickly. Squeezing my eyes shut as much as possible, I waited for the sounds of men in a physical struggle. Instead, I heard Gary speak.

"Dad?"

"Hello, Son."

Gary's voice sounded weak. "So Tom's got you out like a blood hound again?"

"I wasn't about to let my own son leave the community. Not while I can help it."

I cracked my eyes open slightly. Gary's father was an imposing figure, standing tall and strong, even in his late sixties.

"So what happens now?" Gary stood up, and I followed.

"Gary, I don't have time for your questions. Let's go."

I was surprised when Gary didn't argue or fight back, but that was only until I looked at his father more closely and realized he was carrying a handgun. I had never seen one in real life. I didn't think we had them in Deally, but then lots of things were hidden.

Gary and I were escorted downstairs. I didn't see Eric, Beverly, or any of the kids as we walked through the house. I was taking one last glimpse of family life, I told myself. We walked through the kitchen and the smell of pizza hung in the air, being reheated from the night before. Hannah and Joanne had been excited at the prospect of late night pizza. I wondered if I would see them again.

"Alright, things are taken care of here," came a voice behind us. A door closed in the same direction.

"Good," replied Gary's father. "Let's get going."

Marcus caught up to us in the kitchen. I stared at him. My last memory of seeing his face was the police's suspect sketch. This was the brother who played in the mud with me as a child, the same guy who beat Pastor Freeman mercilessly on the steps of his own church. I did not know this man. He gave me a wink and walked over to the oven. "We'd better turn this off."

Gary's father snorted and pointed his pistol in Marcus' direction. "Alright, Marc. You've done your good deed for the day; the house won't burn down. Now, we need to get back. Tom will be waiting."

Marcus rejoined the group as we made our way toward the front door. Gary stopped and gave Marc a cold stare. "So, Marcus, I see you're just another Deally puppet now."

Marc smiled and replied, "Call it what you want, Gary. All I know is I'm not a little boy any more. I don't hatch plans for joining the disgusting outside world or lie to important people," he paused and laughed a little, looking at me. "And I don't spit on plaques."

"You could certainly learn a thing or two from Marcus about growing up, Gary." His father was ushering us out the door as he spoke.

When we got outside there was a huge full moon looming close above us. The still, calm night seemed almost insulting in light of the tumultuous circumstance beneath it. A white cargo van was parked outside. The side door slid open, revealing Priest Liam inside. His arm had a thick cast encapsulating it, but it was obviously the work of some housewife in Deally, not a real doctor. Seeing him only made things worse. I felt my heart rate increase.

"It's just like a family reunion!" Liam shouted with cheer. "Carly, Gary, we thought it would be just wonderful to have your family bring you back to our fair town. Isn't it wonderful?" He exited the van, carefully holding onto his bandaged arm.

"Yeah, it is pretty nice," Marc chimed in. "But Carly is awfully quiet." He wrapped his arm around my waist and looked into my eyes, still smiling. I felt sick. This was not the brother I once knew. I pulled away and stood behind Gary and his father.

"What? Do you not recognize me anymore?" Marcus actually looked hurt.

"Not really," I replied.

"You all will have plenty of time to catch up when we get back," Liam said. He grabbed something out of the van and turned to Gary and I. "But first, you'd better put these on." He held out pillow cases to us. Mine had pink flowers stitched on it.

"What's this for?" Gary asked. "You know we've been to Deally, right? This does nothing for you."

"Believe it or not, this is for your protection," his father answered. "Lots of things changed after you two left. Deally is not the same place, and there are plenty of people who would love to kill either of you for disrupting paradise."

"It's true," Marc said sullenly. "Things are no longer how God planned. Tom Deally's vision has been shredded." He looked at me and shook his head sadly. "Mom and Dad blame you."

I was surprised at how much that stung. Tears started rolling down my cheeks. I waited for that voice to come back and tell me that I shouldn't have left.

"Deally looks more like a military compound every day," Liam confirmed. "Families are asking to leave, and Tom is holed up in his home with the elders and priests trying their best to keep the peace. People are really scared right now. We need to show them we can restore their paradise."

"How do you propose to do that?" Gary asked.

"Forget it," Marcus answered. "Just put on your pillow cases and get in the van."

ELEVEN

We rode in silence back to Deally. I wondered why this was happening. I wondered if Grandma Freedom had seen this too. I waited for that little voice inside me to say I never should have left, but I had a new voice inside of me. I supposed it must be Jesus, since He was now in my heart. He told me just the opposite of the other voice. *You didn't leave in vain.* I wanted to believe it was true, but things were looking grim.

We made it to Deally in what seemed like the dead of night. When the van's engine died out, I heard no signs of life in the air, not the croak of a little tree frog or a chirping cricket. The door rolled open and a hand led me out into the brisk night air. I could tell it wasn't Gary's hand, and I shuttered at the thought of holding on to Liam or Marcus, but I couldn't very well see with a pillowcase over my head. I grasped the mystery hand and walked carefully across what felt like a grassy area. I expected to hit pavement at any moment and to enter a door; I assumed we were going to Tom's house or the church. When I was pushed down what felt like a damp, dirty tunnel, I knew we weren't at Tom's place. This was another one of Deally's secrets.

When the pillowcases came off, Gary and I were in a dusky underground hideout. There were two cells in the room, side by side, made up of rusted looking metal bars, planted into the ground like fence poles. Gary pushed and pulled on them, testing their strength, but they didn't seem to move much. On the other side of the metal bars holding us captive was a small wooden table and chair. Liam sat there, cradling his injured arm. He shot Gary a look of disdain.

"Stop that!"

Gary backed away from the bars and crossed his arms.

"Please, Liam. What did you do with my family?" I had to know if they were okay. I had been praying they weren't dead.

Liam smiled. "Your family is fine. We tied them all up and they're having a nice evening in the bathroom together."

I thanked God for that piece of information. Now, I needed to focus on what was happening to Gary and me. I stood silently, waiting for my eyes to adjust fully to the dim light. Two passageways on either side of where the jail cells were located came into focus. We must have come in one, but the other no doubt took you further into this underground lair. I wondered how we would figure which was which when we needed to make a run for it. Then, I wondered why I had such an optimistic thought. I reminded myself the odds were stacked against Gary and me, and I decided to try to be at peace about it.

Marcus came walking out from the passageway to our left. He clicked off a flashlight as he entered.

"No reason for you to stick around," Marc said to Liam.

Liam glared at Gary, still cradling his bandaged appendage. "I see a couple of reasons behind those bars."

"That may be, but until Tom gives us further orders, you can't touch either of them. You know that."

"Sure," Liam answered. He stood to his feet and laughed. "Tom Deally knows best, as always. Where is he anyway? He's been hiding in his house ever since the police came through here. He's no leader."

"Wait. The police *have* been here?" I blurted out.

"Yeah. They were here three days ago. They tore the whole community apart!" Liam yelled. "They were looking for this idiot!" He motioned toward Marc, who held a look of satisfaction on his face.

"Yeah, well, they could never find me down here. They were pretty close too. I had been outside only an hour before they showed up." He looked at me and explained, "I went to play around with Jon a little. He worries, you know."

I felt a frown stretch across my face. I had missed Jon. I remembered the last time I had seen him, and how he begged me not to leave.

"Yes, he does worry," I mumbled.

Before more could be said, there was stirring in the second jail cell. I hadn't noticed the body lying in the dirt. An anemic looking woman with dirty orange hair sat up and looked over at us all. "When are you all going to be quiet?" she asked, in a whisper.

She then picked up a heavy sounding cup and threw it across the room, yelling, " I'm trying to forget that I'm in this rat hole!"

Liam walked over to her jail cell and replied, "Shut up, Cynthia."

Cynthia laid back down, obediently.

"Well, I for one am not obligated to stay in this rat hole," Liam declared happily. "But, Marcus- and the rest of the prisoners- have a nice night." He began to walk away, then paused in mid-step and turned back. "Oh, and I'll be talking to Tom Deally as soon as I can to get those next orders. See you soon, Gary."

He left out of the right passageway. That would be the way out, I told myself. If we ever left. With the realization Cynthia Fagetti was our fellow prisoner, I wondered if we too would grow old in a jail cell, never seeing the light of day. Marcus opened up a newspaper and settled into the chair outside of our bars. After Liam was gone a few moments, Cynthia sat back up and positioned herself to sit looking at Gary and me.

"So, they finally got you two, huh? I thought maybe you would be able to pull it off. How was your brief freedom, anyway?" She looked frail, but she spoke with no trace of weakness. I wasn't sure what to answer her, and Gary had become quite tight lipped in the last few hours. He sat at the back of the cell in a dark corner, drawing figures in the dirt. I assumed he was either coming up with plans of escape, or else he had finally admitted defeat. I couldn't exactly blame him for the latter.

"Well, even if we never get back out again, I'm glad we had that time of freedom, because I got to meet my family," I replied. "And God," I added.

"God?" Cynthia looked disgusted. "Well, what a wonderful fantasy. If you wanted religion, why did you leave Deally?"

"I didn't want religion. I didn't want God either, not Tom Deally's god anyway. But I guess things sort of changed when I started to see His hand in things." I felt for Grandma Freedom's ring, but it was gone. It had fallen off in all of the chaos of the evening.

"So, you're saying God is orchestrating things, huh? Well, he did a bang up job sending you back here. Which God is this anyway? Don't tell me it's Jesus." She laughed, but without joy. I felt badly for her; she lost everything. She went into Deally a young woman and now sat rotting in front of me, bitter and aged, with no hope for a future. I prayed that would not be my fate as well.

Cynthia cut off my silent prayer. "I knew some Jesus Freaks back home. They were pretty crazy too."

"I don't get it. Who is this God?" Marcus asked. He set down the paper and looked at me with exacting eyes. "You've found a foreign god?"

"Lots of people know Jesus," I told him. "Grandma Freedom, for one. All of Mom's family outside of Deally knows Jesus. He's only *foreign* to people in

Deally."

"I find that hard to believe," he replied. "In training for the priesthood, we learned all about different common faiths, and then we were introduced to-" He stopped himself from saying more.

"You were introduced to what?"

"It's kind of a church secret," he replied. He shifted his weight around in his chair.

"Well, it's not like any of us have anyone to tell the secrets to," Cynthia said, lying back down again. That seemed to be the most comfortable position for her.

"I guess that's true, and to be honest, it didn't work for me anyway." He rubbed his forehead and let out a long breath.

"What didn't work?" I asked.

He shut his eyes tightly and then blinked a few times and crossed his arms. "I don't know that I should confide in you three."

"Do or don't. Who cares?" Cynthia said from her spot on the dirt floor.

"Every priest in training is supposed to receive a visitation of some kind. They're supposed to get introduced to a spiritual guide who will always be with them, guiding them and giving them wisdom." Marc breathed out a slow sigh. Apparently this had been weighing on him.

Cynthia sat up and looked at Marcus with a sideways stare. "No kidding?"

"No kidding," Marc repeated. "Only I never received a guide. I meditated, I prayed, I memorized portions of the sacred texts. I just never had any visitation. And after two weeks, when everyone else in training had their guide and were already getting revelation and secret wisdom from God, I couldn't hide my problem. I talked to Tom, and he suggested I do the doubter's ritual to purge any unconscious doubt. Still nothing."

"It's because Tom Deally is a liar. His religion is a joke," Gary piped up.

"Right. Then explain how I saw Henry Dill's guide enter the room to meet him," Marc muttered. He swore under his breath and looked back to Gary for an answer.

"What?" Gary said defensively. "I don't know how delusional you might be after all the beatings you received. Delusional enough to attack an innocent pastor and then hide in a hole like a coward." With that, Gary emerged from his dark corner to face Marcus through the bars. Marcus didn't seem intimidated by the move. He remained seated.

"Gary, I'm telling you, Tom Deally's Reformed Church is not a joke. The goddesses are real and Tom Deally's God is real. The celestial visitations that inspired Tom and Carmen to write the sacred texts were real. It's all real. Everyone in the priesthood knows it. They've all experienced visitation themselves."

"Except for you!" Cynthia cried out in laughter. She pointed a bony finger Marc's way and laid on her back, her whole body shaking with laughter.

"Be quiet, Cynthia!" Marcus screamed. He stood to his feet and shook on the bars between himself and Cynthia. "You know nothing!"

Cynthia probably would have continued laughing except for that she began to cough violently. Marc stood in silence, staring with an icy glare at Cynthia's crumpled body. "You know nothing."

"Marcus, I don't understand what's happened to you," I said slowly, "but something happened to me. I had a visitation of my own. I met Jesus, and I'm telling you, this Jesus is a real God. And if you're saying Tom Deally's god, and the goddesses, are real, then I will have to believe you. But Jesus…" I trailed off, not knowing what to say next. I looked into Marcus' eyes in the dim light. I remembered they were green once, but now they looked gray.

"Jesus is the God who created everything," I said. "He made *you*. And He loves you, Marcus." I found myself wringing my hands.

"That's interesting," Marc replied quietly. "A God who loves. It's interesting, but it doesn't make any sense, Carly. Why would a God who created everything care about me, or you, or anybody?"

I looked to Gary, hoping he would have something supportive to add. He just looked at me and shrugged his shoulders. Cynthia sat up once more and spoke.

"I told you I knew Jesus Freaks back home. And if one thing was consistent- and annoying too, it was the message of love," Cynthia confirmed. "The Christian God is definitely a lover, if he exists at all."

I was glad for the help, but Marc didn't seem impressed. He looked at me with raised eyebrows. "*Christian*? The *Christian* god? You're telling me that our family on the outside are all Christians and now you are too?"

127

I was surprised at his annoyance. "Yes. I don't understand why-"

"Be quiet, Carly. Just don't say anything, okay? Don't say anything around Tom or Liam or anyone. Don't say a word about Jesus."

"Why?" I asked.

"It was one thing when Tom Deally and the elders thought you and Gary were simple doubters, or even atheists. They have a way of reaching people like that. But Christianity is one of the most dangerous false religions. You know that just as well as I do. Everyone in Deally knows that!"

"I didn't *try* to believe in Jesus. Jesus revealed himself to me, and there's no way I can deny that." I thought of the night Jesus appeared in the painting. I remembered receiving Grandma Freedom's ring. I recalled praying with Gary for salvation. I was convinced. Jesus had revealed Himself to me, and I wasn't about to let being back in Deally change what I knew was truth.

"Carly, listen to me. Just don't say anything. I don't want to see anything bad happen to you." He sounded genuinely concerned as he said this and took a step toward my cell. Before I could say a word, red light filled the room and flashed. Marcus sat in his chair and looked toward the exit passageway attentively.

"What's the flashing light about?" Gary asked.

"The authorities are here again," Marcus said, keeping his gaze down the tunnel passageway.

Gary and I began screaming for help in unison. I imagined Officer Ian and Agent Jones were right above our heads. Marcus broke his concentrated gaze to look at us. "Shut up! No one can hear us down here."

We took his word for it and quieted down.

"This sucks," Gary whispered to me. I nodded in agreement. "But I think God has a plan."

TWELVE

I almost didn't notice the red lights ceasing to flash, they had been going so long, and I had been trying to ignore them.

"I guess the police are gone," I said, blinking away the red stains in my eyes.

Marcus looked at me and laughed. "Yeah, sorry everybody. Your freedom is not near."

"Marc, you're trapped down here, just like us," Cynthia snorted. She was propped up against the dirt wall on her back. Marc didn't retort.

"Is that right, Marc?" Gary asked quietly. "You're a prisoner, too?" He stood beside me in front of the bars that trapped us.

Marc seemed unsure. "I'm down here to be a guard."

"Isn't that beneath the normal duties of a Deally priest?" asked Gary.

"He's no priest," Cynthia said, turning her attention to Gary. "He didn't get a guide. You can't be a priest and not be spiritual. He never got his visitation. Poor thing," she said sarcastically.

"Quiet, Cynthia," Marcus said, without much assertion.

"You seem to know a lot for being trapped down here," Gary said to Cynthia.

"Yeah, well those girls they had down here with me knew a lot of information. I miss them. Where'd you take those girls anyway?" she asked Marcus.

"Cynthia," Marcus said, leaning forward in his seat. "You've got to shut up."

"Girls?" Gary asked. He had a concerned look on his face, and I knew he and I were thinking the same thing. The elders' daughters.

"Yeah, a bunch of girls. They were being held in some secret passageway deal like this one, only it was under Tom Deally's place. They told me they were all taken there when they were little. Tragic, really. They were prisoners just like

129

me. The stories those girls had were…strange."

"Marcus, what is she talking about? Who are these girls?" Gary asked. "Are they the elders' daughters?"

Marc was quiet, sitting back in his chair, looking ignorant.

"Don't lie to me, Marc. I know that the elders give up their first born daughters. Where are they now? Are they safe?"

Marc shook his head. "How do you know about the girls?"

"My father is an elder. How would I *not* know?"

"Well, I just thought that most elders make up some kind of excuse for them. For instance, Linda and Fred, they told their older sons that Sheila got a private school scholarship at another Deally community."

"Are there other Deally communities?" I asked.

Marc smiled slightly. "No, but people will believe anything."

"Are they safe?" Gary asked again. His speech was deliberate and slow, voicing each word clearly. Gary's face was stoic, but I knew the emotion that lie behind the mask. He was worried for his sister.

"They're just a little ways over," Marcus said, motioning toward the passageway beyond where we were being held. "They're just fine."

"I don't understand. Why aren't they at Tom's house?" I asked.

"The outside authorities got a court order to search his home. Tom may not like the outside world, but he realizes he's under their power in many circumstances."

"So they're being hidden more carefully?" Gary asked.

"Yes," Marc replied.

"At least down here they're safe from Tom," Cynthia said bluntly.

"Why? What did they say about Tom?" Gary asked.

"It's probably not something you want to hear," Cynthia replied. "I mean, if one of them was your sister?" She sounded unsure of the information she had gleaned.

"It doesn't matter if I want to hear it." Gary said slowly, "I need to know."

I grabbed Gary's hand. "Are you sure?"

"Yes."

I let go of his hand and listened.

"They're just servants for Tom and Carmen," Marcus interjected. "It's nothing sinister."

"Servants?" Cynthia said, shaking her head. "That's not what they told me."

"And just what did they tell you, Cynthia?" Marcus asked with a laugh.

"Gary," Cynthia started, ignoring Marcus, "these girls told me that they were used in rituals. Some of them wouldn't speak at all. I can't imagine what Tom must have done to those poor girls, but it was all in the name of his religion. One of the older ones said that she was *not a goddess*, and that's all she would say. She just kept repeating it."

"What were the *rituals*?" I ventured a question I knew would have an unpleasant answer.

Cynthia shook her head and cursed under her breath. "You sure you want to know this stuff?"

Gary just nodded.

"There was one girl who talked a lot. She was mad, and I think she wanted to tell her story, you know? Well, she talked about how Tom would feed them drugged food. It made them all feel like they'd die, unable to move and unable to speak."

I watched Gary's face as Cynthia spoke. His eyes narrowed and I could see anger in his countenance.

"This is ridiculous," Marc interrupted. "Cynthia, you need to keep quiet."

Cynthia continued despite Marc, "So they were helpless. Tom would say a lot of prayers, asking the goddess spirits to take over their bodies. Then he-"

"Cynthia, shut up!" Marcus stood from his seat and rushed toward her cell. "Shut up! You know nothing!"

Cynthia stared at Marcus and slowly began to rise up from off the floor. She got on all fours and used the bars to lift herself up onto her feet. Standing she looked even more frail. Everything about her reminded me of the skeleton decorations on front doors during Halloween, which was one of the few holidays Deally observed which the outside world also celebrated. The skeleton spoke. "Marc, you are the one who knows nothing." She pointed her finger close to his

131

face. "If you think that Tom Deally is a genuine guy, just trying to run a nice community, then maybe you should take a second look at where you are right now." Her voice rose and cracked as she continued, "You're in a dirt prison, keeping watch over people whose only crimes were wanting to move to another town. That's not normal!"

Marcus just sat back down. "No, it's not normal. It's God-ordained! But go on, continue your blasphemy. I don't know why I'm so upset- *You're in jail.*"

Cynthia laughed a scoffing laugh and returned to her sitting position. "Okay, Marcus."

"Go on, Cynthia," Gary said.

"Look, the short version of all of the stories are that Tom's a freak. He touches them, he plays with them, he treats them like his personal life sized dolls- and he calls them each by the names of the Deally goddesses. It's messed up."

"I don't believe it," Marcus said flatly.

"Of course not," Gary said. "You're too busy trying to be Tom Deally's good little priest boy. I guess if you get enough good beatings you'll convert pretty easily."

Marc didn't reply.

"Tom has a lot of secrets," Gary said. "He's manipulated everyone to play into his own little fantasy of paradise."

"*Everybody*'s been fooled," I added. "It's really not your fault for wanting to believe in it all, Marc."

Marc looked up. "How is it you all didn't want to believe?"

Cynthia laughed. "What, are we on trial now? Funny how imprisonment comes first in this town."

"No, you're not on trial," Marc replied sharply.

Cynthia's lips curled up in a mocking smile. "So maybe the good little priest boy is struggling with doubts of his own?"

Marc didn't reply. I watched his face, trying to gather what he might be thinking. Was he having doubts? I prayed that was the case. He kept his face downcast, staring at the dirt floor without a word. Maybe the old Marcus was resurfacing inside of him.

"I knew things weren't right when my sister was taken away." I turned to see Gary addressing Marcus. Marc looked into our cell, still silent, as Gary continued. "Brittany was supposed to be a role model, a friend, a big sister. Instead, she's been locked away all her life." Gary shook his head and let out an angry grunt. "But Tom's going down. The police are going to do their job. It's going to be over for Tom."

"Maybe," Marc mumbled.

"As for me," Cynthia said abruptly, "I didn't have any problems with Deally, I just got tired of it. I wasn't made to fit the religious mold. I just wanted to get back to my old life in California."

"That doesn't seem like a jail-able offense," Marc said.

"Yeah, well, Tom Deally wasn't too happy when he heard I was packing up. Turns out, when Tom Deally assaults you in the process of trying to get out of town, and you threaten to tell the police, you go to a dirt jail underground."

"Of course," Gary added. "Nobody leaves Deally."

Marcus stood up suddenly. Someone holding a flashlight was approaching. As they came in to the dimly lit area where we all were I began to see clearly who it was.

"Well, how are my prisoners doing?"

Tom Deally took the liberty of sitting down in the only chair.

"Things are going fine," Marc replied. "What was all of the flashing about earlier? That was longer than usual."

"You just worry about what's going on down here, Marcus. I'll take care of matters up there."

Gary grabbed hold of the bars in front of him and addressed Tom. "Hey, you realize you're not going to be getting away with anything, right? There's a reason the police have been all over this place. They're coming after you. They've finally got the testimonies they need to put you away, you sorry son of a-"

I grabbed Gary's hand and squeezed. The last thing we needed was to get Tom Deally angry. Gary got the hint.

"Go on," Tom insisted. "You were doing really well, telling me all about how I'm going to be imprisoned." He shined his flashlight at Gary. "Funny how you're the one behind bars."

"They're looking for us. There's no way that they're not looking for us.

I'm sure by now that the cops have found Eric and Beverly and the kids, all tied up in the bathroom- And they're looking for us."

Tom laughed. "You think I'd let those people live?"

"I don't think you were the one at the house," Gary said coolly. "According to Marcus, nobody's dead."

Tom turned to Marc. "Is that right?"

"I didn't know about that order, Mr. Deally. I swear."

"I told Liam it had to be done. He didn't report that?"

"No," Marcus replied. His voice was shaking.

"Well, no need to worry. I'll deal with Liam. As for you two," Tom said, turning back toward Gary and me. "They may be looking for you, but I'm quite certain you won't be found. We're planning a little program for you tomorrow; it will be the last time you two ever see daylight. A public shaming is in store for you."

I clasped my hands over my mouth. A sudden memory came to me. I was very young. I was standing in the back of the church with my family. I remembered being excited about a potluck and games that were planned, but something had to happen first. We were waiting for a long time at the back of the church before Tom Deally came onto the church's stage area and stood behind the pulpit. He said a few words. A man was brought up on stage behind him, wearing restraints that held his hands together. Many people came on stage and spoke, they also kicked the man and spat on him. I didn't recognize the man, and I never did see him again.

I felt a surge of emotion spring out of my stomach. A whimper came out. I clasped my hands tighter over my mouth and tried not to let out any more sounds or tears.

Tom stood and faced me, bars between us. He smiled at me and shook his head.

"Carly, I almost made your father an elder at one time."

I felt sick. My feet began shuffling backwards until I was in the dark corner of the cell.

Tom flashed his light back toward me. "It's just too bad he had children who could never play by the rules."

Marc laughed nervously, causing the light to leave me and jump to him. I was grateful to be hidden in the returning darkness. I sat on the dirt floor and prayed silently. *God, show me a way out.*

"Sorry about that difficult streak," Marc said, still laughing. "But praise be to God for showing discipline toward us."

"Yeah, praise God for all of those beatings, huh Marc?" Gary was brazen. The light flashed to him now.

"Gary, your father *is* an elder. Why couldn't you do right?"

"Right according to you and right according to the rest of the world are not the same thing," Gary replied.

"That outside world is nothing but a cesspool," Tom grumbled. "Don't you understand that?"

"You're the one drugging five year old girls so you can do God knows what- Whatever witchcraft it is you call worship!" Gary wildly reached out and swung a fist at Tom. It struck him on the left cheek with enough force to cause Tom to reel backward, almost losing his balance. "Where is my sister?" Gary cried out in anger. Tom was rubbing his cheek. He took a seat at the table again.

"Gary," Tom replied in a quiet voice, "I hope you're not planning on trying anything else like that." Tom placed his flashlight on the table and pulled a pistol from behind his back. "And, I also hope you aren't planning on continuing to blaspheme in my presence." He stroked the pistol, as if to polish the steel.

Gary cleared his throat and began to speak again, in a tone matching Tom's. "Where is my sister? I want to see her."

"I'm afraid I can't make that happen." Tom put the gun behind his back again.

"Why not?" Gary asked indignantly.

Tom grabbed his flashlight and pointed it toward Gary. "Because I don't like you, and I don't owe you any favors, boy."

Gary crossed his arms and kept a steady glare at Tom.

Tom turned to Marc. "I came down here for two reasons, and it's time I wrap it up. Number one: You're not to come up out of here, Marcus. It's too risky now. I will send someone down here to get the prisoners for the shaming tomorrow, but you stay put."

"Okay, I understand."

Tom turned away from Marc.

"Wait. What's the second thing?"

Tom stood at our cell again, risking getting punched with his closeness, but apparently willing to bet that his pistol was insurance enough against it. "The second thing has nothing to do with you, Marcus." Tom pointed the flashlight back into my corner. I had been watching everything, but hoping I was hidden and forgotten in the dark.

"Carly," Tom said, "I have an offer to make. Your parents don't want to see you shamed. The elders have ruled that it is fitting, but I have real respect for your father and mother. I have agreed to make a deal with your father that makes everyone happy."

I felt my heart begin to thrash against the walls of my chest. I pulled my knees up to meet my chin and covered my face with my hands. My breathing became labored. I flashed back to the afternoon in the woods behind Uncle Eric's home. Then I had panicked, imagining Tom Deally was near. Now the danger was real.

"So, here's the arrangement, Carly." Hearing Tom speak my name caused a surge of fear to cascade through my body. It felt like hot poison had been poured down my back. "I'm going to make your father an elder of the church. And you are going to come live with me. You'll be under my care."

It was silent. I kept my eyes squeezed shut, waiting for something to happen.

Gary spoke, breaking the silence with frustration. "Your town is falling apart, Deally. You really think this is going to last? Everything you've made here, the church, everything that-"

"One more word, Gary!" Tom screamed. My eyes popped open and my hands flew to my ears. Tom Deally's face contorted in his rage. "One more word and I promise to kill you right now!"

Now no one would speak.

"Carly, this has to be a choice you make here and now." He paused for a moment and smoothed the front of his shirt. "Come with me and you will live. I can give you a comfortable life. I will ask very little of you."

I felt more poisonous fear pour over my spine. It was like something evil had entered the room, and I was too scared to speak. I just shook my head, no.

"Come now, Carly. What I haven't told you yet is that the elders decided to have a shaming, but they also decreed that you will both be put to death for all of the trouble you've brought on our community. Come with me and you won't have to share Gary's grim fate."

I felt a tremble take hold of my body, the fear was taking its full effect. I heard a buzzing in my brain, like being right inside a beehive. I couldn't think, except to see Jesus. I could see him in my mind, like the night the painting looked at me. He was saying something now, but I couldn't hear the voice over the buzzing. I watched, reading lips, as Jesus spoke the same word over and over. Finally, I grabbed hold of what He was saying.

"Carly?" Tom Deally's voice broke me out of the vision. I looked up at Tom. I felt the fear melt away as I realized the word Jesus was speaking. He had given me a simple answer, and with it I felt a surge of strength. I stood up slowly and took a step out of the corner toward Tom. I stood beside Gary, who looked at me with desperation in his face. He was pleading with me silently. Whether his plea was for me to stay or go I couldn't tell. Neither option was good. I looked from Gary to Tom. Tom was smiling at me. I repeated what Jesus had been saying over and over. "No."

Tom let the light of his flashlight fall to point at his feet. "Then you will both die, and your father will have reason to spit on you tomorrow morning." He walked out quickly with those last words.

Nobody spoke. There had been enough talking. With Gary beside me and Tom Deally now gone, I felt safe again. I allowed myself to put away thoughts of the shaming- and what was to come after. I felt myself become exhausted suddenly. It had been a long night. I decided to take a page from Cynthia's book and lie on the floor. Gary sat beside me, leaning against the dirt wall of our cell.

~~~

"What's going on?"

Marc's voice jolted me out of a terrible nightmare. Back to the reality, which was worse. Gary had been resting his head on my shoulder. I gave him a nudge and he woke up easily. "Something's happening," I whispered to him.

Liam was standing in the tunnel now. He held a shovel in one hand and cradled a handgun between his cast and chest. "There's no more time for the shaming program."

"Wait, what?" Marcus' voice sounded groggy, like he had been asleep as well.

"The police have set up watch all around us. They are refusing to leave.

We need to eliminate the prisoners and block off the entrance."

Marcus looked over at me and his mouth opened slightly. A look of horror appeared on his face as Liam handed him the gun.

"Wait," Marcus whispered to Liam. "Did Tom talk with you?"

"Yes, I just told you he did. Now we don't have much time before daybreak, and Tom wants this finished tonight."

"No, no, no. Did you speak with Tom, face to face?" Marcus was waving the gun in the air and began pacing in front of our jail cells.

"No, I didn't speak to him face to face. He's been all locked up in his house. It was on the phone, okay? Tom wants *you* to do this, but if you can't, I'll trade you for this shovel. I don't know why he thought the guy with the cast should be the one covering the prison entrance anyway." Liam reached toward Marc to grab the gun.

Marcus jumped away from him. "Hey! Tom has asked me to do this, so you just go get started on finding some dirt and rocks to cover this place up."

"Fine," Liam replied defensively. "But you'd better be done with this soon-"

"I know," Marcus interrupted him, "we don't have much time."

"I was gonna say you seem pretty emotional. Just do it, don't chat."

"Don't worry about me," Marcus said angrily. "You're the one who didn't follow orders to kill Eric's family, remember?"

"Don't you worry about my choices in letting a couple of little girls and their family live, okay? This is different."

"Fine. And don't question whether I can follow through! Just go get your dirt. And get it from the park. You can cover up the hole by pulling the sandbox over it." Liam nodded and left.

Marcus stood, staring at the gun in his hand. Gary slowly went toward him, standing as close as possible on our side of the cell bars. "Hey, Marc. What's happening?"

"Tom wants to get rid of the evidence of his crimes," Marc replied, eyes still glued to the gun.

"But what will he do with *you*?" Gary asked.

"What do you mean?" Marc looked at Gary. His eyes looked teary.

"You're going to be taken in for beating up Pastor Freeman. And when the police have you, they're going to ask you a lot of questions. You know a lot. I can't believe Tom's not thinking about getting rid of you too."

Marc's face went from scared to devastated. "Maybe Tom has a plan to protect me."

"Do you really believe that?" Gary asked quietly.

Marcus didn't reply.

I stood beside Gary and looked at my brother. "There's a reason we're all here right now," I told him. "This is your chance to make things right. You can save us and you can bring down Tom Deally."

"Bring him down? He's been good to me."

"He's been good to you?" I asked. "He took you away from your family, and he had you beaten and brainwashed."

"It was for my good," Marcus replied. Tears began to come down his face. "He was just trying to show me the truth, and he was pulling me out of my rebellion. It was good for me."

"Marcus," I said, using my most demanding tone. "Tom Deally is asking you to kill us."

"I know!" He screamed and slammed the gun down on the table. He gripped onto the bars of my jail cell and looked into my eyes. "I just want to please God."

"Tom Deally's god wouldn't give you a visitation, even with all of your devotion. His god doesn't care about you, and I can promise you that if you kill us to please this *god*, you will lose your life tonight." I spoke as clearly and calmly as possible. I felt a lump in my throat, my eyes were stinging and I knew I would cry. Just not yet. "You have to do the right thing, and I can promise you that Jesus will give you a visitation. But you have to choose right now."

I tried to grab his hand through the bars, but he pulled away. He wiped the tears from his face, straightened up, grabbed the handgun from the table and replied, "I'm sorry, but we don't have much time."

Marcus walked determinedly past us and into the passageway which would undoubtedly lead him to the elders' daughters. He gripped the pistol tightly.

Gary yelled after him. "Marcus, rethink this! Do the right thing!" Gary began shaking the jail cell bars vigorously and screaming, "Marcus! Marcus!"

I sat on the ground and placed my hands over my ears. I didn't want to hear the gunshots, the screams, the horror that was soon to take place. I looked over to see Cynthia lying on the floor with her eyes closed. She looked sicker than ever. I wondered if she was already dead or if she was about to sleep through her own murder. Either way, I envied her.

Gary continued yelling and shaking the bars. One of them actually came loose, and then another. He was able to pull them out of the ground and throw them aside. There was just enough room for him to squeeze through. I almost expected him to grab my hand and lead me outside to safety. I should have known better. He went running down the passageway after Marcus. He began calling Brittany's name as he ran.

"God, please help," I whispered into the dank air.

THIRTEEN

Two gunshots rang through the underground labyrinth. I sprang out of the cell, through Gary's newly fashioned doorway, and looked at Cynthia. She was still unmoving, her eyes closed. I thought of trying to wake her and get her out, but there was no key and I very much doubted my strength would aid in loosing the bars to her cell as Gary's had to ours. Besides, she still wasn't moving and I needed to get out of there before another gunshot rang out with a mission to kill me. I made my way out of the jail area and headed through the hallway to what I hoped would be the exit.

I saw some morning light beginning to shine at the end of this tunnel I found myself in. I hadn't known where this underground hideout was located on the property until I peered outside. I could see the front gate of Tom Deally's home about two hundred yards away. A small creek that would lead to the Sadmen River was running just to the right of the opening I was standing in. Dense bushes and a few tall trees separated the hideout from view of the gravel road between it and Tom's home.

I looked more closely at the house. The security gate was closed, and there had been barbed wire added to the top of the cement walls that held the gate doors together. Men stood guard out front. They were elders I recognized from Tom Deally's Reformed Church. They each held massive weapons which I had never seen before. Machine guns and shot guns. I stepped out of the underground cave and took a few steps forward, staring at the men in front of Tom's home.

"Freeze, girl!" A man's voice came from behind me. I did freeze immediately. "Turn around with your hands up."

I obeyed, but with fear. I wished I had the pillowcase over my head. I remembered what Gary and I had been told about everyone blaming us for Deally's problems. As soon as I showed my face, that would be the end for me. I took a deep breath and thanked God for His salvation. I would soon be cashing in for the after life.

When I turned, I saw two men hunkered down in the bushes with long rifles. They were wearing black outfits. A third man stood between them, a man I recognized. Agent Jones! I breathed out, "Thank You, God."

"Carly!" Agent Jones holstered his sidearm and motioned me to come to him. "Where did you just come from?"

"There's a cave. Underground," I replied in shock. Agent Jones was the last person I expected to see. He spoke into a walkie-talkie, demanding another unit to meet him.

"How did we miss this?" The agent said to himself. "Carly, who else is down there? Anyone?"

"Yes. But I'm afraid everyone is dead. Well, except for my brother." My voice cracked.

"Marcus?" Jones asked.

I nodded. I sat down in the grass beside Agent Jones. I tried to speak, but it may have come out in incoherent sobs. "The girls were down there, and Cynthia too. And Gary…"

Agent Jones squatted down beside me. "Okay. We're going to have someone take you out of here. Just hold on." He stood back up straight and spoke to one of the men dressed in black. "Go and do a sweep of the cave. One of our suspects is down there. If he's armed, don't take any chances. Just shoot."

The man nodded and proceeded carefully toward the cave's entryway. I watched him enter and suddenly remembered Liam. I shot to my feet and looked at Agent Jones. "Sir, there's another man who's going to be coming back here any minute."

"Do you know where he's coming from?" Agent Jones asked me.

"Yes, from the playground in town. And he's been gone some time. He was getting dirt to close up the jail entrance." My arms were flailing as I spoke.

The agent kept a calm, controlled look on his face. "That's just fine. We have agents in the community. If he went there, he's being held there."

"Oh, good." My mind raced over the events of the past twenty-four hours. "What happened to my family?" I asked, suddenly concerned.

"I assume they're being held in their home as well as all the other Dealy residents."

"Oh, right. I was thinking about my uncle and his family, though. Are they okay?" I hadn't really thought of my mother, my father or my siblings. They were still my *family*, but the term seemed more suited to Eric, Beverly and their kids.

"Yes, Eric and the family are fine. They were all tied up in their house.

Eric and Jacob were pretty beat up. No broken bones or anything like that, though. They're all at home, waiting for this whole Deally thing to be over."

"What's happening?" I asked.

The man who had gone into the cave emerged from the bushes before Agent Jones could answer. He was alone. I shut my eyes in an attempt to keep back tears. Everyone must be dead, I thought.

"Carly," Agent Jones said. "Carly, open your eyes."

I opened my eyes slowly and looked ahead. Marcus was carrying Cynthia Fagetti in his arms. She looked groggy and sick, but she was alive. Soon, girls were coming out of the opening behind them. There were twelve of them, the oldest looked to be in her thirties. She had a sullen looking, tired facial expression. There were two other older girls, in their twenties or late teens who shared her down trodden face. There were a couple of younger girls as well, maybe seven years old. They looked happy. They must have realized they were being rescued. All the girls followed closely behind the man in black.

I watched in disbelief. I knew I had heard gun shots. Why was everyone alive, and why wasn't Marcus in custody, or dead? I waited for Gary to emerge from the cave. It felt like an eternity of waiting. I held my breath and tried to make my heart stop palpitating. Marcus, Cynthia, the man in black and the girls reached our position and were instructed to wait for someone to come and escort them to a safe location. While Agent Jones was talking with them I kept my eyes fixed on the opening in the earth where Gary would surely emerge from.

"Were there any casualties in there?" Agent Jones asked the man in black who had gone in.

"One," he replied.

I spun around and screamed in terror. "Gary!"

The man in black stared with his mouth open at me. I didn't wait for him to respond. I turned back toward the cave and ran. I sped through the dark, dank hallway and past the jail cells, through another deep hall and into the very back of the hideout where I'd heard the gunshots originate.

I had to stop and wait for my eyes to adjust to the dim light. I looked around desperately, but for almost a minute, all I could see was the color red. I could hear Gary moaning and crying. I dropped to my knees and crawled toward where I heard him. My eyes finally allowed me to see as I reached him. He was sitting on the ground with a woman in his arms. She was dead. I look to Gary in confusion. His eyes were red from tears and his face was pale.

I looked from him to the woman. She had chestnut colored hair that was long and dirty, like it hadn't been washed in a long time. Her face looked like it had been broken and healed back up at least once. Her eyes were sunken in, and her skin looked terribly tired. Her body was very thin. She must have starved to death, I thought. Even in her current condition, though, she resembled her brother.

"I'm sorry, Gary," I said. Tears began to stream down my cheeks.

"She was a fighter," he said with a slight smile. His face was glistening with tears. "I can tell she fought until the very end. Can't you tell?"

"Yes," I replied. "I can tell."

Gary nodded and began to stand up with the body. He hoisted her over one shoulder and motioned for me to follow. He began to go toward the end of the tunnel, toward the outside. Before we stepped out, he took my hand in his.

"She's going to make it out, just like us," he told me.

FOURTEEN

When we emerged from the hideout, we were immediately carted away in an FBI van with the rest of the people who had been inside. We went to a make-shift office that had been set up about a mile away from Deally. We were questioned briefly, but mostly the girls were of interest. After about an hour they were taken in a black SUV to the city for further questioning and, I assume, counseling. I'm sure they needed it. Apparently, Tom Deally had told these girls that they were specially chosen by God to be the housing places of the Deally goddesses. The younger ones wanted to believe this, that they were special, but the treatment they received kept them from accepting that they were. They all felt used. Marcus was arrested for the assault of Pastor Freeman, but was promised leniency if he answered all of the authority's questions about the community and Tom Deally. He agreed without hesitation.

Brittany's body, and a very sick Cynthia Fagetti, were both transported to the nearest city hospital and morgue. Gary was invited to go with his sister's body, but he said he needed to stay with me and make sure I'd be okay. I mourned with him, finding myself in tears every time I saw him break down. I wished we could have gotten to her sooner.

There were people scurrying about all around us, but we seemed to be of little priority in the midst of the authority's current operation. We were under one of three large canopy tents that were working as command central for the FBI's operation. Their plan was to get all of the Deally residents corralled and eventually shipped out for questioning. That part of the plan seemed to be going well, but it was the second part they were having difficulty executing.

They wanted Tom Deally to come out of his home and surrender, but he wasn't even answering their phone calls anymore. Armed Deally clergymen were surrounding Tom's home, most probably ordered not to back down, to defend their paradise, to serve their God.

I prayed that God would continue to do the miraculous and bring Tom Deally out of the house like He'd brought us out of the jail. Then, I remembered the gunshots.

"Gary? Did Marcus try to shoot you?"

Gary smiled. "No. He shot the lock off of the girls' jail cell. I guess he

145

didn't have a key."

"I'm confused." I leaned toward Gary who was sitting on a folding metal chair beside me. "So, Marc didn't try to kill anyone?"

"I guess the things you said got to him, because he was trying to get us all out alive." He paused and his eyes seemed to look somewhere very far away. "He almost succeeded."

My heart hurt for Gary. I knew he had spent most of his life wondering about his sister, and to have found her lifeless body must have been horrible.

"But at least Marcus is going to be okay," Gary said, drawing his eyes back to mine.

"Do you really think so?"

"Yeah, I do. I'm just praying Jesus will visit him, like you promised."

I had forgotten about that.

"I think it'll happen," Gary said with a slight grin. "Maybe it already did. I mean, what exactly makes someone go from brainwashed to suddenly in their right mind, willing to rescue the people they were commanded to kill?"

"You don't think I'm that persuasive?" Gary smiled and shook his head.

"No. I think God had a hand in it."

"You're probably right. I guess there was a reason for us to come back here after all."

Agent Jones walked into our canopy right about then and sat himself in a chair beside us. His usually calm face looked sick.

"Are you okay, Agent Jones?" Gary asked.

"Something happened," Jones replied. "It's..." He rubbed his forehead and pinched the bridge of his nose. "It's not good. Gary, I'm afraid your father has been shot. He's been rushed to the nearest hospital, but things don't look good."

"Wait, what happened?" Gary didn't seem upset so much as curious.

"Tom wouldn't answer our calls, he wouldn't surrender. We didn't want things to happen like this, I assure you. We had a negotiator go to the gate to attempt to meet with Tom. He was shot by one of the men guarding the house. From there, a battle ensued. Some of our people were injured, but all of the elders surrounding Deally's home went down. Most were shot by our snipers, and

146

they're not going to survive..." Agent Jones trailed off and got an angry look on his face. "This shouldn't have happened."

"Well, at least you've got Tom," Gary replied.

"Tom Deally wasn't even in the house! He had those men guarding an empty place. At some point he got away, and we didn't know about it."

"Wow," Gary said. "That's messed up."

"I've got to get my people started on a search now. I just thought you might want to know about your father. He's one of only two men who look like they might actually survive."

Agent Jones shook our hands formally and left the tent.

"Can you believe that?" Gary said to me.

"No. I hope they find Tom fast."

"Me too."

Tom Deally had left the men who knew the most about the inner workings of the community to die for him. I was amazed that anyone could be so cold, and I had never thought Tom Deally was that low. All of the dinners we shared at my home in Deally, all of the church events and services, through them all, I never realized just how sinister Tom Deally was. He thought he could flee and leave everyone who knew anything dead.

Tom had taken his wife with him, but they left their children in Deally. Extensive questioning revealed that Tom's children were almost as clueless about the inner workings of the community as everyone else. It's frightening how two-faced men can be, even in their own homes.

Gary and I were told that Eric and Beverly were coming to pick us up. We waited expectantly at the edge of the FBI's makeshift field office. We watched black FBI vehicles with tinted windows carry loads of Deally residents out of the community as we waited. We couldn't make out their faces through the tinted glass, but we knew they were people we knew, people we'd grown up with. They were people jilted by Tom Deally, but who blamed our rebellion for the end of their paradise.

My heart sank a little every time one of the vehicles drove by. I didn't want to think about my mother and father, staring out at me, thinking I was the reason their happy existence was coming to a sudden and violent end. They always loved Tom and the Deally community. I found myself hiding behind Gary when the vehicles passed by. He didn't seem to mind.

When we saw the shiny red family van pull up in front of us, I think we both sighed in relief. I looked at Gary to catch a glimpse of his facial expression as Eric pulled up. A slight smile appeared and he shut his eyes for a moment. I wondered if he was thanking God.

"Well, are you ready to leave Deally again?" I asked. He laughed.

"Carly, I'm not sure Deally exists anymore."

Eric and Beverly jumped out of the van, leaving it idling. They both rushed over to us, and the hugging began. Beverly was crying. Eric kept his cool, but only until he gathered us to pray. "Come on, everyone. Grab hands."

We stood in a circle and Eric began to pray. "Dear Lord, we thank You for bringing our family safely back together and for bringing these people out of Deally." His voice began to break and he had to pause before continuing.

"God, we ask You to let the truth be known about Tom Deally and all that he has done. Bring Your justice into this situation and let many be saved through it." Eric stopped praying. We stood still, in silence. I opened my eyes and looked around at everyone. Their eyes were still closed, heads bowed in reverence to God, reveling in the moment. Eric had tears rolling down his face now.

"Jesus, please reveal Yourself to Carly and Gary's families," Beverly said, breaking the silence. "Just visit them and comfort them in this time of transition and uncertainty. Let the scales fall from their eyes, Lord." I remembered my promise to Marcus, that Jesus would visit him. I closed my eyes quickly and whispered, Amen. Everyone else followed, and the prayer was over.

"I feel warm all over," I observed aloud. We dropped each other's hands and headed for the van. Beverly laughed at my comment. "I get that too, Honey. It's just the presence of God. Hannah calls it the *warm and fuzzies*."

"I felt it too," Gary said with satisfaction. We climbed in the back of the van and buckled ourselves in. "Where are the kids, anyway?" Gary asked.

"They're waiting at the house with Officer Ian and a couple of deputies," Eric informed us. "They wanted to come, but it took a lot of persuading just for Bev and I to leave the house."

"We could have had one of the FBI agents bring you two home, but we wanted to come ourselves," Beverly added.

"I'm glad you did," I said.

Beverly turned around to look at me. "I almost forgot. I found this in the doorway as we were leaving the house."

I took Grandma Freedom's ring in my hand and held it tightly before slipping it on my finger. "I'm so happy to see this."

Beverly smiled.

"I think I'm starting to see it now," I said to her. Beverly's smile widened and she turned back to face the front. No one spoke the rest of the ride home. I had plenty of thoughts to fill the time with, and I suppose everyone else did too.

A warm welcome, and more tears, awaited us at home. Jacob had been watching everything on the news and was happy to see us safe. The girls didn't know exactly what had gone on, and they were still in shock from the "bad men" breaking into the house. They cried with joy to see their parents, because they didn't want them to leave home at all; after seeing Eric and Beverly were safe they greeted Gary and me. The policemen who were there retreated to their posts. There were seven of them with orders not to leave the property until Tom Deally was in custody.

When they left us alone, we all joined Jacob in watching the news. It wasn't too long before the authorities were able to figure out where Tom Deally and Carmen were going. They didn't announce this on the news, but they did tell viewers that the FBI were aware of their destination and were waiting for them there. It reminded me of being confronted by Liam on the bus to Carl Hill, being told that our pursuers were waiting for us at the end of the line. That seemed like bad news, but God was on our side. I didn't see it then, but as I watched the coverage on the "Fall of the Deally Cult Commune", I saw what I was blind to before. God was always with us, shaping things for our good. As for Tom Deally, he would face justice after all.

We were eating our previously neglected pizza when the news broadcast showed us what we wanted to see.

"Tom Deally is being taken in police custody here at the international airport in Phoenix, Arizona. We're told Deally was actually here for a lay-over before he would be boarding a flight to an undisclosed location in Europe. I guess just this once we can be glad for airport lay-overs," a female reporter said over the live footage being shown.

Tom and Carmen were both put in handcuffs right on the tarmac. The images were fuzzy; the cameras were far away. I could make out Tom and Carmen clearly, though. I let a satisfied smile spread across my face.

"Hey, is that Agent Jones?" Gary said, excitedly, pointing to a man dressed in black at the corner of the screen.

"I think it is," I replied. "He must be really happy right now."

"You know it! This is awesome," Gary replied. "I wish I could be there to see the look on Tom's face."

"Yeah," I agreed.

"I'm sure both of you will get a chance to see the look on his face when he's sentenced," Eric assured us.

"You think they'll air the trial on the news?" Beverly asked.

"Probably. But I'm fairly certain Carly and Gary will be a part of it."

"Yeah. That's probably true," Beverly replied. She glanced at the clock and her eyes widened. "It's time for you girls to get to sleep," she said, herding Hannah and Joanne out of the room. They were both more than ready for bedtime, totally submissive to their mother's command.

As the night dragged on, Jacob got bored of the news coverage and went to his room. Eric followed suite around midnight, saying he was too old to stay up, but he would catch up on the story in the morning.

Gary and I watched the news silently into the early morning hours. There was no break in the story. The news networks, locally and nationally, were putting all of their airtime toward the story. There was no lack of information. People were calling in with comments and even stories of being in the town. Several people were interviewed who had tried to move into Deally over the past years and were rejected for various, and sometimes ridiculous, reasons. One woman told of how she was almost allowed to relocate her family to the community, but when Tom Deally suspected her hair was dyed, and she told him it was, her family was turned away. She ended the interview by thanking her hairdresser from saving her from the biggest mistake of her life. "I was ready to give up everything for what I thought was paradise," she said. "I just thank my beautician every time I go in for my hair appointment. I will never stop dying my hair."

Around four in the morning the coverage began to lose momentum. The same interviews and information were being repeated. At this point, it began to hit me. The magnitude of what had happened in the last months was hard to even believe. I looked at Gary. "Can you believe this?"

"What? The hair dye thing?" Gary asked. That interview had just been shown again.

"Sure, that and everything else that's gone on."

Gary nodded slowly. "It's been wild."

We sat in silence for several minutes before I asked a question that had been on my mind. "Do you think Marcus will do the right thing?"

Gary folded his arms. "I'd like to think so."

"And do you think it could be possible, if he doesn't go to prison, for he and I to have a relationship again?" I wanted my big brother back. Despite all that Marcus had done, I wanted to believe he could be my brother again.

"He didn't kill anybody in that cave, and I believe that had to do with what you said to him. I think he still cares about you."

I nodded. "I hope everything works out for him."

"What about the rest of your family?" Gary asked.

"I don't know. Maybe Jon will want to have something to do with me. He's still young, and I doubt he realizes what's going on. But everybody else-" My throat choked up suddenly. I felt my eyes sting as tears pushed their way out. I tried to speak but my throat was throbbing. I shook my head in frustration and cried.

Gary leaned toward me and put an arm around my shoulder. "It's going to be okay, Carly."

"You don't know that," I managed to squeak out. I grabbed a throw pillow and buried my face. Gary didn't say a word, and I probably wouldn't have been able to hear him through my blubbering if he had. Instead, he left his arm around my shoulder, a silent gesture of support. I wished I was as strong as he seemed to be.

I'd ruined my parents lives, and even though the Deally community was one of seedy inner workings, they would look past it to blame me for wrecking paradise. I left Deally with the notion that I would never have to face my family again, but now that we were all outside of Deally, I was beginning to believe otherwise. I feared the day I might certainly face my family. I had replaced them in my mind with Eric and Beverly, Jacob and the girls. In my heart, however, my own parents and my own siblings were deeply rooted as my family. I couldn't change that. I wished I could.

"Carly? It's late. Maybe you should just go to sleep. Rest will do you good."

I pulled my face out of the pillow and nodded. "You're probably right."

I studied Gary's face more closely now and saw that it was glistening. He had been crying. I felt selfish. Who did Gary have to lean on? "Are *you* okay?"

Gary looked away and laughed. Not a laugh out of joy, but a laugh out of pain, a laugh to cover up whatever raw emotion was pent up beneath the surface. "I will be fine, Carly."

I gave him a moment of silence, hoping he would open up.

"You're worried about your family, but the fact is you've got a family right here." Gary waved his arm in the air demonstratively. "All of this is here for you. It's all for *you*."

"I know. I know what you're saying, Gary."

"Yeah. Meanwhile, I've got a dead sister and parents who never had much to do with me anyway- and my father is in the hospital. I doubt if he'll make it."

"Why do you doubt it?" My own pain was pushed aside. I would let no more tears fall for my problems, not while Gary was venting his own.

"I just have a bad feeling." He pulled his feet off the ground and onto the sofa between us. "There's no reason why he should live. I mean, I don't think that he sees a reason. His whole life was wrapped up in Deally. He was willing to die for Tom. I don't think my father is going to try too hard to live."

"Wow," I replied in a whisper. I was astonished. "Well, maybe if he knew he had a reason-"

Gary cut me off in mid-sentence. "I know. I know what you're thinking." He looked into my eyes and shook his head. "But I don't think I can do that."

"Do you mean going to talk with him?" Gary nodded and looked away. Fresh tears fell.

"Yeah."

"Well, why not?" I asked.

"Because I'm pretty sure my dad would have killed us if Tom asked him to."

I wasn't sure what to say to that.

"I thought a lot about what Marc did for us. He decided to save our lives. He decided to be a good brother to you, to do the right thing for your sake. If it had been my father in there with orders, he would have followed through."

Gary wiped the tears away and looked me squarely in the eye. "The funny part is, no matter how much I tell myself I won't go see him, I keep hearing this little voice inside telling me it's the right thing to do."

FIFTEEN

Agent Jones made it his business to walk us through all of the pre-courtroom training. He was there every step of the way, which I must admit did put me at ease. Familiar faces were nice, especially trustworthy ones. The police headquarters where we went through all of this happened to be a few blocks from where Gary's father was in the hospital.

Agent Jones informed Gary that he was free to visit him, but he had to be escorted by an officer and probably a lawyer, just in case. His father was in a stable condition and would be well enough to lend his testimony to the trial, and depending on evidence, be prosecuted himself. Gary would have to be coached on what he could and could not discuss with his father.

On the other hand, I was not allowed to speak with my family. I was too young, I was told. There was a risk that my testimony could be compromised by the emotion of seeing them, or of hearing whatever they had to say. I didn't argue this point. When Jones told me, I nodded and thanked God. I didn't want to speak with my family. I did wish Gary would see his father, however. I knew God wanted him to go. He knew that too. It only took a few days of prodding before Gary gave in, called Agent Jones, and went to visit his father.

Gary went to see his dad early in the day, before anyone in the house was awake. Agent Jones escorted him there, along with a lawyer and another police officer. He came home around noon. It was a few weeks before the school year was to start, so Jacob and Eric were in the city taking care of Jacob's registration. The girls were both at a birthday party; they brought a police officer along too. Meanwhile, Beverly was on the phone. I waited for Gary in the kitchen.

When he finally returned home, Gary sat down beside me at the kitchen counter. He looked more dressed up than usual, wearing dress pants and a dull green colored polo shirt. The outfit reminded me of being back in Deally, the dull semi-formal fashion on display. I wondered if he had dressed this way on purpose. He let out a shaky breath.

"How is your dad?"

"Not good." He ran his fingers through his hair and crossed his arms. "He could barely speak. He had a lot of tubes and wires and stuff all over. I guess I expected him to look better from what Jones said."

"Yeah. He said he was stable."

"Well, he's got surgery in a couple of days, and that's supposed to get him going again."

"So, did you two talk?"

"We did. Just a little. Like I said, he couldn't really talk much. He was shot by the SWAT team right up by his neck and it shocked his vocal cords," he said, placing his hand over his own throat. "But, I think that might have been a good thing. Him not being able to speak too much, I mean." His eyes focused on mine. "I was able to tell him about Jesus."

Gary shrugged his shoulders. "I mean, I don't know if any of it resonated in him, but I sort of knew that was why I was there."

"Well, did he say anything about it?" I asked.

"No. I left the room on that note, so I didn't really give him a chance. You think I should have?"

"I don't know. Either way, he's got something to think about."

"Yeah." Gary nodded. "I hope he realizes the truth about Tom Deally. My father was willing to die for him, but he knows now that Tom wasn't in the house when all of the elders were protecting it."

"Did you tell him that?"

"No. I wanted to, but I asked Agent Jones ahead of time and found out he was already told. They've been telling him things to try to sway his loyalty away from Deally. I was told not to bring it up, though."

"That makes sense, I guess."

"Yeah." Gary nodded.

"Was your mother there?"

"She was." He let out a sigh. "But she didn't really want to speak with me."

"You didn't talk at all?"

"She was sitting in a chair outside of my dad's room. I went to give her a hug. She let me, but she didn't hug back. I pretty much got the picture at that point, so I didn't try to talk to her. She was never that loving anyway...But, she never shied away from hugs either."

"I'm sorry, Gary."

Gary gave me a weak smile, climbed off the kitchen stool and walked away. Normally I wouldn't have let him leave in the middle of a conversation, but he needed a pardon. He was obviously in need of time to himself, time to think.

A few hours later, I found him sitting in the upstairs hallway. He had a sheet of paper in his hands.

"What's that?" I asked, sitting down beside him on the carpet.

He looked a little startled. "Oh. Here."

He handed the paper to me and I looked over it. It was the death announcement for Gary's sister, Brittany. I handed it back to him and sat quietly. I wasn't sure if he'd want to talk about it.

"The funeral is tomorrow," Gary said. "I'm hoping Eric will take me. You can go if you want." I was surprised by the invitation. I was also surprised that Gary wanted to go to the funeral. He wasn't one to show emotion, and a funeral wasn't a great place for masking feelings.

"Sure, I'll go."

"It's going to be small, hidden away from the press. That's the plan anyway." Gary folded the paper in half and smoothed down the crease methodically. "I'm not sure how it will be. Have you ever been to a funeral?"

"Once," I replied. "My Grandpa Sid's funeral in Deally. But I was too young to remember."

"I've got to tell you something," Gary said suddenly.

"What is it?" I felt my eyes searching his countenance. I was trying to find some flicker of happiness in his expression. He looked so sad. I suppose it was a sad circumstance, his father being in the hospital and his sister's funeral coming up.

"I wanted to let you know what's going on before I told anyone else. I figure I owe that much to you."

"What is it?"

"I'm going to be leaving soon."

"Are you going back to the hospital or something?"

Gary shook his head. "No, I mean I'm moving out. I won't be living here

157

much longer."

I suddenly felt a headache coming on. "What do you mean?"

"I was talking with the police today. One of the officers has a wife who works as a professor at a college a few towns away. The college is going to give me a full scholarship. They have a GED program, so I can catch up on the education I missed out on in Deally's school. Then, I'll have four years allotted toward pursuing whatever degree I'd like. It's actually a really great opportunity." He smiled, and I was glad to see some joy flicker in his eyes.

"When do you have to leave?"

Gary's smile faded, but his eyes retained their cheer. "I will be leaving next month."

I nodded and pretended to examine a scuff on my sneaker.

"There's a scholarship for you too. Of course, you'll have to wait until you're old enough. I think Beverly's been looking into your attending grade school, or Junior High. I'm not sure."

"It depends on how I do on some tests," I informed him, still rubbing at my shoe with my thumbs. "I guess I didn't think about *you* going to school." I looked up from my shoe. "But it's great." I shot him a smile, which I hoped looked authentic. I hated the idea of Gary going away. It hadn't crossed my mind at all.

"So, you're going to be gone for four years?"

Gary shrugged. "Probably more like five. I mean, it might take someone else less time to get ready for the GED test, but I've missed more education than most. I'm not even sure if the basic stuff we were taught in Deally was right or not. It's going to be a mess trying to straighten out what I really know and what I don't."

"So, *five* years then?" I felt my headache intensifying. I rested my head in my hands.

"Yeah, but there will be summer breaks and holidays. I'll be back sometimes."

"I guess that's true," I replied, lifting my head from my palms. "And five years isn't so long… I mean, if I'm in school and keeping busy, it could fly by, right?"

"Yeah," Gary laughed.

158

"What's so funny?"

"I'm just surprised that you're so distraught over my leaving."

"Well, you're part of my family now..." I trailed off and let my thoughts stay in my head. Gary couldn't possibly understand how much he meant to me. Not only had he been a protector to me, but he had helped me accept Jesus, he had filled the role Marcus had left empty, and he had been my first crush. He had been my first fiancé! He meant the world to me, but he didn't seem to notice.

Gary smiled and held me in a hug. "I'm glad to be a part of your family, Carly."

It was just about that time that crunching gravel was heard outside. Eric was home. Gary and I went downstairs. Beverly was almost finished making lunch, when Hannah and Joanne ran in to see her.

"Mommy!" Joanne screeched. "The birthday was so fun and we got baggie goods!" She held up a pink gift bag.

"Oh, *goodie bags*," Beverly corrected.

"Yes, goodie bags," Joanne replied. "Look, Carly!" She held the gift bag up for me to see.

I opened my eyes wide to look surprised. "Joanne! What did you get in there?"

"I don't know yet," she said with an excited smile. I grabbed the bag out of her hand and sat her at the kitchen counter beside me.

"Let's see," I said, dumping out the bag. "Nail polish!" I held up a tiny pink bottle. "Candy!" I held up a handful of Hershey's Kisses. "And a necklace!" I showed her the plastic beaded necklace, clearly handcrafted by whoever held the birthday party. Joanne lifted her arms into the air.

"What a great goodie bag," she cried out. "Put the necklace on!"

I reached over to put the necklace over her head.

"No! On *you*, silly!" Joanne laughed.

"Oh, you want me to wear it?" She nodded her head vigorously.

"Yes. You wear the necklace and then do nails," she said. She grabbed the nail polish bottle and pushed it into my hand. Hannah came and sat on the other side of me at the counter.

"Let's see what I've got too," she said. She spilled the contents of her purple goodie bag onto the counter.

"Well," I said, "You've got the same things as Joanne, but your nail polish is purple!" I mocked excitement, showing Joanne and Hannah the two colors. "Now we can do pink *and* purple!"

"That's great," Joanne said through a huge smile. "Let's go do nails."

Beverly leaned over the counter across from us and smiled. "Girls, let's have lunch first, okay?"

Joanne's lower lip jetted out suddenly. "Are you sure?"

Beverly gave her a motherly look, raising one eyebrow.

"Okay, Mommy. We can wait to have lunch first."

"Thanks, sweetheart," Beverly replied. "Everyone, let's gather for prayer before we eat."

Eric, Jacob and Gary gathered with us girls around the counter. We joined hands and Beverly prayed,

"Father, we thank You for all You've done for us in these past weeks and we are anxious to see what you will do in the future. God, we ask for a speedy end to all of this Deally business and for peace to return to our home and our community. In Jesus' name we pray. Amen." The amen was echoed around the circle.

~~~

Brittany's funeral was an especially sad event. Gary and I were dropped off at a local funeral home, along with our police escort, of course. We sat at the back of the church with Officer O'Neil. The church where the funeral was held was decorated with yellow roses. I wondered if anyone realized the Deally symbolism, but decided not to say anything. After all, Deally had been dissolved. Yellow roses were just yellow roses now.

Besides the man facilitating the funeral, there were about twelve other people in the building. One woman sitting ahead of us had a tape recorder in her hand, and a note pad with some words scribbled on it sat beside her on the pew. I wondered if she was a reporter trying to be discreet. I don't think Gary noticed her, and this was another observation I didn't bring up. I also didn't bring up the fact Gary's parents were not in attendance. I figured he had probably already made that observation for himself.

A man approached the cream colored podium at the front of the room and

160

began to pray. "Heavenly Father, we give You thanks this day for life. Though it ends in this world, it is eternal in Your Son, Jesus Christ. God, we ask You to have mercy on Brittany's soul, knowing her life on this earth was deprived of the truth of Your gospel. Show her the love that You have for her by taking her into Your Kingdom, and give peace to those who she has left behind in this world, that they might see her in the next. In Jesus' name we pray. Amen."

The preacher allowed a short time for anyone to speak. Most of the people in the church were strangers. I'm not sure why they were there, maybe the church asked its congregants to come, simply to fill seats. I did recognize a small cluster of girls in the front, girls who lived with Brittany under Tom Deally's home.

One of the girls from the group went up to speak first. She was a thin brunette who looked to be about twenty years old. She walked slowly to the front and kept her arms rigidly straight at her sides. At the podium she looked unsure of herself, scanning the faces in the room before speaking. Her expression softened slightly when she looked at Gary and me. She must have remembered us from the day Marcus spared all of our lives.

"My name is Stella," she said. "And I knew Brittany for a long time. She was only a few years older than me, I think. She and I used to tell stories to the younger girls who stayed with us. She was a better storyteller than me." Stella paused and her eyes dropped. She didn't make any more eye contact or look out to the crowd. "Brittany had a way of helping the younger girls to get through the days. She was always full of hope. But, after a while…" Stella's voice broke and she left the stage quickly, rejoining the other girls.

"I'll finish for you," one of the girls told Stella. Stella nodded and her younger friend walked up to the pulpit. She was not as nervous as Stella; she seemed almost confident. "Hello," she said, addressing everyone. "I'm Kelly. Brittany didn't do so well at the end of her life. Like so many of us who were used by Tom Deally for his evil religious activities, she was at the end of herself. She wanted to regain control. One way to do this was by refusing to eat or drink. She was left alone, because she couldn't be drugged if she didn't eat. We were always drugged for the ceremonies…" Kelly took a deep breath and dabbed at the corners of her eyes with a tissue before continuing.

"But Brittany got her way. She was left alone. Her accomplishment couldn't last, though. She died only a day before we all got out of Deally. She was really strong, even to the end, but her body couldn't keep up with her spirit. She will be missed." I was surprised at Kelly's bluntness. It felt inappropriate somehow. I was glad when she flipped her hair and walked back to her seat.

161

Gary went up next, which I did not expect. He trudged up to the front, looked out at everyone and spoke. "My sister is one of the many reasons that Tom Deally is going to be put away for the rest of his life. He was a liar and a horrible man. It may be that God will have mercy on him, but it will be from behind bars and he will never step foot outside of prison for the rest of his life. Brittany did not die in vain." Gary repeated his point before returning to his seat, "I might have lost a sister, but it wasn't in vain."

SIXTEEN

Gary came home every weekend at first. It was a two hour drive. He had received a rarely driven 1990 Buick from Eric and Beverly only a day before he left. He drove that Buick home each Friday afternoon and stayed for Sunday dinners. After a month or so, however, he apparently got used to college life and no longer felt the need to come home each weekend. He had made friends at school and was even working part time at a convenience store. I was happy for him, but I missed him a lot. I began to find myself thinking about him more and more every day.

Gary was pulled away from his classes to testify in the Deally trial toward the end of his first year. When I was told Gary would be returning home, I listened to my heart and did something a little irrational. I wrote him a letter. It started out thanking him for everything he'd done for me and welcoming him home. As I continued to write, my feelings poured out. I confessed all. I wrote that even though age was a limitation for the moment, I was willing to wait.

I felt my heart rate increase as I scribbled my feelings down as quickly as they came to my mind. I was willing to wait until age was of no consequence. I was nearing fifteen! Then, he would have my hand in marriage. And, after all, we *were* once engaged.

I left the letter on top of Gary's dresser that night, knowing he would find it when he came home the following day. My head told me it was a bad idea, my heart told me to let out my feelings, and my stomach told me I should go vomit.

~~~

We pulled up in a black SUV, with Agent Jones, and we were met with a sea of news vans and the people they had carried there. This was the day we had been waiting for. It was going to be a day remembered by all, and the news cameras and reporters were going to make sure of it.

There were many men and women, dressed in their best professional outfits, but acting less than professional, pushing and shoving each other for shots and sound bites. It was overwhelming, but Agent Jones pushed through the crowds and guided us safely inside the building. Gary and I had never made a televised appearance before this, which had all of the reporters asking us who we were. Agent Jones kept repeating the same sentence to the swarm: "Back up, back up! We have no statement!"

When we got inside there was one network, which apparently had exclusive access to the case. Their camera people were set up in the halls outside of the courtroom.

Gary and I were seated toward the back of the court chamber, where we could see almost everyone. Tom Dealy sat at a large table at the front, facing the judge's elevated podium seat and the witness stand. I recognized the back of his head, but I would not see him fully until I faced him from the witness platform. Gary's testimony came before mine.

The way Gary walked, slowly and decisively, to the front reminded me of Brittany's funeral. I knew he must have been thinking of her, thinking about his promise that she did not die in vain. His face was emotionless, but there was a determinedness to his movements that let me know he intended to do and say all he could to send Tom Dealy away for the rest of his life.

When Gary returned from the witness stand to his seat beside me, he whispered to me,

"Whatever you do, keep your eyes on the lawyers. Don't look at the other people. Don't look at the cameras. Don't look at Tom." I nodded and folded my hands together in my lap. I knew that would be a difficult task.

When my turn to stand witness came, I answered as best I could, but I remember being at a loss for the most part. I had more questions than I did answers about Dealy. My left leg bounced continually on nervous toes as I did my best to follow Gary's advice and keep my eyes only on the lawyers standing before me.

When the first attorney finished his round of questions, before the second one reached my podium, I looked around at all of the people. I looked at the cameras and the news people. I looked at Marcus in the crowd. He smiled at me, a brotherly look of support on his face. The rest of my family was not there, and I must say, I was relieved by this. I continued to look around at the different faces, most unfamiliar. Finally, my eyes landed on Tom Dealy. He was studying a document on the table before him. He looked up and smiled at me. My eyes darted away from his and landed on the approaching legal representative.

Gary was right, I shouldn't have looked at Tom Dealy. All I could think about through the rest of my questioning was Tom Dealy, smiling at me from the large defendant's table. That was all I seemed to think about for the rest of the day, in fact. His face wasn't joyful by any means, but it wasn't sorrowful either. He looked calm, peaceful, almost happy.

Gary and I were making our way through the halls, attempting to get outside of the courthouse after proceedings were over for the day. The crowded hallway was flowing like a river, everyone streaming together toward the doors. When Tom Deally came into the hall and began speaking with a reporter, the river stopped flowing. We stood and listened.

"The dissolution of Deally is regrettable. I'm certainly going to miss that place," Tom said to a female reporter. The woman held her microphone out for him to speak into. He grabbed hold of it for himself and continued to speak, looking into the camera.

"I would like to applaud all of the noble men who sacrificed their service to the cause of the community. But, we all knew this would happen." Tom paused for a moment, adjusting his tie.

The reporter moved beside Tom and spoke into the microphone he now held, "What do you mean by that?"

Tom looked up from his tie and smiled at the reporter. "Well, I'm no fool. All great religious thinkers endure persecution. Few true movements of God succeed in the wake of sinful humanity. But I have no doubt that God will raise up another behind me who will continue this legacy of pure religion." His eyes went back to addressing the camera. "I make no apologies for the things Deally stood for, or for my own actions in relation to the Reformed Church. I answer to a higher authority than these on the earth, and while this life is fleeting, eternity is indeed eternal." He paused and gave a chuckle at his statement. "In eternity, I will be honored, and all who have raised a hand against me will find their humility-" He rose a hand and then made a flourish toward the ground. "At my feet."

My stomach churned as I listened to Tom Deally's final statement. His words held such conviction. I linked arms with Gary and looked at him. He shook his head and returned the look.

"He really thinks he's not at fault here."

"And that we'll all bow before him," I added. Gary shook his head again and turned us away from Tom Deally's position. We found Agent Jones in the crowded corridor and he led us through the courthouse and out a back door.

SEVENTEEN

"So, who is this girl I've been hearing about?" asked Beverly.

The whole family was seated for dinner. Gary looked up at Beverly, then at Jacob.

"Girl?" Gary asked. "I guess you're talking about Wendy." He twirled his fork deep into a plate of spaghetti and continued, "It's not anything serious. We've just been hanging out. I'm surprised Jacob said anything." He shot Jacob a hard look.

"Well, maybe you'll let us meet her some time," Beverly said.

"Sure."

I watched Gary give Jacob another look, eyebrows raised, eyes questioning. He obviously didn't want us all knowing about this Wendy girl. I took a long drink from my water glass and tried to appear calm.

"Is she a Freshman too?" Beverly asked.

"Yes," Gary replied. "She's a Business Management major."

"A smart girl," Eric said, suddenly interested.

"A smart girl," Joanne echoed, using her hands to build a tower of red noodles on top of her French bread. Beverly noticed her project and removed her from the table.

When dinner was finished, Jacob pulled Gary away to watch videos on his computer. I went upstairs, wondering if perhaps Gary hadn't seen my letter yet. He hadn't spoken to me about it, and he was so busy with school work since he got home. Maybe, just maybe, he had missed it. I made my way to Gary's room and turned the doorknob slowly. I took a quick look left and right before jerking open the door and jumping into the room, shutting it behind me.

It was slightly tidier than I imagined it might be. Everything was in it's place. I felt my heart rate quicken suddenly. *I shouldn't be in here.*

I surveyed the dresser top. The letter. *Oh, thank You, God.* It hadn't moved. I snatched it from its place. My fingers felt frayed edges. The envelope was torn open at the end. The envelope had looked untouched, but it had been neatly opened and the contents removed. I let out a grunt and placed the envelope back on the dresser.

I took a walk out to the creek. The creek, after I stopped fearing it, had become a sanctuary for me. I would spend hours there alone, breathing in the quiet. I used to take Beverly's old easel there and paint. It was very relaxing. Towering conifer trees that littered the ground with green and brown needles veiled my sanctuary on every side from unwanted eyes.

I sat on a grassy slope where my feet could dangle into the brook. Feeling the water babble over my toes brought my soul into a state of relaxation. I closed my eyes and focused on the sound of the water. My mind wandered, and I began to think of Gary and Wendy. I imagined Wendy was a tall, beautiful woman with wavy golden hair and an infectious laugh. Gary looked at her with passion in his eyes and talked to her about his past. She listened with interest, and they shared their dreams for the future. I opened my eyes.

"God, this isn't right," I said aloud. "Is this part of Your plan?" I waited for an answer. It was quiet. I knew God was with me, but I could not understand His plan in that moment. I was wearing Grandma Freedom's ring, as always. Looking at the piece of aged jewelry, I reminded myself that it takes time to see what an artist is painting.

"What about the plan for *me*?" I sighed and shut my eyes again.

The sound of the brook was suddenly muffled by the sound of approaching footsteps. My breathing stopped. I fully expected to open my eyes and see Gary approaching.

"Carly." The footsteps got closer. I opened my eyes to see Beverly coming near.

"Hi. You scared me," I told her.

"Sorry, Sweetheart. What are you up to out here?" She sat down beside me and started untying her sneakers.

"Nothing. I'm just hanging out."

"I see." Beverly peeled off her socks and dipped her feet into the stream. "You know, there used to be fish in here."

"Really?"

"Yeah. When we first moved here. But a few years ago they built a dam upstream from here. This brook used to be a river, if you can believe it."

"That must have been great for swimming in."

"Oh, yeah. Jacob learned how to swim back here," Beverly laughed. "He loved it."

I found myself smiling at the thought of a little Jacob paddling around with water wings on his arms. "That's great. Too bad they built the dam."

"Yeah, it made the property different, for sure. But this is nice, too."

Beverly and I sat quietly for a while before she broke the silence.

"So, Carly..." She hesitated with her words and looked at me with an awkward smile.

"What?"

"Well, Gary showed me and Eric the letter you wrote him."

She spoke slowly, looking straight into my eyes. I was mortified.

"He wasn't trying to be disrespectful toward you, Carly. He just wasn't sure how to handle it."

"I don't know what to say." I took my feet out of the water and stood up.

"Carly, please sit. Let's talk about this."

I shut my eyes. *Oh God, help me.*

I sat back down and gave Beverly an exaggerated smile. "Okay."

"Thank you." She waited for me to speak, but I was tight lipped. She gave me a motherly look of concern. Head tilted forward, eyes locked on mine.

"Fine," I said. "So, I wrote him a letter. Did I do something so wrong?" I felt my shoulders raise up and touch my ears.

"You put Gary in a very awkward position."

"Is this why you were so insistent about talking about *Wendy* at dinner?" I asked with a sneer.

"No. In fact, I didn't know about your letter until after dinner." Her voice rose, "Now, drop the attitude, please."

"I'm sorry." She wasn't my enemy. Neither was Wendy. My shoulders dropped, and so did my eyes.

"I understand, Carly. I understand that you're in an awkward position too, and if you get a little huffy I can take it."

169

"Okay," I laughed softly. I dipped my toes into the brook and looked up into Beverly's eyes. I suddenly realized how embarrassing it was that she read the letter, and Eric too.

"Why did I have to give him that letter?"

"Sometimes we do crazy things when our emotions are high."

"It wasn't just crazy. It was stupid," I said, putting my hands over my face.

"Well, yes," Beverly said with a laugh. "Gary loves you like a sister, you know? And you are quite a bit younger than him."

"I know, I said that in the letter," I reminded her. I pulled my hands down from my face and waved them dramatically. "I'm not asking him to date me right now. Just to consider…" I knew it sounded dumb. I crossed my arms and looked at Beverly. "Forget it."

"Carly, the problem is that Gary doesn't feel that way about you, and there's no guarantee that time will change that. It's not fair to put this burden of expectations on him."

"What burden does he have? I'm the one who's in love with the guy who's in love with *Wendy*." I couldn't help but say that name with disdain. *Wendy*. I knew I should have good Christian love toward this girl, but I felt a whirlwind of emotions surging all around me. None of them were love.

"I just don't see how this changes anything for Gary," I said.

"Honey, don't you see what I mean?" Beverly took a long breath and folded her hands in her lap. "What if Gary does end up in love with Wendy? Is it fair that he should feel guilty about that?"

I stared into the brook. "Can I help how I feel?" The water sparkled in the dimming sunlight. "Should I have hidden my feelings forever?"

"I don't know…" I looked up at Beverly. She was staring into the brook too. "I would like to tell you that there are clear answers when it comes to matters of the heart. Honestly, though, there aren't any."

"I know," I muttered.

"But, look, Gary is very upset. He doesn't want to hurt you."

I nodded. "I know. I really should have thought this whole letter thing through a little better."

170

"I guess so."

"What do I do?"

Beverly let out a little sigh. "My advice is to apologize quickly and then don't bring it up again."

"That sounds embarrassing," I replied. "Shouldn't we discuss what I wrote?"

"If he wants to talk about it, fine, but let him decide if it gets discussed. I'm not sure he feels comfortable with the idea." She placed a hand on my shoulder. "I could be wrong, but leave the ball in his court." Beverly splashed her feet a bit and continued, "Meanwhile, you're going to have to be careful how you interact with Gary."

"Yeah. I get it." I felt a frown burrowing in, beyond my face and into my soul. I sure had messed things up. From then on, I knew Gary and my relationship would be watched closely. I was suddenly looking forward to him going back to school.

I accepted Beverly's advice as sound. I found Gary in the living room, reading out of some thick textbook with notebooks and loose papers scattered on the coffee table in front of him. He looked up and smiled awkwardly when I walked into the room. No one else was around at the time.

"Hey, Carly."

I returned the awkward smile and stood still before him. "I wanted to apologize for that letter I wrote," I said quickly, tripping over my words. "It was out of line, and it was unfair."

Gary nodded. "Thanks, Carly."

He looked back into his textbook. I stood still for a moment, expecting more from the generally talkative Gary. When it became clear he had nothing to say on the matter, I turned to leave.

"Wait," Gary called after me. I cringed, but turned back to face him.

"I'm sorry, too." He shut the textbook on his lap and rubbed his chin. "I have been thinking, and I have also had it pointed out to me that I may have been leading you on."

"Leading me on?"

"Yeah." Gary sighed. "Like, doing and saying things that made you feel like our relationship was more than it actually was."

171

"And what *was* our relationship?" As soon as I asked, I regretted pressing the issue.

Gary shook his head and let out a sound of exasperation. "We were friends- we *are* friends."

"I knew that," I replied. "And I'm sorry for thinking anything else." My eyes were drawn to the floor, and I figured that was my cue to walk away, but once again I was called back.

"Carly, I want you to understand that it's not your fault. It's all on me, okay? I know, I held your hand, I gave you hugs, I asked for your hand in marriage for goodness sake."

I had to laugh, and my giggles seemed to break the bout of awkwardness. Gary laughed too.

"I guess that counts as leading a girl on," I said.

Gary reopened his textbook and stated finally, "I think I was just trying to protect you, and I realize you're not my sister." He paused for a moment and blinked back what must have been tears. "I always wished I could have protected Brittany."

Gary went back to reading his textbook. I felt my legs carry me out of the room, but my mind was elsewhere.

EIGHTEEN

A blonde anchorwoman in the courtroom corridor informed the watching public of what was presently taking place. "We are here at the court house in Salem, Oregon, where one of the biggest federal cases we've seen take place in our state has just come to a head. Thomas Irving Deally, founder of the Deally Reformed Church and the isolated community with the same name, has plead No Contest to charges of Assault, Battery, Conspiracy, Molestation, Menacing, and really, the list goes on and on. The Deally commune has been called a cult by the local religious leaders, and in fact there are no religious organizations backing Tom Deally in any way. All of the religious organizational leaders that we've interviewed have emphatically opposed the practices of the Deally Reformed Church and lend their support instead to the survivors of what has been called a polytheistic, highly syncretic religious order that seems to have come out of nowhere."

The screen went from the woman on site to the newsroom. A man with graying brown hair sat behind a huge desk. "Thank you for keeping us updated on the scene there. Now, sentencing is to be handed down today, is that right?"

Back to the blonde. She held a sound piece close to her ear for a moment before responding. "That's right, Steve. The court has been in recess for just a few minutes now. Both the defense and the prosecution have given their final statements, so now it's just a waiting game as the jury meets to go over evidence and testimony. If the jury finds Deally guilty, he is facing Life in maximum security prison. His rap sheet is so extensive, even if the sentence is lessened or he gets time off for good behavior, he will still live the rest of his days in prison."

Gary gave a short round of applause as the camera shot back into the studio.

"Shauna, you've been watching all of this go on, what has been the most condemning piece of evidence that's been presented thus far?"

The blonde woman nodded and furrowed her brow. "You know, Steve, there have been so many things. But the Victim Impact Statements from what have been called *Deally's Goddesses*, a group of twelve females ranging in age from seven to thirty one- Well, Steve what they had to say alone was enough to condemn this man if any of those jurors have a heart."

173

"And the footage of those statements can be found exclusively on our website," Steve told his audience. "All of the court proceedings and interviews from outside of the courtroom are on that site, as well as a blog from our very own Shauna Yates."

"That's right," Shauna said, coming back into view. "And the Community Board is also up on that site, so you can add your comments and get in on the conversation. So far we have had over two thousand posts and people are getting pretty heated, debating what exactly it means to have freedom of religion in this country and if in fact Tom Deally should be on trial at all."

"What?" Gary sat up straight. "Can you believe that?" He looked at all of us in the room, but there was no time for a conversation, as Anchorman Steve began speaking again.

"When is the jury due to be back in?"

"It will take as long as it takes," Shauna replied. "There's honestly no way to tell, and like I said before, it's just a waiting game at this point. But we will be on the scene and Breaking News will air as soon as the jury is in. Until then, this is Shauna Yates, live and on location. Back to you, Steve."

"Thanks, Shauna. And I'd just like to remind you all that you can only see the in-court room drama unfold here, so stay tuned."

The anchor went on to the normal news of the day, and Gary stood to his feet in frustration. "I thought the jury was supposed to be in already!"

"Yeah, old Steve there said we'd have a verdict *today*," Jacob confirmed.

"That's why they say not to believe everything you hear on TV," Eric replied.

"This is so lame," Jacob muttered. "How are we supposed to know when the jury is ready?"

"I'll call Agent Jones," Eric said. "Don't worry about it. We'll get an update if we ask, I'm sure." He walked to the phone hanging on the living room wall. It rang before he picked up.

"Maybe that's someone from the court," Jacob said.

Eric answered the phone with a chipper hello. After a brief moment he repeated his hello. Then again. "Hello? Hello? Who is this?" Eric looked back at us all and shrugged. The phone was still at his ear when he explained, "Prank call, I guess."

Jacob stood up. "Who would-"

Eric put a finger up to his lips and waited in silence a moment. "Hey, I can hear you breathing. Who is this?"

"What's up?" Jacob whispered, walking toward him. Eric waved him off.

"Hello? Yes, who is this?" A pause. "Well, I'm not handing the phone over without an answer." Eric listened for a minute or two longer, with an annoyed look on his face. "Goodbye," he finally said, slamming the receiver back onto it's holding place on the wall.

"Who was that?" Gary and Jacob asked at the same time, smiling at the coincidence.

Eric crossed his arms and looked squarely at me. "It was my sister. Emma."

"My mother?" I was dumbstruck. I felt my jaw fall open and I couldn't seem to get it to return to its place.

"Apparently she wanted to talk to you," Eric said, looking over at Gary.

"What? She wanted to talk to me?" Gary stood from his seat on the couch. "What did she say?"

"It's not important," Eric replied.

"Well, what was the gist of it? I don't need details."

Eric looked at me and shook his head. His arms uncrossed and he walked out of the room slowly, without another word.

"What just happened?" Jacob wondered aloud.

I felt my eyes burning, tears finding their way out suddenly. Gary and Jacob both left the room as well, no doubt to track down Eric and get him to talk. Meanwhile, I sat on the couch, wondering why my mother had called and why she didn't want to talk to me. Perhaps wondering was better than knowing.

NINETEEN

Thomas Deally was convicted, with a guilty verdict on all counts against him. We were all sitting at the breakfast table when Eric got the call from the ever faithful Agent Jones. Eric and Beverly excused Jacob, Gary and myself to abort breakfast in favor of television. When we went to the exclusive coverage, there was no banter between anchor people, but a straight live feed of footage from inside the courthouse.

When the verdict came, a close shot of Tom Deally showed he was stifling a grin, shaking his head. He cursed under his breath as he was led away. He was sentenced to 100 years in prison, or life. I couldn't help but notice how old Tom looked, older than he had looked little over a year prior. He was in his seventies, but he'd always seemed young and energetic while in Deally. The real world wore on him. His countenance was a mess of wrinkles and anger.

The rest of the men involved in Tom's crimes would receive trials soon as well, though none of them would receive sentences nearly as severe as what Tom was facing. They wouldn't be televised either.

When court let out, Tom Deally appealed to the cameras that followed him outside to a police convoy. He waved his hands expressively and shouted above the crowd around him. "God cares for his servants! Serve God, and not men! I will be avenged, I will not be forgotten! God exalts those who serve him, who don't back away from trouble, who stray not far from the place of holiness!"

His last statement was a quote that I remembered from Deally's Reformed Church. *God exalts those who serve him, who don't back away from trouble, who stray not far from the place of holiness.* It was mandatory for all children of age seven to memorize that portion of the sacred texts. We were all taught that it meant we were better off staying in the community and suffering trouble than leaving to live a life of leisure. It made me think of the elders who died in Deally. They lived out that philosophy. I glanced at Gary, and he returned a knowing look.

"Maybe God will have mercy on his soul." Gary muttered, "I don't know anyone else who will."

After the cameras watched Tom Deally get hauled away, there was still ongoing news coverage for the rest of the day and into the rest of the week as well. Immediately following what we had just watched, there were a series of interviews, live on the street, asking people what they'd thought of the case.

Most of the people they interviewed were glad to have Tom Dealy behind bars. Most of them made comments about the *Dealy goddesses*. Their stories had been what really sealed Dealy's fate in the eyes of the public. We watched the interviews that afternoon.

"Those girls- the girls that Thomas Dealy thought were goddesses- he must have been out of his right mind!" A caramel colored woman with lots of jewelry on was speaking to some unseen journalist. "He poisoned them. He knocked them around. I hope he gets poisoned and knocked around, I hope some big guy in prison thinks Thomas Dealy is a goddess and messes with him!" She looked into the camera now and pursed her lips before adding, "Watch your back, Thomas Dealy! Watch your back."

TWENTY

Gary threw his orange duffel bag into Eric's van. Eric was already in the driver's seat, warming the engine. Jacob sat in the front seat to keep them company on the long drive.

"We will miss you, Gary." Beverly gave him a quick hug and handed him a plate of cookies. "Here, don't eat these all on the way." Gary smiled warmly and placed the cookies in the van.

"Thanks for everything, Beverly. You've been like a mom to me." He paused. "...But no need to get all mushy. I will be back in a few months."

"*Months*?" Beverly asked, "You're not coming back for summer break?"

Gary shrugged. "I don't think so. I just want to get away for a while."

"Well, I certainly understand."

Gary and I said our goodbyes, but for the first time in history, refrained from hugging. He told me to enjoy high school and I told him not to enjoy college too much, because we did want to see him again. He just nodded and climbed into the van.

~~~

I went to my room and shut the door when I called Marcus. I knew I would have to be brief, since he was in police custody, but Agent Jones assured me I would be able to speak with him. I was given a number to reach him; I was also given a number to reach my parents.

"Carly, it's so nice to hear your voice. How are you?"

A smile spread across my face. He sounded optimistic. "I'm fine, Marc. How about you?"

"I'm going to make it. I realize I have to face the consequences of my actions, and I'm willing to do that. For the most part things are going well. That pastor isn't even pressing charges."

"*Really*? That's amazing. But, then why are you still in custody?"

"I'm being charged with other things," he replied with a sigh.

179

"Deally things?"

"You've got it." He tone was even, calm.

"I'm surprised you're taking this so well…" I paused to swallow a lump that seemed to have developed in my throat. "So, did you get any kind of- you know, a visitation?" I squinted my eyes closed, bracing myself for his reply.

"Oh," Marcus laughed. "You mean from *Jesus*?"

"Yeah," I exhaled. I thought I detected some sarcasm.

"Well, that pastor- what's his name?"

"Pastor Freeman?"

"Yes, yes. Pastor Freeman came to visit me. He let me know he was dropping the charges and then he talked to me about Jesus for quite a while."

"Really?" I felt my smile return.

"Yeah. I mean, it wasn't Jesus, but it was a visitation nonetheless," he chuckled.

Marcus told me about the whole conversation. Pastor Freeman had gone over the entire gospel message with him. Marc had been thinking a lot about Jesus, since the day he had found out that I was a Christian, but had very little knowledge of who Jesus was. For nearly two hours, the jailer allowed Pastor Freeman to speak with Marcus, uninterrupted. They even discussed the validity of Tom Deally's religion, including the spiritual guides. Pastor Freeman explained to him that he wasn't crazy for believing in the guides, because there are evil spirits that involve themselves in the lives of men, trying to deceive and lead people away from God. When Marcus shared his frustration with never receiving a guide, Pastor Freeman assured him that God was protecting him, probably because of the prayers of his Christian family. It sounded like a wonderful conversation.

"At the end of it all, he asked me if I would like to accept the gift of salvation. Of course I said yes. Who doesn't want that, right?" He gave a light laugh and went on. "He also asked me if I would like to *know* Jesus, and I have to admit, that threw me off a little, but I figured if it's possible to know the Savior, then I'd better find out. So, Pastor Freeman prayed with me."

"That's so great, Marc!" My excitement was suddenly uncontainable. "I am so happy for you."

"Me too. But I didn't tell you the best part yet."

"Then go on," I urged.

"Well, you asked if I had a visitation. I don't know if this counts, but it felt like a touch from God…I don't know if you'll understand what I mean, but it was like… *electricity*?" There was an air of uncertainty in his voice.

"*Electricity*," he repeated. "Pastor Freeman prayed that Jesus would come into my heart, and it was like *electricity* went through my whole body." Marcus laughed nervously. "I mean, it was like I felt Him come into me. And then, I just felt warm."

"Hannah calls that the *warm and fuzzies*!" I shouted. My hand clamped onto my mouth quickly and I began to laugh.

"What?" Marcus sounded genuinely confused.

"I'm sorry," I laughed. "What you felt was the presence of God. My cousin- *our cousin*, Hannah, calls that feeling *warm and fuzzies*."

"That's appropriate. It was warm, and *fuzzy* as well, I suppose." We both laughed.

Before we said goodbye, I asked if he had talked to our parents since the infamous fall of Deally. He hadn't, and he knew nothing about our mother's odd phone call. That bothered me.

~~~

Marc's trial came and went. He was sentenced to a year for his crimes. Mostly, he was an accessory to other more heinous crimes than his own. He was essentially a lackey in Deally, doing the work of other people's imaginations. He was willing to please, however, so he did his tasks well. Agent Jones had been faithful to inform me about all of the happenings with Marcus' case.

TWENTY ONE

It was ten o'clock in the evening now, but I couldn't help myself. Eric had put me on his family's cell phone plan when I started at high school. I had a blue flip phone sitting on top of my dresser, and it was beckoning me to call. So, I did. I dialed, I pressed Talk, and I waited.

The first ring sent the blood coursing through my veins. All at once I wanted to hang up, possibly vomit- but I stood firmly and waited for the ringing to cease and someone to greet me with hello.

It was my father's voice. I took in a deep, silent breath and tried to say hello. Empty wind escaped my lips, no words would come.

"Hello? Is anyone there?" My father's voice evoked deep emotion in me. I felt my eyes well with tears. His voice was distant, as he addressed someone in the room with him. "I just don't understand these tele-" The line went silent.

He had hung up. I placed the cell phone back on top of my dresser. I worried for a moment that my father's line might have caller ID, that I might suddenly receive a phone call back. Then, I laughed aloud. Even if he did have caller ID, he would likely have no interest in using it. He obviously had no affection for the telephone.

My smile curved further upward as my thoughts jumped from my father and mother to my siblings. My sisters would be well into their teen years. Jon would no longer be like a baby, but more like a little boy, I thought. It had been two years since I laid eyes on any of them. I reached again for my cell phone. Grandma Freedom's ring looked up at me from my tanned finger. I closed my eyes and remembered her as best I could. She stood before me, surrounded by nothingness in my mind. Wrinkled nose, silver hair, a smile eternally on her face.

I left for the same reason Grandma Freedom had to leave Dealy years before I had. A conviction that it was the right thing, the only thing, to do. As an adult, her conviction was certainly more refined, nevertheless it was the same. I never recalled her speaking to me about Dealy, even when I asked her to come live with us there as a child. She would just smile and say she would see me again soon enough. I had loved her more than my parents, and had she asked me to stay with *her*, I would have left Dealy in a moment.

I looked again at Grandma Freedom's ring. It was a consistent reminder of how God had changed my life. I didn't understand it, but I had to believe there was some sense to it all. I had to believe that God was creating some masterpiece with my life, and if I waited long enough, it would come into focus. The brushstrokes would suddenly form something meaningful and beautiful. I longed for that day of clarity. Clarity like Grandma Freedom must have had when she declared that her ring should be given to me. Somehow, she caught a glimpse of what God was creating- not just in her own life, but in mine. He was working things together for my good. There was nothing to fear.

I felt my hand reach again for the phone, and I didn't stop it. I pressed Redial and waited again for the ringing. My mother answered this time. She said hello with a rather shrill tone of voice.

"Hi, Mom." I was doing it! I felt a strange boldness come over me.

"I was wondering what your call was about the other day." I allowed a smile to spread over my face, satisfied with my directness.

My mother didn't answer right away, but I knew better than to think she had hung up. She was never one to back out of any situation, no matter how tense or awkward. I waited for her reply, still smiling.

"Carly, I suppose?"

Who else would it be? "Yes."

"You sound different. Look different too."

"You've seen me?"

"I saw you on the television."

"You're watching television now?"

"Yes. We've been locked up in a hotel room with little else to do. We watched the whole dreadful occurrence with the court case." I heard a sigh. "Poor Tom." My mother didn't usually put on such a passionate tone of voice.

"So you saw me in court then?"

"Yes, we did see you. We're not very pleased."

My smile had faded by now. I had no desire to discuss poor Tom Deally, or disappointing Carly. I just wanted to know why my mother called Eric's home. I decided to be direct again, and asked what was on my mind.

"So, you called here at Eric's home, looking for me?"

"I did not call for you, Carly," she answered with a snort. "I called for Gary. You're but a child, and I know he answers for you. Is he there now?"

Gary answers for me? In Deally, that would have been true, but in the outside world- the real world- I could answer for myself! Even with Deally abolished, my mother's mind was still there.

"Mother. Gary is not in charge of me." I used the most assertive, responsible tone I could.

"Well, then, answer me this: Why did you choose to follow Gary into rebellion? Why did you follow him into sin?"

"I didn't follow Gary into anything." I focused on keeping my tone of voice assertive and responsible. "I left Deally willingly. I would have set off on my own, even if Gary was never around. That's the truth."

"Then I suppose I've held a grudge against Gary for little reason." Her voice cracked, and it sounded as if she had begun to cry. I tried to recall a time that had ever happened before, and I drew a blank. She was silent for some time. All I could hear was the choppy breathing pattern of a woman trying to compose herself. I waited for her to say more, but no words came.

"Are you angry with me, then?"

There was a pause. I could hear my mother take a deep breath and exhale.

"Are you happy at my brother's home?" The strength of her voice was back.

"Yes," I replied truthfully.

"Then I see no reason for further talk. Goodbye, Carly."

She hung up.

I didn't attempt to contact my parents again.

After a few months had passed, I found out that they were being relocated to Idaho, where my father would be given a job on a farm. The farm owner had heard of the Deally commune, and he offered housing and work for a displaced family on his land.

When I told Marcus over the phone about the farm in Idaho, he decided to move as well. After his prison sentence was fulfilled, he planned to leave immediately and reunite with the family. They hadn't known about his conversion to Christianity, or the fact he spent his prison sentence getting acquainted with the Bible.

TWENTY TWO

"When is Gary supposed to get here?" I was sitting at the kitchen counter, watching Beverly put together a homemade tomato salsa.

She turned to face me and a blue streamer fell from the ceiling into her bowl of salsa. We both laughed. We would be celebrating both Gary's graduation and mine. He was ready to start thinking about the real world. I was ready to start thinking about college. He always seemed to be a step ahead of me. That was something I had learned to accept. Our lives had been in sync for the briefest time. Now, our lives were no longer intertwined.

"Well, hopefully he'll get here before all of Eric's decorations fall apart," she answered. "But when I spoke with him he said two o'clock."

I looked at the digital numbers on the microwave. "It's already two o'five."

"Any minute now, then." Beverly tore down the fallen streamer and tossed it in the trash. Hannah and Joanne ran into the kitchen, sliding on their socks.

"Girls, I told you not to slide around in here anymore," Beverly scolded. I winced. My sisters and I used to slide on our socks in Deally. All of our floors were slick linoleum there. I taught Hannah to slide and she taught Joanne. They were sliding nonstop since then, until Hannah fell, causing Beverly to put a stop to the fun.

"Sorry, Mom!" Joanne yelled with overdone emotion. "We were too excited."

"Yeah. Gary just got here!" Hannah shouted with a huge smile.

My heart leapt. I felt a smile burst onto my face. No, our lives weren't in sync anymore. But we would have this summer. He would be back home with me, getting things prepared for his moving into the real world. I would be home, getting things prepared for college. This summer, we would be back in sync again! I began to cross the room toward the door.

"Come on! Gary is outside with Dad and Jacob and some pretty lady." Hannah smiled and ran back with Joanne from where they came.

187

"Some pretty lady?" I stopped walking and looked at Beverly. The girls were already gone. Bev looked at me with a frown.

"I don't know what they're talking about. Maybe one of the neighbors came by for something."

I followed Beverly outside to see exactly what the girls had described. Gary was pulling luggage out of his car as Eric and Jacob spoke to *some pretty lady*. She was a tall, pale girl with red, tightly curled hair. She was smiling and holding her long hair against her shoulder to keep it from catching in the wind.

Her name was Wendy, and she was coming to stay with us for the summer.

~~~

I had spent the day acting busy. I politely greeted Gary and Wendy both when they came, but I made myself scarce as soon as I could get away. It was strange. I had been so excited for Gary to come home, but when he finally did, I couldn't do enough to stay out of his way. Of course, I couldn't avoid him, or Wendy, all day. Dinner time was like a trap.

We sat down for a beautiful meal of chicken, potatoes and a tossed salad, all accompanied by homemade dressings- Eric's specialty. It smelled and tasted great, but I found myself rushing through the meal, drowning every bite with water to increase speed. Wendy interrupted my rhythm when a lull in conversation occurred at the table.

"So, Carly, you were living in Deally before it got busted up?"

I swallowed a mouthful of food and nodded. "Yeah, I was." What a dumb question. I forced a smile.

"I can't even imagine," she replied. "I bet you're glad Gary came along with a plan to get out of there, though, huh? I mean, even though it was all you knew, you also knew there was more, right?" She giggled slightly for some unknown reason and gave Gary a playful punch on the arm. He seemed to like it.

"Yeah, I guess that's true." I shoveled the last bite of my meal and looked around the table. Everyone else was well behind me in finishing. "May I be excused?"

Beverly looked at me with a raised eyebrow. "Sure, honey. Why don't you pull out the air mattress and get that ready for Wendy."

I had briefly forgotten that I would be having a slumber party with this Wendy girl all summer. I felt myself sigh, but covered my melancholy with a quick smile. "Oh, yeah, sure."

"It will be fun, Carly!" Wendy smiled at me. Without trying, she was beautiful. She had red hair and green eyes; all of her features were bright. I had dark hair and dark eyes, nothing extraordinary at all.

"Great," I replied, removing my plate from the table.

I washed up my dishes and hurried upstairs to find the air mattress. It was stuffed in the back of the linen closet. I lugged it out of the closet and into the privacy of my room.

"Jesus, help me," I prayed aloud. "I don't want to hate Wendy. I don't want to be miserable all summer. God, change my attitude, please."

I spent the next few hours reading my Bible, trying to refresh my memory on things like love and patience. It felt like not much time had passed when I heard a knock on the door. Wendy's head popped in and she laughed cheerily, "Hi, roomie!"

I looked at my alarm clock. It was already 10 PM. "Oh, hey. I didn't realize it was so late."

She entered the room slowly and looked around. "Nice place you've got here."

"Thanks." I had some of my artwork on one wall. Wendy walked over to stand before them and seemed to stare at a particularly bright piece.

"This is great," she said, staring at the painting. It was an orange cat looking into a koi pond. I had spent a month working on that one, and Beverly and Eric were so proud of it they had it framed.

"Thank you. I was inspired by one of Jacob's skateboards. It had a koi fish on the bottom."

"That's neat-o," she laughed. "I had a little orange cat like that once. Her name was Velvet, and she used to love to paint."

"To *paint*?" I felt my eyes widen.

"Yep. Just dipped her tail in paint and went to town," Wendy replied, still looking at the painting.

"No way."

Wendy spun around, laughing, "I'm totally kidding!"

I let out a laugh at the absurdity of her story.

"Can you imagine?" Wendy asked, laughing still. "I wish that cat did something cool like that, but all she ever did was sleep."

"I can't believe I fell for that," I told her.

"Me either…" Wendy took another look at the painting before sitting beside me on my bed. "You are a really great artist, though, have you ever tried to sell your work?"

"I've definitely thought about the idea. But I've never really had an opportunity."

"Well, I think people would like it. My uncle owns a gallery, you know? I might be able to get you a space, at least put something up and see if anyone's interested."

"Wow, really?" I looked at my art and wondered if it could really become a career.

Wendy and I continued to talk about my art, and lots of other things as well. God had changed my attitude toward Wendy, and the summer was finally looking up.

TWENTY THREE

Jacob was out the door for work before I was even out of bed. He worked at a shoe store, and it seemed they didn't want to miss the 5AM crowd. Eric and Beverly took the girls to the city after finishing breakfast. They were getting haircuts.

Gary and Wendy washed up the breakfast dishes while I wiped down the table. I was attempting to get some mysterious crayon markings off. It was a green crayon, probably in the hand of Joanne, that had caused the mess. Just when I had scrubbed the table top clean I noticed more markings running down the leg of the table. I sat down on the floor and began scrubbing the dark wooden leg, wondering all the while how Joanne had gotten away with so much graffiti without being noticed.

Halfway through the crayon cleaning job I noticed the clanking of dishes had stopped. I looked up. Gary was holding Wendy close, his lips pressed against hers, right in front of the sink full of dishes. Their eyes were closed, and I stood quickly, wanting to escape without being noticed.

My foot caught on a chair as I attempted to dash away and it went tumbling down. My legs went to mush, and I fell too, landing with a loud thud. Gary and Wendy both called after me, but I kept moving until I was upstairs and in my room. I shut the door behind me. My face felt hot. I sat in the wicker chair beside my bed and took a breath. Had I really just run away like that? I tried to compose myself before Wendy or Gary would surely be coming in after me.

I found a stale glass of water on my nightstand and gulped it down. My mind flashed back to Deally. The night Gary had stood beside me and washed dishes. The night his pinky finger had brushed my hand and I'd suddenly had feelings for him. But for us, washing the dishes never developed into a kiss. Tears began blurring my vision. This was supposed to be *our* summer! I was finally old enough. I was finally mature enough. Gary and I had this one summer for things to go right.

"Stop!" I scolded myself out loud. "It's obviously not meant to be." I stood to my feet and crossed my arms. I was not going to cry over something so stupid. I began pacing the floor, and I heard footsteps in the hallway. I stood still now.

191

Gary and Wendy were both in the hall. I heard them bicker briefly about who should talk to me. Then, footsteps walking away. A knock on the door. I wondered who had won the right to talk to the embarrassed little girl. "No," I whispered to myself. "You are not a little girl who needs taken care of. You are an adult now. Act like it."

I whipped open the door. Gary was standing there with a dumb, anxious look on his face.

"Are you okay?" He reached his arm toward me. His hand landed on my shoulder gently. I shrugged it off.

"I'm fine, Gary!" The offense was thick in my voice.

Gary crossed his arms and looked down grimly. "I'm sorry, Carly. I didn't know you were in the room when I-"

"What?" I butted in. "You think I didn't know you might kiss your girlfriend sometimes? Give me some credit, Gary. Seriously."

"I just know that you-"

"You know that I *what*? You know that I'm just a little kid who needs their feelings protected? You know I had hopes of marrying you when I was *fourteen*? Look, you haven't been around since then, so don't try to act like you know anything about who I am now."

Gary's eyes cut into me. I could see anger flare in them for a moment. He let out a sigh, and I watched his eyes calm.

"You're right, Carly. You aren't a little kid anymore."

"Nope," I replied with anger.

"But you are still my best friend, and I *do* know you."

"If I'm your best friend, why haven't you come around here? Almost five years of school, and you barely come home, even on breaks?"

"I didn't want to see you," he stated bluntly. "Is that what you want to hear? Do you want it to be about you?"

I glared at him and crossed my arms to match his stance. "You didn't want to see your *best friend*?"

"I had other things that I just-" He was getting visibly frustrated. "Carly, I was in school! I was concentrating on-"

"Just drop the act, Gary. You stayed away from here to be with Wendy.

192

She can be your *best friend* now, ok?"

"Carly-"

"Wendy is great," I said. "Gary, I want you to move on. *I* am moving on." I slowed down and took a breath. I had to stop being angry. Wendy really *was* great. I had to admit defeat. "Just go and be with her and don't worry about chasing me down every time I leave the room."

Gary tilted his head a little. "I just worry about you."

"I know," I said. "But you and I are going to have different lives. You don't have to feel any obligation to me anymore. I can take care of myself. We're not in Deally anymore."

Gary was silent. His head shook back and forth slightly. He stared at his shoes. I had the distinct feeling he wanted to say more.

I turned and went back into my room, shutting the door behind me. I waited at the door, listening for footsteps. Why was he just standing there? *Please, go away.*

Footsteps. Voices. Wendy had sought Gary outside of my door. They began speaking in whispered tones. Soon Wendy laughed with what sounded a lot like scorn. I hadn't heard her be anything but bubbly since I'd known her, so it troubled me. I almost went back into the hall to see what was wrong, but there was sudden silence. Then, stamping feet. Someone had stormed off, and the other followed the first.

Loud voices were coming up from the floorboards. Downstairs, Wendy and Gary were apparently in a fight. How fickle their relationship had to be to go from a passionate dishwater embrace to a shouting match. I wanted to laugh about Gary's fickle relationship, but I felt tears come. "Honestly, Carly?" I whispered to myself. "You still can't let this go?"

I heard a crash downstairs. Something or someone had fallen. Instinctively, I ran out of the room, down the hall, and descended the stairs. I saw a strange scene before me. Wendy was flying out the front door, keys in hand. Gary was placing a small table upright. It was a table that held a vase and a lamp Beverly had gotten on a missions trip years ago. The lamp was broken, but the vase looked okay. I rushed over to Gary and asked what had happened.

He placed the broken lamp and the vase back onto the table and looked at me with an angry groan. "Carly! Just stop. Stop getting in the middle of things!"

I stepped backwards and looked at Gary. He was arrayed in full

193

frustration. Neither of us spoke, and I heard a car's engine start up outside. Gary's eyes widened. "My car!"

I did laugh now. Gary paused halfway to the door and turned to me.

"If you really want to know what just happened, here it is." He handed me a crumpled piece of paper, gave me a quick glare, and went out the door. I stood in amazement for a moment and then went to the window. Wendy was already gone in Gary's Buick, and he was pulling Eric's car out of the driveway to go after her.

I stared at the crumpled piece of notebook paper. It seemed innocent enough. I almost threw it away before it occurred to me to uncrumple the thing and take a closer look. I sat on the couch and looked at a faded message on the yellowed sheet of paper. When my eyes focused fully on the writing, my mouth dropped open. It was my handwriting. My message. My letter, professing my love for Gary and my hopes for marrying him one day. I thought he had thrown it away years ago. It had fragile crease lines from being folded and opened back up many times. He had to have kept it. My heart was beating too fast suddenly.

~~~

It was almost 2AM when Gary made it home. Wendy did not return with him. I stood outside of my room and waited for him to come upstairs. I clenched the letter tightly in my hands. My heart started palpitating when I heard footsteps on the stairs. When he appeared before me in the hall I cleared my throat.

"Uh, hey." He looked at me nervously, shoving his hands in his pockets. "You're up late."

"I couldn't sleep."

"Well, laying in bed might help," he replied dully.

"Sure," I laughed. "I wanted to-"

"I'm sick of talk, Carly. Can't this wait? I just had three hours of listening to Wendy talk."

"That's what I wanted to talk about- partly. What happened with Wendy today? And what does this have to do with it?" I held out the letter.

Gary took the letter from me and sighed. "Fine. Let's talk."

"Well, what happened today?" I persisted. "Why is Wendy gone?"

"That's pretty simple," he replied. "We broke up."

"...Oh. Is that because you-"

Gary cut me off and said plainly. "I honestly don't want to have this discussion right now."

He looked tired and frustrated. His brow was furrowed. Both hands were in his pockets again.

"Please. Just at least tell me what the letter had to do with it. You sort of left me wondering, shoving it in my face like that."

"Fine, fine." Gary rubbed his face and put a hand through his hair. "Wendy found it in my backpack. Apparently she was putting her own love letter in it for me to find, and instead she found your little ditty. Kind of ironic, right?"

I was silent.

Gary looked at me. "Well, is that enough explanation for you? She just felt weird about the letter, and it made things strained, and then we broke up. Ok?"

I smiled and thought for a moment, wanting to speak the right words. "Gary, I'm eighteen now. I mean, it's ok if-"

"What? No, it's not that. It's not... It's just not." I laughed at Gary's lack of confidence. His face was turning red. "The fact is it wasn't going to last. I was fooling myself."

"What do you mean? She's great and you two were together for like three years."

Gary let out a long, slow breath. "Well, yeah, but-" He crossed his arms and shrugged. "She's not a Christian, and I don't suspect after three years that she was ever going to change that for me."

"I tried to convince myself I could build a life with her. She's moral, but she doesn't know Jesus... Don't ever do that, Carly. Don't try to date someone who doesn't know Him, it just makes you stay up late worrying." He let out a dry laugh. "It improves your prayer life, sure. But it's more heartache than it's worth."

I smiled. "Well, increased prayer life is good."

"Yeah. So, does that answer your questions?" Gary turned to go to his room, apparently unconcerned with my answer.

"Wait." My stomach flipped as I watched Gary turn back toward me. "Tell me we have a chance."

Gary was quiet.

"Please, Gary. Why did you carry that letter around all this time?"

"Alright," Gary conceded. "I did carry around your letter. And I read it over and over and I-" His jaw tightened and I noticed his hands ball into fists. "And I didn't want to have this conversation…"

"You said that already," I reminded him. "But we're having it."

"You asked me why I never came back home during school. It was all about the letter. It was about *you*."

"I knew it," I said, bursting into tears. "You hate me."

Gary rushed to my side and put his arm around me. "No, no. That's not it."

"Well what?" I stepped away from him and tried to stifle my tears.

Gary let out a groan. "I don't hate you, Carly." Gary took a step back and crossed his arms. He looked right into my eyes. Then his eyes dropped to his feet. He shifted his weight back and forth, from foot to foot. His eyes came back up to meet mine. "I *love* you."

He looked at the floor again. I stared at him and my jaw fell open slightly. Gary continued to look at the ground. I wiped my face of tears, but more came behind them.

"I don't understand. Why won't you look at me?"

He didn't answer, just shook his head in silence. Still looking at the floor.

"You can't look at me? You don't love me." He kept his eyes down. "Stop playing games with me, Gary. Look at me." I wanted to yell, but I knew I might wake someone, so I tried to keep my voice level and quiet.

I waited for Gary to look up, but he continued to look down and shake his head.

"Gary. What's wrong?"

Gary sighed. "You were fourteen when you wrote me that letter. A little kid. When I couldn't stop looking at it, couldn't stop thinking of you, I knew it was wrong." His shoulders raised in a shrug. "I knew I couldn't be here…"

I watched his face as he grappled with old emotions.

"I didn't want to be around you, I wanted to forget about you for a while.

196

Does that make sense? I just wanted some time away. Then..." He paused and folded his arms. "Then, I met Wendy, and I finally felt okay. I fell for her so hard that I finally got your words out of my head." He laughed now and I saw a softness in his countenance that wasn't there before. "It was great."

"I'm glad forgetting about me was all you needed to get some peace," I said, trying to put on a light tone of voice. This was turning into a horrible story.

"Wendy is great. You were right about her." Gary rubbed his eyes. "But the fact is, I never stopped thinking about you."

"So, what does that mean?" My mind was struggling to understand.

Gary looked up and searched for something invisible on the ceiling above us. "It means..." His eyes returned to mine again. "It means that we have a chance to start over. You're not fourteen and I'm in not with Wendy anymore."

I felt a warmth cover my face. Surely, I was blushing. "Oh."

"But it's going to take time. I mean, I just got out of a relationship," Gary said. He laughed through a frown, something I had never seen before.

I allowed just the smallest version of a smile to spread across my face. "That's okay with me."

FREEDOM'S LEGACY

It had been almost ten years since the evacuation of Deally when Marcus showed up unannounced at my door. We hadn't spoken for a while, only exchanging occasional letters over the years.

"What are you doing here?" I ushered him in the front door. He looked so much older now. His forehead had horizontal lines permanently engraved across it.

"Let me take your bag, Marcus!" Gary said, coming in from another room. Marc handed over a leather duffel bag.

"Thanks, Gary. This is a great place you've got here." He looked around, smiling. What Marc was admiring was simply the "mud room", a tiny foyer area furnished with old boots, a coat rack, and a washing machine.

"What are you doing here, Marc?" I repeated my question.

Gary disappeared for a moment, placing Marcus' bag somewhere.

"Thanks, Gary," Marc called after him. He looked at me and said nothing.

Gary came back into the mud room. "Come on, let's go sit down. I've got some sodas in the fridge. You want one, Marc?"

"Oh, yeah." Marcus followed Gary out of the room and through a narrow hallway, emerging into the living room. I trailed behind, my question still unanswered.

"It just gets nicer, Carly! This place is great," Marcus said.

"Thanks." I watched Gary usher Marcus onto the brown leather couch, run into the adjoining kitchen, and return quickly with an arm full of soda cans.

I took a seat on the matching love seat across from Marc. Gary distributed drinks and sat beside Marcus. A long glass coffee table separated us.

"So, how are you? How is the kid?" Marcus said, rushing his words into each other.

"Well, fine. We're all fine," I replied. "And, Frieda is due to be with us in about six weeks now." I looked down at my enlarged stomach.

199

"You're naming her after Grandma Freedom?" Marcus cracked open his soda can.

"We feel like we owe her a lot," Gary said. "Without her prayers, I don't think things would have turned out so well for us."

Marcus sipped his soda slowly. "Well, that's probably true."

"So, Marcus. What's going on here? You haven't answered my question."

Marc took another long sip of soda pop. He squared his eyes and looked at me with a frown. "And what question's that?"

"Well, why are you here?" I was beginning to wonder if something terrible had happened. Why would he show up without a phone call and hesitate so much to give a reason?

"Oh, that question." The lines in his forehead seemed to deepen. He sat his can of pop on the coffee table, leaned forward, and positioned his elbows on his knees. "I have some bad news. I didn't want to tell you over the phone or anything like that."

"What's up?" Gary asked, leaning forward to match Marc's posture.

"It's about our dad," he said, looking from Gary to me. "He's been in poor health for a while. He wouldn't go to a hospital. Too steeped in the old ways." Marc paused to clear his throat. "I mean, they're all just doing what they know, trying to be independent of the outside world. But, last week he fell asleep and didn't wake up."

I felt my heart rate speed slightly. My father had died? I cut off Marc's next sentence. "What? What happened? Why did you leave in the middle of all of this? How is everyone?"

"You don't understand, Carl-"

"No," I cut him off again. "You should be there to help them deal with this. Why are you *here*?"

"Carly, Carly." Marc's hands were up now, trying to block my interruptions. "Dad's not dead."

"Okay… So, what's going on?"

"I tried to get a doctor in the house, but Mom chased him off before he could get in the door."

"So, you're saying, what? He never woke up?… He's in a coma. Is that what you're saying?" I asked.

Marc nodded. "I don't know how much longer he will have, and I wanted you to know-"

"Why didn't you call, Marcus? You should have called right away."

"She's right," Gary said. "What if he's passed away in the time you've been gone?"

"No," Marcus said insistently. "No. He's not gone yet. He's not going to die, at least not until…" Marcus trailed off and began staring at the floor.

Gary stood up. "Come on, Marcus. You can't be here. You should be with your family."

"I know, I know." Marcus looked up at me. "You've got to come back with me, Carly."

"What?" I instinctively clutched my stomach. "I can't go now." I looked to Gary. He sat back down and put a hand on Marcus' shoulder.

"Marc, what do you mean? What's going on here?"

Marcus let out a sigh. "I don't know if I'm crazy or what, but I had to come here." His voice was getting higher with each syllable until his voice cracked.

"I had to tell you." Marcus squeezed his eyes shut and took a breath.

"What is it, Marcus?" I reached my hand toward him over the table. Marc grabbed our hands and looked back and forth between us.

"You've got to believe me." He paused for another breath. Gary and I exchanged worried glances.

"I had been praying over Dad everyday. Whenever I had the chance. Mom would shower or go cook a meal. And I would be in there praying. She didn't like it, but after a few days without any improvement, she finally stopped scolding me about it and let me just be in there by him. Praying."

"Okay," I said, not knowing what else to say. Obviously, this was leading up to something. Something Marcus was worried that we wouldn't believe.

"Alright," Marcus said. "I was praying two nights ago. It was late, and Mom had fallen asleep in another room. So it was just me and Dad. I stopped for a minute. I was just watching Dad breath, wondering what it all meant. Why God would let him die before he got to know Jesus. Wondering how this was going to work out."

A sheepish smirk came across Marcus' face. He looked into my eyes. "And then I heard God's voice, and He said 'Carly has to come and pray'…"

Gary and I exchanged looks again, and Marcus continued, "And I knew that Dad wasn't going to die. Not yet. Not until you came and prayed for him." Marcus shifted in his seat and released our hands. "So, you've got to believe me. You've got to come back to Idaho with me. You've got to pray, Carly."

I sank back into my chair. I wasn't sure what to think, or what to say.

"There's a train leaving tomorrow morning. It just takes a couple of hours to get there."

My eyes felt heavy suddenly. It was late. I wasn't prepared to process this information.

"You know what, let's sleep on all this," Gary said.

I let my eyes fall closed. I was grateful for Gary's suggestion.

"Okay," I heard Marc say.

"Let me show you to the guest room. It's painted pink, but it is going to be the baby's room soon." Gary and Marcus laughed, sort of strained chuckles. They left me without saying a word.

~~~

I must have passed out right then in my chair, because the next thing I remember is waking up. There was a blanket draped over me and only a dim lamp in the corner of the room penetrated the darkness of night all around me.

I reached toward the coffee table where I'd sat my cell phone earlier that evening. In addition to laying a blanket over me, Gary had plugged it in to the wall to charge. I clicked the power button. The screen illuminated, revealing the time. It was exactly midnight. I felt a chill run through my body. Suddenly, a memory came to me. No. A dream. I had been dreaming, and now the memory flooded to my conscious mind.

~~~

I was standing outside the front entrance of a dilapidated old building. It towered above me, casting a long shadow down the whole street. At first, I thought it was night. Everything was so dark. As I looked around more, however, I realized that if I looked straight up, above the old building, the sun was shining. It was the middle of the day, but this building was casting a huge shadow. There were little houses up and down the street as far as I could see, but they were all in the shadow of the old building. I felt nauseous standing in front of the old building, a thick, gaseous poison was filtering from it. I knew I had to get away from this place. I began walking down the street. As I passed the houses, I noticed people peeking through windows. They were hiding their faces. Only eyes appeared in windows. I knew they were staying inside because of the poison in the air. I wondered why they didn't all just leave. As I had this thought, I heard a voice up ahead. It was a little boy dressed in all white. He was standing on the porch of one of the houses, calling out. I wasn't close enough to hear him yet. I kept walking. He kept calling out.

I got up to his house and stopped to listen. He was crying. Between sobs, he would repeat the same phrase. "Who will save us? Who will bring us daylight?"

I tried to explain to the boy that he could come with me, but he didn't seem to even see me standing there. He just kept weeping, calling out, "Who will save us? Who will bring us daylight?"

"Please, come with me. You don't have to live here anymore!" I started to climb the porch steps toward the boy. I looked down to see two large, diamond shaped, yellow eyes looking up at me from beneath the porch. They belong to a black spider. I froze. First, the eyes emerged, then the torso, and finally, the legs unfolded from beneath the porch. This insect stood almost as tall as the houses.

The boy continued to weep, but his cries for help became muffled and quiet with this spider standing between us. I tried to run. I tried to scream. Inside my being, I was yelling for help. Inside my body, I was pumping my leg muscles. No words came from my throat. No movement came from my body. I was frozen.

The spider's fangs dropped from its mouth. They were dripping something black. It dipped its body low to the ground. Now its face was close to mine. Hot breath beat upon my cheeks. I could smell the poison that had been coming from the old building. It was strong on the beast before me. I screamed inside. I tried again to run. Still nothing. The spider tilted its head back and readied its fangs to sink into my chest. I squeezed my eyes shut and waited for two javelins to pierce my body through.

"Who will save us? Who will bring us daylight?" The boy's cry rang out louder than before. It shattered some invisible restraint. My own scream was released now. My legs were moving now. I was running faster than I'd ever run before. I opened my eyes. Looking back, the spider was now turned toward the boy. I tripped to my hands and knees. My palms had landed hard and slid against the pavement. They began to bleed profusely. My hands were covered with blood in moments. I began to weep, watching the boy on the porch. He was quiet now, the spider looming over him, threatening to strike.

I lifted my blood-covered hands in the air and raised a cry. "*Jesus!*"

Immediately, I heard a crash. I turned toward the noise to see the old building. It was crumbling, falling to the ground in a heap of rubble. Its shadow was shortening. Sunlight was rushing toward all of the houses. I looked back toward the boy. The sunlight hadn't quite reached his home yet, but it was quickly approaching. Closer and closer. I watched the spider. As the sunlight reached it, the bug began to shrivel up and shrink down until I couldn't see it any more.

The boy stood on his porch, now bathed in sunlight. He was stunned, standing there silently. I looked all around. The old building was now a heap of bricks and sheet rock, a fine dust coated the rubbish. I breathed in the air. The poison was gone.

~~~

One booming thought came to me as I remembered the closing moments of my dream. *Carly has to come and pray.* Marc's words. Or, God's words. It was just a little past midnight now, and I knew what had to be done. I would go and pray for my father.

~~~

"I'm going with you, Carly."

Gary had been trying to convince me that we should both go to Idaho with Marc. I wasn't so sure. After all, the last time I spoke with my mother I had made it clear that Gary didn't speak for me, that I was my own person.

Gary had sent Marcus on an errand to pick up lunch, so we had a few minutes to discuss travel plans. We were standing in the kitchen.

"I just don't think you should go alone. I want to be there for you," Gary said, grabbing me around the waist for an embrace. "And, you're carrying our baby. I want to be there for both of you." He smiled and pressed his forehead against mine.

"Gary…" I felt my defenses melting. "I'm just not sure."

Gary kissed me quickly and fled to the fridge to retrieve three sodas. "*I'm sure*, Sweetheart. It's going to be a volatile time. If I don't go, you're going to wish I had." He sat the sodas on the countertop. He stood like a superhero, hands placed firmly on his hips, and faced me. "Trust me. I don't know what it is, but I've got to go with my gut here. I need to come with you."

"Okay," I said. "I won't deny your gut feeling."

~~~

Arriving on the farm in Idaho was strange. The place was nestled in a little valley, hills surrounding green pastures. It was far from any neighbors, about five miles outside of the nearest town. I imagined my parents liking that and trying to keep as self-sufficient on the farm as they could. The house my family was living in was an old three story building, white paint peeling all over. A large vegetable garden was growing in front of the house, looking a little overgrown.

When we pulled up to the house and began unloading our bags from the rental car, my mother and all of my siblings silently filtered out of the house and stood watching.

"They knew we were coming, right?" Gary asked Marcus.

"Yeah, they knew." Marc pulled the last bag from the trunk and latched it shut. "Let's go say hi."

I felt myself hesitate. I just wanted to look for a moment. My mother had gray hair now. My youngest sibling, Jon, whom I remembered as pudgy and childlike, was now tall and thin, standing taller than our mother and sisters.

"Come on, Sweetie." Gary extended a hand to me from a few steps ahead. I took it and walked with him. We followed Marcus, who greeted each of them with a hug. That was encouraging to me. Hugs were all too rare in Deally. Perhaps even more things had changed than that. I hoped.

I reached the group and put on my best smile. "Hi everyone. It's been a while."

Before anyone could respond with a kind word, my two sisters announced that they were taking the family car for a day in the city. Then, they were all going to spent the night at a mutual friend's house and be back late the next day. I would be gone before they returned. I wasn't feeling welcomed. I found myself gripping Gary's hand more tightly.

"Well, you girls be safe," my mother said. They didn't reply, but went straight for the silver Sedan parked beside our rental car. They were in their late twenties now. I watched them leave, wondering who they had grown up to become. They wore modern clothing and makeup, and obviously had friends

205

outside of the farm. That was all I would know of them.

"Well, there's no use in us standing around outside all day. Let's go inside." My mother led the way inside, Jon following close behind her. They were both wearing handmade clothing, like what would be worn back in Deally. Dull, brown clothing. I didn't miss the fashion of Deally.

When we got inside the house, I was surprised to see that much of the furniture inside was from the house in Deally. I hadn't considered that they would recover any of their belongings from the community. Mom led us to the living room, where I sat with Gary on the same yellow couch that had once been in the sitting room of my parent's home in Deally. Jon was sent upstairs with our bags, to put them in the room we would share for the night. Our plan was to stay for only one night. I wasn't comfortable with the idea of outstaying my welcome, and I had already done it with my sisters.

There was a large, stout wooden coffee table in front of us, filled with platters of homemade treats. A vegetable platter boasted of the garden outside, a plate of still warm chocolate chip cookies filled the room with a sugary scent, and oven crisped tortilla chips completed the table.

Mother sat in a rocking chair in the corner of the room, and Marcus took a seat on a second couch from the Deally days which was on the other side of the coffee table.

"You can help yourselves to any of the snacks. Drinks are in the kitchen if you're feeling thirsty." My mom began a slow, melodic rock in her chair.

"Thank you, Mrs. Samson," Gary said. She nodded.

"So…" I began to ease into conversation. "How have you all adjusted to life here on the farm?"

She shook her head back and forth. "Well, we sure don't like the circumstances that brought us here. And just about the time I start liking it here, I remember the circumstances."

I chewed on a celery stick, trying to think of something more pleasant to bring up. Marcus spoke up before I thought of anything. "You know, you're going to have a grandchild before too long, Mom."

She stopped rocking and looked at Marcus. "I didn't know you were courting anyone, Marcus. You know, there's a way these things are supposed to take place! I just don't-"

"No, it's not by me," Marcus said. "Carly is pregnant."

206

She began rocking again. "Well, that's nice, isn't it?" She looked over toward Gary and I. "Congratulations." Her face was stoic, her tone of voice dry.

"Thank you, Mom."

Jon came in just then. He stood in the door way and cleared his throat. We all looked. "Your room is ready. It's just the third door on the left upstairs. The second floor."

"Thanks, Jon!" I was actually excited to speak with Jon. "How have you been? Aren't you going to sit down with us for a while?"

He looked at his feet. "You know, I should probably check on Dad. He has to be looked after, you know."

"Right. Can I come with you? I wanted to see him."

Jon looked up to make eye contact with me, and then with Mom. She just kept rocking, looking off into nowhere now. He looked back at me. "I suppose that would be okay."

I followed Jon through the doorway, down a long hall, and into a large bedroom. The room was dark, with only a small table lamp in the corner of the room. There was a large bed, on which my father slept. Jon and I stood beside him.

"I thought Dad was going to get better. It seemed like he was getting stronger and talking more, but he just didn't wake up one day."

"I'm so sorry, Jon." I found myself whispering. "I came to pray for him. Did Marc tell you that?"

Jon looked at me, frowning. "He said that Jesus could heal Dad. But he's been saying that, ever since Dad got sick. I don't know why nothing has happened yet. He's always coming in here and praying." Jon looked back to Dad. "But he told me that he thought maybe you should be here."

Jon had a point. Why was God waiting? Why did I need to be there? I looked at my father. He looked like a corpse, face frozen in sleep, gray hair disheveled from lying on his pillow so long. My father's chest was rising and falling, and that seemed to be the only indicator of the life hanging on inside him.

What are You going to do, Lord?

I kneeled beside my father's bed and grabbed hold of his hand gingerly. "I'm here, Dad. It's Carly." I watched his eyes, hoping they'd open with recognition of my voice. His eyelids were sealed shut. "Dad…" I searched my heart, remembering the love that God had for this poor man, and the few moments of love I had felt for him in childhood. "You're going to be okay..." What a thing to promise to a man in a coma. My mind was calling my heart a liar, but I ignored the accusation. "I'm going to be here until tomorrow, and hopefully we can talk before I go..." My heart spoke up again, "I love you, Dad."

I had decided to love my father at that moment. The Lord knew I had so many reasons, so many memories, to excuse me from loving him. Those things were in the past, though, and I could feel the love of God within me spurring me onward toward love. I would love this family of mine, regardless of how they felt about me.

I took a deep breath and prayed silently. *Jesus, please do what only You can do. Reveal Your love to my family. Bring healing. Wake up my father. Wake up my whole family.*

"Dad, I'm going to pray for you. I know Marcus has been telling you about Jesus-" I laughed. "Well, He's real. And He loves you, Dad. He wants you to be well, and He wants you to know Him." My father's eyes were moving rapidly beneath the sealed lids. I closed my eyes too and began to pray aloud.

"Lord Jesus, thank You for Your love. God, You love us endlessly. You don't consider our past, because You loved us before it happened. From before the foundation of the world You loved us." My heart began burning intensely with the love of God, causing tears to stream from my eyes. "...God, thank You for Your love. Demonstrate Your love now by bringing healing to my father, and-" My words were choked off with sobs. What was this great, suffocating love? I couldn't speak any more words. I felt these waves of warmth and compassion crashing over me. Sobs were all that I could let out.

A hand was on my shoulder now. I opened my eyes and looked back to see Marcus standing beside me. His eyes were closed and his free hand was extended toward the bed. I closed my own eyes again and listened as he spoke, "We claim healing for our father in the name of Jesus. Thank You for Your faithfulness, God."

Gary's voice came from behind me. "Amen."

I kept my eyes closed and drank in the presence of God. It was warm and peaceful. I whispered, "Amen."

I heard a sound in front of me. I looked at my father. His lips were smacking together as if he were parched. Then, his eyes opened and looked at me.